Hezekiah Butterworth

In the Boyhood of Lincoln

Hezekiah Butterworth

In the Boyhood of Lincoln

ISBN/EAN: 9783337342852

Printed in Europe, USA, Canada, Australia, Japan

Cover: Foto ©Andreas Hilbeck / pixelio.de

More available books at **www.hansebooks.com**

IN THE
BOYHOOD OF LINCOLN

A Tale of the Tunker Schoolmaster and the Times of Black Hawk

BY

HEZEKIAH BUTTERWORTH

AUTHOR OF THE LOG SCHOOL-HOUSE ON THE COLUMBIA

Let us have faith that right makes might, and
in that faith as to the end dare to do our duty.
PRESIDENT LINCOLN.

ILLUSTRATED

SEVENTH EDITION

NEW YORK
D. APPLETON AND COMPANY
1896

LIST OF ILLUSTRATIONS.

CONTENTS

(vii)

IN THE BOYHOOD OF LINCOLN.

CHAPTER I.

INTRODUCED.

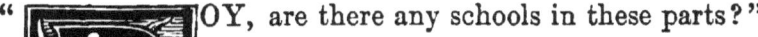

"OY, are there any schools in these parts?"

"Crawford's."

"And who, my boy, is Crawford?"

"The schoolmaster, don't yer know? He's great on thrashing—on thrashing—and—and he knows everything. Everybody in these parts has heard of Crawford. He's great."

"That is all very extraordinary. 'Great on thrashing, and knows everything.' Very extraordinary! Do you raise much wheat in these parts?"

"He don't thrash wheat, mister. Old Dennis and young Dennis do that with their thrashing-flails."

"But what does he thrash, my boy—what does he thrash?"

"He just thrashes boys, don't you know."

"Extraordinary—very extraordinary. He thrashes boys."

"And teaches 'em their manners. He teaches manners, Crawford does. Didn't you never hear of Crawford? You must be a stranger in these parts."

"Yes, I am a stranger in Indiana. I have been following

the timber along the creek, and looking out on the prairie islands. This is a beautiful country. Nature has covered it with grasses and flowers, and the bees will swarm here some day; I see them now; the air is all bright with them, my boy."

"I don't see any bees; it isn't the time of year for 'em. Do you cobble?"

"You don't quite understand me. I was speaking spiritually. Yes, I cobble to pay my way. Yes, my boy."

"Do you preach?"

"Yes, and teach the higher branches—like Crawford. He teaches the higher branches, does he not?"

"Don't make any odds where he gets 'em. I didn't know that he used the higher branches. He just cuts a stick anywhere, and goes at 'em, he does."

"You do not comprehend me, my boy. I teach the higher branches in new schools—Latin and singing. I do not use the higher branches of the trees."

"Latin! Then you must be a *wizard*."

"No, no, my boy. I am one of the Brethren—called. My new name is Jasper. I chose that name because I needed polishing. Do you see? Well, the Lord is doing his work, polishing me, and I shall shine by and by. 'They that turn many to righteousness shall shine like the stars of heaven.' They call me the Parable."

"Then you be a Tunker?"

"I am one of the wandering Brethren that they call 'Tunkers.'"

"You preach for nothin'? They do."

"Yes, my boy; the Word is free."

" Then who pays you ? "

" My soul."

" And you teach for nothin', too, do ye ? "

" Yes, my boy. Knowledge is free."

" Then who pays you ? "

" It all comes back to me. He that teaches is taught."

" You don't cobble for nothin', do ye ? "

" Yes—I cobble to pay my way. I am a wayfaring man, wandering to and fro in the wilderness of the world."

" You cobble to pay yourself for teachin' and preachin'! Why don't you make *them* pay you? I shouldn't think that you would want to preach and teach and cobble all for nothin', and travel, and travel, and sleep anywhere. Father will be proper glad to see you—and mother; we are glad to see near upon anybody. I suppose that you will hold forth down to Crawford's; in the log meetin'-'ouse, or in the school-'ouse, may be, or under the great trees over Nancy Lincoln's grave. Elkins he preached there, and the circuit-rider."

" If I follow the timber, I will come to Crawford's, my boy ? "

" Yes, mister. You'll come to the school-'ouse, and the meetin'-'ouse. The school-'ouse has a low-down roof and a big chimney. Crawford will be right glad to see you, won't he now? They are great on spellin' down there—have spellin'-matches, and all the people come from far and near to hear 'em spell—hundreds of 'em. Link—he's the head speller—he could spell down anybody. It is the greatest school in all these here new parts. You will have a right good time down there; they'll treat ye right well."

"Good, my boy; you speak kindly. I shall have a good time, if the people have ears."

"Ears! They've all got ears—just like other folks. You didn't think that they didn't have any ears, did ye?"

"I mean ears for the truth. I must travel on. I am glad that I met you, my lad. Tell your father and mother that old Jasper the Parable has gone by, and that he has a message for them in his heart. God bless you, my boy—God bless you! You are a little rude in your speech, but you mean well."

The man went on, following the trail along the great trees of Pigeon Creek, and the boy stood looking after him. The water rippled under the trees, and afar lay the open prairie, like a great sun sea. The air was cool, but the light of spring was in it, and the blue-birds fluted blithely among the budding trees.

As he passed along amid these new scenes, a singular figure appeared in the way. It was a woman in a linsey-woolsey dress, corn sun-bonnet, and a huge cane. She looked at the Tunker suspiciously, yet seemed to retard her steps that he might overtake her.

"My good woman," said the latter, coming up to her, "I am not sure of my way."

"Well, I am."

"I wish to go to the Pigeon Creek—settlement—"

"Then you ought to have kept the way when you had it."

"But, my good woman, I am a stranger in these parts. A boy has directed me, but I feel uncertain. What do you do when you lose your way?"

"I don't lose it."

" But if you were—"

" I'd just turn to the right, and keep right straight ahead till I found it."

" True, true; but this is a new country to me. I am one of the Brethren."

" Ye be, be ye? I thought you were one of them land agents. One of the Brethren. I'm proper glad. Who were you lookin' for?"

" Crawford's school."

" The college? Am you're goin' there? I go over there sometimes to see him wallop the boys. We must all have discipline in life, you know, and it is best to begin with the young. Crawford does. They say that Crawford teaches clear to the rule of three, whatever that may be. One added to one is more than one, according to the Scriptur'; now isn't it? One added to one is almost three. Is that what they call high mathematics? I never got further than the multiplication-table, though I am a friend to education. My name is Olive Eastman. What's yourn?"

" Jasper."

" You don't? One of the old patriarchs, like. Well, I live this way—you go *that*. 'Tain't more'n half a mile to Craw-ford's—close to the meetin'-'ouse. Mebby you'll preach there, and I'll hear ye. Glad I met ye now, and to see who you be. They call me Aunt Olive sometimes, and sometimes Aunt Indiana. I settled Pigeon Creek, or husband and I did. He was kind o' weakly; he's gone now, and I live all alone. I'd be glad to have you come over and preach at the 'ouse, though I might not believe a word on't. I'm a Methody; most people

2

are Baptist down here, like the Linkuns, but we is all ready to listen to a Tunker. People are only responsible for what they know; and there are some good people among the Tunkers, I've hern tell. Now don't go off into some by-path into the woods. Tom Lincoln he see a bear there the other day, but he wouldn't 'a' shot it if it had been an elephant with tusks of ivory and gold. Some folks haven't no calculation. The Lincolns hain't. Good-by."

The Tunker was a middle-aged man of probably forty-five or more years. He had a benevolent face, large, sympathetic eyes, and a patriarchal beard. His garments had hooks instead of buttons. He carried a leather bag in which were a Bible and a hymn-book, some German works of Zinzendorf, and his cobbling-tools. We can not wonder that the boy stared after him. He would have looked oddly anywhere.

My reader may not know who a Tunker was, as our wandering schoolmaster was called. A Tunker, or Dunker, was one of a sect of German Baptists or Quakers, who were formerly very numerous in Pennsylvania and Ohio. The order numbered at one time some thirty thousand souls. They called themselves Brethren, but were commonly known as "Tunkards," or "Dunkards," from a German word meaning to *dip*. At their baptisms they dip the body of a convert three times; and so in their own land they received the name of Tunkers, or *dippers*, and this name followed them into Holland and to America. A large number of the Brethren settled in Germantown, Pa. Thence they wandered into Ohio, Indiana, and Illinois, preaching and teaching and doing useful work. Like the Quakers, they have now nearly disappeared.

Their doctrines were peculiar, but their lives were unselfish and pure, and their influence blameless. They believed in being led by the inner light; that the soul was a seat of divine and spiritual authority, and that the Spirit came to them as a direct revelation. They did not eat meat or drink wine. They washed each other's feet after their religious services, wore their beards long, and gave themselves new names that they might not be tempted by any worldly ambitions or rivalries. They thought it wrong to take oaths, to hold slaves, or to treat the Indians differently from other men. They would receive no payment for preaching, but held that it was the duty of all men to live by what they earned by their own labor. They traveled wherever they felt moved to go by the inward monitor. They were a peculiar people, but the prairie States owe much that was good to their influence. The new settlers were usually glad to see the old Tunker when he appeared among them, and to receive his message, and women and children felt the loss of this benevolent sympathy when he went away. He established no church, yet all people believed in his sincerity, and most people listened to him with respect and reverence. The sect closely resembled the old Jewish order of the Essenes, except that they did not wear the garment of white, but loose garments without buttons.

The scene of the Tunker's journey was in Spencer County, Indiana, near the present town of Gentryville. This county was rapidly being occupied by immigrants, and it was to this new people that Jasper the Parable believed himself to be guided by the monitor within.

Early in the afternoon he passed several clearings and

cabins, where he stopped to receive directions to the school-house and meeting-house.

The country was one vast wilderness. For the most part it was covered with gigantic trees, though here and there a rich prairie opened out of the timber. There were oaks gray with centuries, and elms jacketed with moss, in whose high boughs the orioles in summer builded and sang, and under which the bluebells grew. There were black-walnut forests in places, with timber almost as hard as horn. The woods in many places were open, like colonnades, and carpeted with green moss. There were no restrictions of law here, or very few. One might pitch his tent anywhere, and live where he pleased. The land, as a rule, was common.

Jasper came at last to a clearing with a rude cabin, near which was a three-faced camp, as a house of poles with one open side was called. Spencer County was near the Kentucky border, and the climate was so warm that a family could live there in a house of poles in comfort for most of the year.

As Jasper the Parable came up to the log-house, which had neither hinged doors nor glass windows, a large, rough, good-humored-looking man came out to the gate to meet him, and stood there leaning upon a low gate-post.

"Howdy, stranger?" said the hardy pioneer. "What brings you to these parts—lookin' for a place to settle down at?"

"No, my good friend—I'm obliged to you for speaking so kindly to a wayfarer—peace be with you—I am looking for the school-house. Can you direct me there?"

"I reckon. Then you be going to see the school? Good for ye. A great school that Crawford keeps. I've got a boy and a girl in that there school myself. The boy, if I do say it now, is the smartest fellow in all the country round—and the laziest. Smart at the top, but it don't go down. Runs all to larnin'. Just reads and studies about all the time, speaks pieces, and preaches on stumps, and makes poetry, and things. I don't know what will ever become of him. He's a queer one. My name is Linkem " (Lincoln)—" Thomas Linkem. What's yourn ? "

" They call me Jasper the Parable—that is my new name. I'm one of the Brethren. No offense, I hope—just one of the Brethren."

" Oh, you be—a Tunker. Well, we'll all be proper glad to see you down here. I come from Kentuck. Where did you come from ? "

" From Pennsylvania, here. I was born in Germany."

" Sho, you did ? From Pennsylvany ! And how far are you going ? "

" I'm going to meet Black Hawk. My good friend, I stop and preach and teach and cobble along the way,"

" What ! Black Hawk, the chief ? Is it him you're goin' to see ? You're an Indian agent, perhaps, travelin' for the State or the fur-traders ? "

" No, I am not a trader of any kind. I am going to meet Black Hawk at Rock River. He has promised me a young Indian guide, who will show me all these paths and act as an interpreter, and gain for me a passage among all the Indian tribes. I have met Black Hawk before."

" You've been to Illinois, have ye ? Glad to hear ye say so. What kind of a kentry is that, now ? I've sometimes thought of going there myself. It ain't over-healthy here. Say, stranger, come back and stop with us after you've been to the school. I haven't any great accommodations, as you see, but I will do the best I can for you, and it will make my wife and Abe and the gal proper glad to have a talk with a preacher. Ye will, won't ye, now? Say yes."

"Yes, yes, if it is so ordered, friend. Thank you, yes. I feel moved to say that I will come back. You are very good, my friend."

"Yes, yes, come back and see us all. I won't detain ye any longer now. You see that there openin'? Well, you just follow that path as the crow flies, and you'll come to the school-'ouse. Good-day, stranger—good-day."

It was early spring, a season always beautiful in southern Indiana. The buds were swelling; the woodpeckers were tapping the old trees, and the migrating birds were returning to their old homes in the tree-tops. Jasper went along singing, for his heart was happy, and he felt the cheerful influence of the vernal air. The birds to him were prophets and choirs, and the murmur of the south winds in the trees was a sermon. A right and receptive spirit sees good in everything, and so Jasper sang as he walked along the footpath.

The school-house came into view. It was built of round logs, and was scarcely higher than a tall man's head. The chimney was large, and was constructed of poles and clay, and the floor and furniture were made of puncheons, as split logs were called. The windows consisted of rough slats and oiled paper. The door was open, and Jasper came up and stood before it. How strange the new country all seemed to him!

The schoolmaster came to the door. He affected gentlemanly and almost courtly manners, and bowed low.

"Is this Mr. Crawford, may I ask?" said Jasper.

"Andrew Crawford. And whom have I the honor of meeting?"

"My new name is Jasper. I am one of the Brethren. They call me the Parable. I am on my way to Rock Island, Illinois, to meet Black Hawk, the chief, who has promised to assist me with a guide and interpreter for my missionary journeys among the new settlements and the tribes. I have come, may it please you, to visit the school. I am a teacher myself."

"You do us great honor, and I assure you that you are very welcome—very welcome. Come in."

The scholars stared, and presented a very strange appearance. The boys were dressed in buckskin breeches and linsey-woolsey shirts, and the girls in homespun gowns of most economical patterns. The furniture seemed all pegs and puncheons. The one cheerful object in the room was the enormous fireplace. The pupils delighted to keep this fed with fuel in the chilly winter days, and the very ashes had cheerful suggestions. It was all ashes now, for the sun was high, and the spring falls warm and early in the forests of southern Indiana.

It was past mid afternoon, and the slanting sun was glimmering in the tops of the gigantic forest-trees seen from the open door.

"We have nearly completed the exercises of the day," said Mr. Crawford. "I have yet to hear the spelling-class, and to conduct the exercises in manners. I teach manners. Shall I go on in the usual way?"

"Yes, yes, may it please you—yes, in the usual way—in the usual way. You are very kind."

"You do me great honor.—The class in spelling," said Mr. Crawford, turning to the school. Five boys and girls stood up, and came to an open space in front of the desk. The recitation of this class was something most odd and amusing to Jasper, and so it would seem to a teacher of to-day.

"*Incompatibility*," said Mr. Crawford. "You may make your manners and spell *incompatibility*, Sarah."

A tall girl with a high forehead and very short dress gave a modest and abashed glance at the wandering visitor, blushed, courtesied very low, and thus began the rhythmic exercise of spelling the word in the old-time way:

"I-n, in; there's your in. C-o-m, com, incom; there's your incom; incom. P-a-t, pat, compat, incompat; there's your incompat; incompat. I-, pati, compati, incompati; there's your incompati; incompati. B-i-l, bil; ibil, patibil, compatibil, incompatibil; there's your incompatibil; incompatibil. I-, bili, patibili, compatibili, incompatibili; there's your incompatibili; incompatibili. T-y, ty, ity, bility, ibility, patibility, compatibility, incompatibility; there's your incompatibility; *incompatibility*."

The girl seemed dazed after this mazy effort. Mr. Crawford bowed, and Jasper the Parable looked serene, and remarked, encouragingly:

"Extraordinary! I never heard a word spelled in that

way. This is an age of wonders. One meets with strange things everywhere. I should think that that girl would make a teacher one day; and the new country will soon need teachers. The girl did well."

"You do me great honor," said Mr. Crawford, bowing like a courtier. "I appreciate it, I assure you; I appreciate it, and thank you. I have aimed to make my school the best in the country. Your commendation encourages me to hope that I have not failed."

But these polite and generous compliments were exchanged a little too soon. The next word that Mr. Crawford gave out from the "Speller" was *obliquity*.

"Jason, make your manners and spell *obliquity*. Take your hands out of your pockets; that isn't manners. Take your hands out of your pockets and spell *obliquity*."

Jason was a tall lad, in a jean blouse and leather breeches. His hair was tangled and his ankles were bare. He seemed to have a loss of confidence, but he bobbed his head for manners, and began to spell in a very loud voice, that had in it almost the sharpness of defiance.

"O-b, ob; there's your ob; ob." He made a leer. "L-i-k, lik, oblik; there's your oblik—"

"No," said Mr. Crawford, with a look of vexation and disappointment. "Try again."

Jason took a higher key of voice.

"Wall, O-b, ob; there's your ob; ain't it? L-i-c-k, and there's your lick—"

"Take your seat!" thundered Mr. Crawford. "I'll give you a *lick* after school. Think of bringing obliquity upon the school in the presence of a teacher from the Old World! Next!"

But the next pupil became lost in the mazes of the improved method of spelling, and the class brought dishonor upon the really conscientious and ambitious teacher.

The exercise in manners partly redeemed the disaster.

"Abraham Lincoln, stand up."

A tall boy arose, and his head almost touched the ceiling. He was dressed in a linsey-woolsey frock, with buckskin breeches which were much too short for him. His ankles were exposed, and his feet were poorly covered. His face was dark and serious. He did not look like one whom an unseen Power had chosen to control one day the destiny of nations, to call a million men to arms, and to emancipate a race.

"Abraham Lincoln, you may go out, and come in and be introduced."

It required but a few steps to take the young giant out of the door. He presently returned, knocking.

"James Sparrow, you may go to the door," said Mr. Crawford.

The boy arose, went to the door, and bowed very properly.

"Good-afternoon, Mr. Lincoln. I am glad to see you. Come in. If it please you, I will present you to my friends."

Abraham entered, as in response to this courtly parrot-talk.

"Mr. Crawford, may I have the honor of presenting to you my friend Abraham Lincoln?—Mr. Lincoln, Mr. Crawford."

Mr. Crawford bowed slowly and condescendingly. Abraham was then introduced to each of the members of the school, and the exercise was a very creditable one, under the untoward

THE TUNKER SCHOOLMASTER'S CLASS IN MANNERS.

circumstances. And this shall be our own introduction to one of the heroes of our story, and, following this odd introduction, we will here make our readers somewhat better acquainted with Jasper the Parable.

He was born in Thuringia, not far from the Baths of Liebenstein. His father was a German, but his mother was of English descent, and he had visited England with her in his youth, and so spoke the English language naturally and perfectly. He had become an advocate of the plans of Pestalozzi, the father of common-school education, in his early life. One of the most intimate friends of his youth was Froebel, afterward the founder of the kindergarten system of education. With Froebel he had entered the famous regiment of Lutzow; he had met Körner, and sang the "Wild Hunt of Lützow," by Von Weber, as it came from the composer's pen, the song which is said to have driven Napoleon over the Rhine. He had married, lost wife and children, become melancholy and despondent, and finally fallen under the influence of the preaching of a Tunker, and had taken the resolution to give up himself entirely, his will and desires, and to live only for others, and to follow the spiritual impression, which he believed to be the Divine will. He was simple and sincere. His friends had treated him ill on his becoming a Tunker, but he forgave them all, and said: "You reject me from your hearts and homes. I will go to the new country, and perhaps I may find there a better place for us all. If I do, I will return to you and treat you as Joseph treated his brethren. You are oppressed; you have to bear arms for years. I am left alone in the world. Something calls me over the sea."

He lived near Marienthal, the Vale of Mary. It was a lovely place, and his heart loved it and all the old German villages, with their songs and children's festivals, churches, and graves. He bade farewell to Froebel. "I am going to study life," he said, "in the wilderness of the New World." He came to Pennsylvania, and met the Brethren there who had come from Germany, and then traveled with an Indian agent to Rock Island, Illinois, where he had met Black Hawk. Here he resolved to become a traveling teacher, preacher, and missionary, after the usages of his order, and he asked Black Hawk for an interpreter and guide.

"Return to me in May," said the chief, "and I will provide you with as noble a son of the forest as ever breathed the air."

He returned to Ohio, and was now on his way to visit the old chief again.

The country was a wonder to him. Coming from middle Germany and the Rhine lands, everything seemed vast and limitless. The prairies with their bluebells, the prairie islands with their giant trees, the forests that shaded the streams, were all like a legend, a fairy story, a dream. He admired the heroic spirit of the pioneers, and he took the Indians to his heart. In this spirit he began to travel over the unbroken prairies of Indiana and Illinois.

CHAPTER II.

HE red sun was glimmering through the leafless boughs of the great oaks when Jasper again came to the gate of Thomas Lincoln's log cabin. Mr. Crawford had remained after school with the tall boy who had brought "obliquity" upon the spelling-class. Tradition reports that there was a great rattling of leather breeches, and expostulations, and lamentations at such solemn, private interviews. Mr. Crawford, who was "great on thrashing," no doubt did his duty as he understood it at that private session at sundown. Sticks were plenty in those days, and the will to use them strong among most pioneer schoolmasters.

Abraham Lincoln and his sister accompanied Jasper to the log-house. They heard the lusty cry for consideration and mercy in the log school-house as they were going, and stopped to listen. Jasper did not approve of this rugged discipline.

"I should not treat the boy in that way," said he philosophically.

"You wouldn't?" said Abraham. "Why? Crawford is a great teacher; he knows everything. He can cipher as far as the rule of three."

"Yes, lad, but the true purpose of education is to form character. Fear does not make true worth, but counterfeit character. If education fails to produce real character, it fails utterly. True education is a matter of the soul as much as of the mind. It should make a boy want to do right because it is the right thing to do right. Anything that fails to produce character for its own sake, and not for a selfish reason, is a mistake. But what am I doing—criticising? Now, that is wrong. I seemed to be talking with Froebel. Yes, Crawford is a great teacher, all things considered. He does well who does his best. You have a great school. It is not like the old German schools, but you do well."

Jasper began a discourse about Pestalozzi and that great thinker's views of universal education. But the words were lost on the air. The views of Pestalozzi were not much discussed in southern Indiana at this time, though the idea of common-school education prevailed everywhere.

Thomas Lincoln stood at the gate awaiting the return of Jasper.

"I'm proper glad that you've come back to see us all," said he. "Wife has been lookin' for ye. What did you think of the school? Great, isn't it? That Crawford is a big man in these parts. They say he can cipher to the rule of three, whatever that may be. Indiana is going to be great on education, in my opinion."

He was right. Indiana, with an investment of some ten million of dollars for public education, and with an army of well-trained teachers, leads the middle West in the excellence of her schools. Her model school system, which to-day would delight a Pestalozzi or a Froebel, had its rude beginning in schools like Crawford's.

"Come, come in," said Thomas Lincoln, and led the way into the log-house.

"This is my wife," said he to Jasper.

The woman had a serene and benevolent face. Her features were open and plain, but there was heart-life in them. It was a face that could have been molded only by a truly good heart. It was strong, long-suffering, sympathetic, and self-restrained. Her forehead was high and thoughtful, her eyes large and expressive, and her voice loving and cheerful. Jasper felt at once that he was in the presence of a woman of decision of character.

"Then you are a Tunker," she said. "I am a Baptist, too, but not your kind. But such things matter little if the heart is right."

"You have well said," answered Jasper. "The true life is in the soul. We both belong to the same kingdom, and shall have the same life and drink from the same fountain and eat the same bread. Have you been here long?"

"Yes," said Thomas Lincoln, "and we have seen some dark days. We lived in the half-faced camp out yonder when I first came here. My first wife died of milk-sickness here. She was Abraham's mother. Ever heard of the milk-sickness, as the fever was called? It swept away a great many of the early inhabitants. Those were dark, dark days. I shall never forget them."

"So your real mother is dead," said Jasper to Abraham.

"I try to be a mother to him, poor boy," said Mrs. Lincoln.

"Abraham is good to me and to everybody; one of the best boys I ever knew, though I ought not to praise him to his face. He does the best he can."

"Awful lazy. You didn't tell that," said Thomas Lincoln; "all head and books. He is. I believe in tellin' the whole truth."

"Oh, well," said Mrs. Lincoln, "some persons work with their hands, and some with their heads, and some with their hearts. Abraham's head is always at work—he isn't like most other boys. And as far as his heart— Well, I do love that boy, and I am his step-mother, too. He's always been so good to me that I love to tell on't. His father, I'm thinkin', is rather hard on him sometimes. Abe's heart knows mine and I know his'n, and I couldn't think more on him if he was my own son. His poor mother sleeps out there under the great trees; but I mean to be such a mother to him that he will never know no difference."

"Yes," said Thomas Lincoln, "Abraham does middlin' well, considerin'. But he does provoke me sometimes. He would provoke old Job himself. Why, he will take a book with him into the corn-field, and he reads and reads, and his head gets loose and goes off into the air, and he puts the pumpkin-seeds in the wrong hills, like as not. He is great on the English Reader. I'd just like for you to hear him recite poetry out of that book. He's great on poetry; writes it himself. But that isn't neither here nor there. Come, preacher, we'll have some supper."

The Tunker lifted his hand and said grace, after which the family sat down to the table.

"We used to eat off a puncheon when we first came to these parts," said Mr. Lincoln. "We had no beds, and we slept on a floor of pounded clay. My new wife brought all of this grand furniture to me. That becreau looks extravagant— now don't it?—for poor folks, too. I sometimes think that she ought to sell it. I am told that in a city place it would be worth as much as fifty dollars."

There were indeed a few good articles of furniture in the house.

The supper consisted of corn-bread of very rough meal, and of bacon, eggs, and coffee.

"Do you smoke?" asked Mr. Lincoln, when the meal was over.

"No," said Jasper. "I have given up everything of that kind, luxuries, and even my own name. Let us talk about our experiences. There is no news in the world like the news from the soul. A man's inner life and experience are about all that is worth talking about. It is the king that makes the crown."

But Thomas Lincoln was not a man of deep inward experiences and subjective ideas, though his first wife had been such a person, and would have delighted Jasper. Mr. Lincoln liked best to talk about his family and the country, and was more interested in the slow news that came from the new settlements than in the revelations from a higher world. His former wife, Abraham's mother, had been a mystic, but there was little sentiment in him.

"You said that you were going to meet Black Hawk," said Mr. Lincoln. "Where do you expect to find him? He's everywhere, ain't he?"

3

"I am going to the Sac village at Rock Island. It is a long journey, but the Voice tells me to go."

"That is away across the Illinois, on the Mississippi River, isn't it?"

"Yes, the Sac village looks down on the Mississippi. It is a beautiful place. The prairies spread around it like seas. I love to think of it. It commands a noble view. I do not wonder that the Indians love it, and made it the burial-place of their race. I would love it myself.

"You favor the Indians, do you?"

"Yes. All men are my brothers. The field is the world. I am going to try to preach and teach among the Sacs and Foxes, as soon as I can find an interpreter, and Black Hawk has promised me one. He has sent for him to come down to Rock Island and meet me. He lives at Prairie du Chien, far away in the north, I am told."

"Don't you have any antipathy against the Indians, preacher?"

"No, none at all. Do you?"

"My father was murdered by an Indian. Let me tell you about it. Not that I want to discourage you—you mean well; but I don't feel altogether as you do about the red-skins, preacher. You and Abe would agree better on the subject than you and I. Abe is tender-hearted—takes after his mother."

Thomas Lincoln filled his pipe. "Abe," as his oldest boy was called, sat in the fireplace, "the flue," as it was termed. By his side sat John Hanks, who had recently arrived from Kentucky—a rough, kindly-looking man.

Abraham Lincoln
his hand and pen.
he will be good but
god knows When

LINES WRITTEN BY LINCOLN ON THE LEAF OF HIS SCHOOL-BOOK
IN HIS FOURTEENTH YEAR.

Preserved by his Step-mother.

Original in possession of J. W. Weik.

" Wait a minute," said great-hearted Mrs. Lincoln—" wait a minute before you begin."

" What are you going to do, mother (wife) ? "

" I'm just going to set these potatoes to roast before the fire, so we can have a little treat all by ourselves when you have got through your story. There, that is all."

The poor woman sat down by the table—she had brought the table to her husband on her marriage ; he probably never owned a table—and began to knit, saying :

" Abraham, you mind the potatoes. Don't let 'em burn."

" Yes, mother."

" Mother "—the word seemed to make her happy. Her face lighted. She sat knitting for an hour, silent and serene, while Thomas Lincoln talked.

THOMAS LINCOLN'S STORY.

" My father," began the old story-teller, " came to Kentucky from Virginia. His name was Abraham Lincoln. I have always thought that was a good, solid name—a worthy name— and so I gave it to my boy here, and hope that he will never bring any disgrace upon it. I never can be much in this world ; Abe may.

" This was in Daniel Boone's day. On our way to Kentucky we began to hear terrible stories of the Indian attacks on the new settlers. In 1780, the year that we emigrated from Virginia, there were many murders of the settlers by the Indians, which were followed by the battle of Lower Blue Licks, in which Boone's son was wounded.

" I have heard my mother and the old settlers talk over that battle. When Daniel Boone found that his son was wounded, he tried to carry him away. There was a river near, and he lifted the boy upon his back and hurried toward it. As he came to the river, the boy grew heavy.

"'Father, I believe that I am dying,' said the boy.

"'We will be across the river soon,' said Boone. 'Hold on.'

"The boy clung to his father's neck with stiffening arms. While they were crossing the river the son died. Oh, it was a sight for pity—now, wasn't it, preacher? Boone in the river, with the dead body of his boy on his back. Our country has known few scenes like that. How that father must 'a' felt! You furriners little know these things.

"The Indians swam after him. He laid down the body of his son on the ground and struck into the forest.

"It was in this war that Boone's little daughter was carried away by the Indians. I must tell ye. I love to talk of old times.

"She was at play with two other little girls outside of the stockade at Boonesborough, on the Kentucky River. There was a canoe on the bank.

"'Let us take the canoe and go across the river,' said one of the girls, innocent-like.

"Well, they got into the boat and paddled across the running river to the opposite side. They reached shallow water, when a party of Indians, who had been watching them, cunning-like, stole out of the thick trees 'n' rushed down to the canoe 'n' drew it to the shore. The girls screamed, and their cries were heard at the fort.

"Night was falling. Three of the Indians took a little

girl apiece, and, looking back to the fort in the sunset, uttered a shriek of defiance, such as would ha' made yer flesh creep, and disappeared in the timber.

"That night a party was got together at the fort to pursue the Indians and rescue the children.

"Well, near the close of the next day the party came upon these Indians, some forty miles from the fort. They approached the camp cautiously, coyote-like, 'n' saw that the girls were there. -

"'Shoot carefully, now,' said the leader. 'Each man bring down an Indian, or the children will be killed before we can reach them.'

"They fired upon the Indians, picking out the three who were nearest the children. Not one of the Indians was hit, but the whole party was terribly frightened, leaped up, 'n' run like deer. The children were rescued unharmed 'n' taken back to the fort. You would think them was pretty hard times, wouldn't ye?

"There was one event that happened at the time about which I have heard the old folks tell, with staring eyes, and I will never forget it. The Indians came one night to attack a log-house in which were a man, his wife, and daughter, named Merrill. They did not wish to burn the cabin, but to enter it and make captives of the family; so they cut a hole in the door, with their hatchets, large enough to crawl through one at a time. They wounded Mr. Merrill outright.

"But Mrs. Merrill was a host in herself. Her only weapon was an axe, and there never was fought in Kentucky, or any-

where else in the world, I'm thinkin', such another battle as
that.

"The leader of the Indians put his head through the hole
in the door and began to crawl into the room, slowly—slowly
—so—"

Mr. Lincoln put out his great arms, and moved his hands
mysteriously.

"Well," he continued, "what do you suppose happened?
Mrs. Merrill she dealt that Indian a death-blow on the head
with the axe, just like *that*, and then drew him in slowly,
slowly. The Indians without thought that he had crawled
in himself, and another Indian followed him slowly, slowly.
That Indian received his death-blow on the head, and was
pulled in like the first, slowly. Another and another Indian
were treated in the same way, until the dark cabin floor presented an awful scene for the morning.

"Only one or two were left without. The women felt that
they were now the masters in the contest, and stood looking
on what they had done. There fell a silence over the place.
Still, awful still everywhere. What a silence it was! The two
Indians outside listened. Why were their comrades so still?
What had happened? Why was everything so still? One of
them tried to look through the hole in the door into the
dark and bloody room. Then the two attempted to climb
down the chimney from the low roof of the cabin, but Mrs.
Merrill put her bed into the fireplace and set it on fire.

"Such were some of the scenes of my father's few years
of life in Kentucky; and now comes the most dreadful memory of all. Oh, it makes me wild to think o' it! Preacher,

as I said, my father was killed by the Indians. You did not know that before, did you? No; well, it was so. Abraham Lincoln was shot by the red-skins. I was with him at the time, a little boy then, and I shall never forget that awful morning—never, never!—Abraham, mind the potatoes; you've heard the story a hundred times."

Young Abraham Lincoln turned the potatoes and brightened the fire. Thomas Lincoln bent over and rested his body on his knees, and held his pipe out in one hand.

"Preacher, listen. One morning father looked out of the cabin door, and said to mother:

"'I must go to the field and build a fence to-day. I will let Tommy go with me.'

"I was Tommy. I was six years old then. He loved me, and liked to have me with him. It was in the year 1784—I never shall forget the dark days of that year!—never, never.

"I had two brothers older than myself, Mordecai and Josiah. We give boys Scriptur' names in those days. They had gone to work in another field near by.

"We went to the field where the rails were to be cut and laid, and father began to work. He was a great, noble-looking man, and a true pioneer. I can see him now. I was playing near him, when suddenly there came a shot as it were out of the air. My poor father reeled over and fell down dead. What must have been his last thoughts of my mother and her five children? I have often thought of that—what must have been his last thoughts? Well, Preacher, you listen.

"A band of Indians came leaping out of the bush howling like demons. I fell upon the ground. I can sense the fright

now. A tall, black Indian, with a face like a wolf, came and
stood over me, and was about to seize hold of me. I could hear
him breathe. There came a shot from the house, and the
Indian dropped down beside me, dead. My brother Mordecai
had seen father fall, 'n' ran to the house 'n' fired that shot that
saved my life. Josiah had gone to the stockade for help, and
he returned soon with armed men, and the Indians disappeared.

"O Preacher, those were dark days, wasn't they? Dark,
dark days! You never saw such. They took up my father's
body—what a sight!—and bore it into the cabin. You should
have seen my poor mother then. What was to help us? Only
the blue heavens were left us then. What could we do? My
mother and five children alone in the wilderness full of savages!

"Preacher, I have seen dark days! I have known what it
was to be poor and supperless and friendless; but I never
sought revenge on the Indians, though Mordecai did. I'm glad
that you're going to preach among them. I couldn't do it,
with such memories as mine, perhaps; but I'm glad you can, 'n'
I hope that you will go and do them good. Heaven bless those
who seek to do good in this sinful world—"

"Abraham, are the potatoes done?" said a gentle voice.

"Yes, mother."

"Then pass them 'round. Give the preacher one first; then
your father. I do not care for any."

The tall boy passed the roasted potatoes around as directed.
Jasper ate his potato in silence. The stories of the hardships
of this forest family had filled his heart with sympathy, and
Thomas Lincoln had *acted* the stories that he told in such a
way as to leave a most vivid impression on his mind.

"These stories make you sad," said Mrs. Lincoln to Jasper. "They are heart-rendin', and I sometimes think it is almost wrong to tell them. Do you think it is right to tell a story that awakens hard and rebellious feelin's? 'Evil communications corrupt good manners,' the Good Book says. I sometimes wish that folks would tell only stories that are good, and make one the better for hearin'—parables like."

"My heart feels for you all," said Jasper. "I feel for everybody. This life is all new to me."

"Let us have something more cheerful now," said Mrs. Lincoln.—"Abraham, recite to the preacher a piece from the English Reader."

"Which one, mother?"

"The Hermit—how would that do? I don't know much about poetry, but Abraham does. He makes it up. It is a queer turn of mind he has. He learns all the poetry that he can find, and makes it up himself out of his own head. He's got poetry in him, though he don't look so. How he ever does it, puzzles me. His mother was poetic like. It is a gift, like grace. Where do you suppose it comes from, and what will he ever do with it? He ain't like other boys. He's kind o' peculiar some.—Come, Abraham, recite to us The Hermit. It is a proper good piece."

The tall boy came out of "the flue" and stood before the dying fire. The old leather-covered English Reader, which he said in later life was the best book ever written, lay on the table before him. He did not open it, however. He put his hands behind him and raised his dark face as in a kind of abstraction. He began to recite slowly in a clear voice, full of a peculiar sympathy that gave color to every word. He seemed as though he felt that the experience of the poet was somehow a prophecy of his own life; and it was. He himself became a skeptical man in religious thought, but returned to the simple faith of his ancestors amid the dark scenes of war.

The poem was a beautiful one in form and soul, an old English pastoral, by Beattie. How grand it seemed, even to unpoetic Thomas Lincoln, as it flowed from the lips of his studious son!

THE HERMIT.

At the close of the day, when the hamlet is still,
  And mortals the sweets of forgetfulness prove;
When naught but the torrent is heard on the hill,
  And naught but the nightingale's song in the grove:
'Twas thus, by the cave of the mountain afar,
  While his harp rung symphonious, a hermit began;
No more with himself or with Nature at war,
  He thought as a sage, though he felt as a man:

" Ah, why, all abandoned to darkness and woe,
  Why, lone Philomela, that languishing fall?
For spring shall return, and a lover bestow,
  And sorrow no longer thy bosom inthrall.
But, if pity inspire thee, renew the sad lay,
  Mourn, sweetest complainer, man calls thee to mourn;
O soothe him whose pleasures like thine pass away:
  Full quickly they pass—but they never return.

" Now gliding remote, on the verge of the sky,
  The moon, half extinguished, her crescent displays:
But lately I marked when majestic on high
  She shone, and the planets were lost in her blaze.
Roll on, thou fair orb, and with gladness pursue
  The path that conducts thee to splendor again:
But man's faded glory what change shall renew?
  Ah, fool! to exult in a glory so vain!

" 'Tis night, and the landscape is lovely no more :
    I mourn : but, ye woodlands, I mourn not for you ;
For morn is approaching, your charms to restore,
    Perfumed with fresh fragrance, and glitt'ring with dew.
Nor yet for the ravage of winter I mourn ;
    Kind Nature the embryo blossom will save :
But when shall spring visit the moldering urn ?
    Oh, when shall day dawn on the night of the grave ?

" 'Twas thus by the glare of false science betrayed,
    That leads to bewilder, and dazzles to blind ;
My thoughts wont to roam, from shade onward to shade,
    Destruction before me, and sorrow behind.
' Oh pity, great Father of light,' then I cried,
    ' Thy creature who fain would not wander from thee !
Lo, humbled in dust, I relinquish my pride :
    From doubt and from darkness thou only canst free.'

" And darkness and doubt are now flying away ;
    No longer I roam in conjecture forlorn :
So breaks on the traveler, faint and astray,
    The bright and the balmy effulgence of morn.
See truth, love, and mercy, in triumph descending,
    And Nature all glowing in Eden's first bloom !
On the cold cheek of death smiles and roses are blending,
    And beauty immortal awakes from the tomb."

Mrs. Lincoln used to listen to such recitations as this from the English Readers and Kentucky Orators with delight and wonder. She loved the boy with all her heart. In all the biographies of Lincoln there is hardly a more pathetic incident than one told by Mr. Herndon of his visit to Mrs. Lincoln after the assassination and the national funeral. Mr. Herndon was the law partner of Lincoln for many years, and we give the incident here, out of place as it is. Mrs. Lincoln said to her step-son's friend :

" Abe was a poor boy, and I can say what scarcely one

woman—a mother—can say, in a thousand : Abe never gave
me a cross word or look, and never refused, in fact or appearance, to do anything I requested him. I never gave him a
cross word in all my life. . . . His mind and my mind—what
little I had—seemed to run together. . . . He was here after
he was elected President." Here she stopped, unable to pro-
ceed any further, and after her grateful emotions had spent
themselves in tears, she proceeded : " He was dutiful to me
always. I think he loved me truly. I had a son, John, who
was raised with Abe. Both were good boys ; but I must say,
both being now dead, that Abe was the best boy I ever saw or
ever expect to see. I wish I had died when my husband died.
I did not want Abe to run for President, did not want him
elected ; was afraid, somehow—felt it in my heart ; and when
he came down to see me, after he was elected President, I felt
that something would befall him, and that I should see him
no more."

Equally beautiful was the scene when Lincoln visited this
good woman for the last time, just before going to Washington
to be inaugurated President.

"Abraham," she said, as she stood in her humble backwoods cabin, " something tells me that I shall never see you
again."

He put his hand around her neck, lifted her face to heaven
and said, " Mother ! "

CHAPTER III.

THE OLD BLACKSMITH'S SHOP AND THE MERRY STORY-TELLERS.

JOHNNIE KONGAPOD'S INCREDIBLE STORY.

HE country store, in most new settlements, is the resort of story-tellers. It was not so here. There was a log blacksmith-shop by the way-side near the Gentryville store, overspread by the cool boughs of pleasant trees, and having a glowing forge and wide-open doors, which was a favorite resort of the good-humored people of Spencer County, and here anecdotes and stories used to be told which Abraham Lincoln in his political life made famous. The merry pioneers little thought that their rude stories would ever be told at great political meetings, to generals and statesmen, and help to make clear practical thought to Legislatures, senates, and councils of war. Abraham Lincoln claimed that he obtained his education by learning all that he could of any one who could teach him anything. In all the curious stories told in his hearing in this quaint Indiana smithy, he read some lesson of life.

The old blacksmith was a natural story-teller. Young Lincoln liked to warm himself by the forge in winter and sun himself in the open door in summer, and tempt this sinewy man to talk.   The smithy was a common resort of Thomas Lincoln, and of John and Dennis Hanks, who belonged to the family of Abraham's mother.   The schoolmaster must have liked the place, and the traveling ministers tarried long there when they brought their horses to be shod.   In fact, the news-stand of that day, the literary club, the lecture platform, the place of amusement, and everything that stirred associated life, found its common center in this rude old smithy by the wayside, amid the running brooks and fanning trees.

The stories told here were the curious incidents and adventures of pioneer life, rude in fact and rough in language, but having pith and point.

Thomas Lincoln, on the afternoon of the next day, said to Jasper:

" Come, preacher, let's go over to the smithy.   I want ye to see the blacksmith.   We all like to see the blacksmith in these parts; he's an uncommon man."

They went to the smithy.   Abraham followed them.   The forge was low, and the blacksmith was hammering over old nails on the anvil.

" Hello! " said Thomas Lincoln; " not doin' much to-day.   I brought the preacher over to call on you—he's a Tunker—has been to see the school—he teaches himself—thought you'd want to know him."

" Glad you come.   Here, sit down in the leather chair, and make yourself at home.   Been long in these new parts? "

" No, my friend; I have been to Illinois, but I have never been here before.   I am glad to see you."

" What do you think of the country? " said the blacksmith.

STORY-TELLING AT THE SMITHY.

"Think it is a good place to settle in? Hope that you have come to cast your lot with us. We need a preacher; we haven't any goodness to spare. You come from foreign parts, I take it. Well, well, there's room for a world of people out here in the woods and prairies. I hope that you will like it, and get your folks to come. We'll do all we can for you. We be men of good will, if we be hard-looking and poor."

"My good friend, I believe you. You are great-hearted men, and I like you."

"Brainy, too. Let me start up the forge."

"Preacher, come here," said Thomas Lincoln. "I haven't had no edication to speak of, but I've invented a new system of book-keepin' that beats the schools. There's one of them there. The blacksmith keeps all of his accounts by it. I've got one on a puncheon at home; did you notice it? This is how it is; you may want to use it yourself. Come and look at it."

On a rough board over the forge Thomas Lincoln had drawn a number of straight lines with a coal, as are sometimes put on a blackboard by a singing-master. On the lower bars were several cloudy erasures, and at the end of these bars were initials.

"Don't understand it, do you? Well, now, it is perfectly simple. I taught it to Aunt Olive, and she don't know more than some whole families, though she thinks that she knows more than the whole creation. Seen such people, hain't ye? Yes. The woods are full of 'em. Well, that ain't neither here nor there. This is how it works: A man comes here to have his horse shod—minister, may be; short, don't pay. Nothin' to pay with but funeral sermons, and you can't collect them all the time. Well, all you have to do is just to draw your finger across one of them lines, and write his initials after it. And when he comes again, rub out another place on the same lines."

."And when you have rubbed out all the places you could along that line, how much would you be worth?" said the blacksmith.

"I call that a new way of keeping accounts," continued Thomas Lincoln, earnestly. "Did you ever see anything of the kind before? No. It's a new and original way. We do a great lot o' thinkin' down here in winter-time, when we haven't much else to do. I'm goin' to put one o' them new systems into the mill."

The meetings of the pioneers at the blacksmith's shop formed a kind of merry-go-round club. One would tell a story in his own odd way, and another would say, "That reminds me," and tell a similar story that was intended to exceed the first in point of humor. One of Thomas Lincoln's favorite stories was " GL-UK ! " or, as he sometimes termed it—

" HOW ABRAHAM WENT TO MILL.

" It was a mighty curi's happenin'," he would say. " I don't know how to account for it—the human mind is a very strange thing. We go to sleep and are lost to the world entirely, and we wake up again. We die, and leave our bodies, and the soul-memory wakes again ; if it have the new life and sense, it wakes again somewhere. We're curi's critters, all on us, and don't know what we are.

" When I first came to Indiana I made a mill of my own—

Abe and I did. 'Twas just a big stone attached to a heavy pole like a well-sweep, so as to pound heavy, up and down, up and down. You can see it now, though it is all out of gear and kilter.

"Then, they built a mill 'way down on the river, and I used to send Abe there on horseback. Took him all day to go and come: used to start early in the mornin', and, as he had to wait his turn at the mill, he didn't use to get back until sundown. Then came Gordon and built his mill almost right here among us—a horse-mill with a windlass, all mighty handy: just hitch the horse to a windlass and pole, and he goes round and round, and never gets nowhere, but he grinds the corn and wheat. Something like me: I go round and round, and never seem to get anywhere, but something will come of it, you may depend.

"Well, one day I says to Abraham:

"'You must hitch up the horse and go to Gordon's to mill. The meal-tub is low, and there's a storm a-brewin'.'

"So Abe hitched up the horse and started. That horse is a mighty steady animal—goes around just like a machine; hasn't any capers nor antics—just as sober as a minister. I should have no more thought of his kickin' than I should have thought of the millstones a-hoppin' out of the hopper. 'Twas a mighty curi's affair.

"Well, Abe went to Gordon's, and his turn come to grind. He hitched the horse to the pole, and said, as always, 'Get up, you old jade!' I always say that, so Abe does. He didn't mean any disrespect to the horse, who always maintained a very respectable-like character up to that day.

"The horse went round and round, round and round, just

4

as steady as clock-work, until the grist was nearly out, and the sound of the grindin' was low, when he began to lag, sleepy-like. Abe he run up behind him, and said, 'Get up, you old jade!' then puckered up his mouth, so, to say 'Gluck.' 'Tis a word I taught him to use. Every one has his own horse-talk.

"He waved his stick, and said 'Gl—'

"Was the horse bewildered? He never did such a thing before. In an instant, like a thunder-clap when the sun was shinin', he h'isted up his heels and kicked Abraham in the head, and knocked him over on the ground, and then stopped as though to think on what he had done.

"The mill-hands ran to Abraham. There the boy lay stretched out on the ground just as though he was dead. They thought he was dead. They got some water, and worked over him a spell. They could see that he breathed, but they thought that every breath would be his last.

"'He's done for this world,' said Gordon. 'He'll never come to his senses again. Thomas Lincoln would be proper sorry.' And so I should have been had Abraham died. Sometimes I think like it was the Evil One that possessed that horse. It don't seem to me that he'd 'a' ever ha' kicked Abe of his own self—right in the head, too. You can see the scar on him now.

"Well, almost an hour passed, when Abe came to himself—consciousness they call it—all at once, in an instant. And what do you think was the first thing he said? Just this—'uk!'

"He finished the word just where he left it when the horse kicked him, and looked around wild-like, and there was the critter standin' still as the mill-stun.' Now, where do you think the soul of Abe was between 'Gl—' and 'uk'? I'd like to have ye tell me that."

A long discussion would follow such a question. Abraham Lincoln himself once discussed the same curious incident with his law-partner Herndon, and made it a subject of the continuance of mental consciousness after death.

It was a warm afternoon. A dark cloud hung in the northern sky, and grew slowly over the arch of serene and sunny blue.

"Goin' to have a storm," said the blacksmith. "Shouldn't wonder if it were a tempest. We generally get a tempest about this time of year, when winter finally breaks up into spring. Well, I declare! there comes Johnnie Kongapod, the Kickapoo Indian from Illinois—he and his dogs."

A tall Indian was seen coming toward the smithy, followed by two dogs. The men watched him as he approached. He was a kind of chief, and had accepted the teachings of the early missionaries. He used to wander about among the new settlements, and was very proud of himself and his own tribe and race. He had an honest heart. He once composed an epitaph for himself, which was well meant but read oddly, and which Abraham Lincoln sometimes used to quote in his professional career :

> " Here lies poor Johnnie Kongapod,
> Have mercy on him, gracious God,
> As he would do if he was God,
> And you were Johnnie Kongapod."

The Indian sat down on the log sill of the blacksmith's shop, and watched the gathering cloud as it slowly shut out the sky.

"Storm," said he. "Lay down, Jack; lay down, Jim."

Jack and Jim were his two dogs. They eyed the flaming forge. One of them seemed tired, and lay down beside his master, but the other made himself troublesome.

"That reminds me," said Dennis Hanks; and he related a curious story of a troublesome dog, perhaps the one which in its evolutions became known as "SYKES'S DOG," though this may be a later New Salem story. It was an odd and a coarse bit of humor. Lincoln himself is represented as telling this, or a like story, to General Grant after the Vicksburg campaign, something as follows:

"'Your enemies were constantly coming to me with their criticisms while the siege was in progress, and they did not cease their ill opinions after the city fell. I thought that the time had come to put an end to this kind of criticism, so one day, when a delegation called to see me and had spent a half-hour, and tried to show me the great mistake that you had made in paroling Pemberton's army, I thought I could get rid of them best by telling the story of Sykes's dog.

"'Have you ever heard the story of Sykes's dog?' I said to the spokesman of the delegation.

"'No.'

"'Well, I must tell it to you. Sykes had a yellow dog that he set great store by; but there were a lot of *small boys* around the village, and the dog became very unpopular among them. His eye was so keen on his master's interests that there arose prejudice against him. The boys counseled how to get rid of him. They finally fixed up a cartridge with a long fuse, and put the cartridge in a piece of meat, and then sat down on a

fence and called the dog, one of them holding the fuse in his
hand. The dog swallowed the meat, cartridge and all, and
stood choking, when one of them touched off the fuse. There
was a loud report. Sykes came out of the house, and found
the ground was strewed with pieces of the dog. He picked up
the biggest piece that he could find—a portion of the back with
the tail still hanging to it—and said :

"' Well, I guess that will never be of much account again—
as a dog.'—' I guess that Pemberton's forces will never amount
to much again—as an army.' By this time the delegation were
looking for their hats."

Like stories followed among the merry foresters. One of
them told another "That reminds me"—how that two boys
had been pursued by a small but vicious dog, and one of them
had caught and held him by the tail while the other ran up a
tree. At last the boy who was holding the dog became tired
and knew not what to do, and cried out:

"Jim !"

"What say?"

"Come down."

"What for ?"

"To help me let go of the dog."

This story, also, whatever may have been the date of it,
President Lincoln used to tell amid the perplexities of the war.
In the darkest times of his life at the White House his mind
used to return for illustration to the stories told at this backwoods smithy, and at the country stores that he afterward came
to visit at Gentryville, Indiana, and New Salem, Illinois.

He delighted in the blacksmith's own stories and jokes.

The man's name was John Baldwin. He was the Homer of Gentryville, as the village portion of this vast unsettled portion of country was called. Dennis Hanks, Abraham Lincoln's cousin, who frequented the smithy, was also a natural story-teller. The stories which had their origin here evolved and grew, and became known in all the rude cabins. Then, when Abraham Lincoln became President, his mind went back to the quaint smithy in the cool, free woods, and to the country stores, and he told these stories all over again. It seemed restful to his mind to wander back to old Indiana and Illinois.

The cloud grew. The air darkened. There was an occasional rustle of wind in the tree-tops.

" It's comin'," said the blacksmith. " Now, Johnnie Konga-pod, you tell us the story. Tell us how Aunt Olive frightened ye when you went to pilot her off to the camp-meetin'."

" No," said Johnnie Kongapod. " It thunders. You must get Aunt Olive to tell you that story."

" When you come to meet her," said the blacksmith to Jasper. " Kongapod would tell it to you, but he's afraid of the cloud. No wonder."

A vivid flash of lightning forked the sky. There followed an appalling crash of thunder, a light wind, a few drops of rain, a darker air, and all was still. The men looked out as the cloud passed over.

" You will have to stay here now," said the blacksmith, " until the cloud has passed. Our stories may seem rather rough to you, edicated as you are over the sea. Tell us a story —a German story. Let me put the old leather chair up here before the fire. If you will tell us one of those German stories, may be I'll tell you how Johnnie Kongapod here and Aunt Olive went to the camp-meetin', and what happened to them on the way."

There was a long silence on the dark air. The blacksmith enlivened the fire, which lit up the shop. Jasper sat down in the leather chair, and said:

" Those Indian dogs remind me of scenes and stories unlike anything here. The life of the dog has its lesson true, and there is nothing truer in this world than the heart of a shepherd's dog. I am a shepherd's dog. I am speaking in parable; you will understand me better by and by.

" Let me tell you the story of ' THE SHEPHERD DOG,' and the story will also tell a story, as do all stories that have a soul; and it is only stories that have souls that live. The true story gathers a soul from the one who tells it, else it is no story at all.

" There once lived on the borders of the Black Forest, Germany, an old couple who were very poor. Their name was Gragstein. The old man kept a shepherd dog that had been faithful to him for many years, and that loved him more than it did its own life, and he came to call him Faithful.

" One day, as the old couple were seated by the fire, Frau Gragstein said:

" ' Hear the wind blow ! There is a hard winter comin', and we have less in our crib than we ever had before. We must live snugger than ever. We shall hardly have enough to keep us two. It will be a long time before the birds sing again. You must be more savin', and begin now. Hear the wind howl. It is a warning.'

" ' What would you have me do ? ' asked Gragstein.

"'There are three of us, and we have hardly store for two.'

"'But what would you have me do with *him?* He is old, and I could not sell him, or give him away.'

"'Then I would take him away into the forest and shoot him, and run and leave him. I know it is hard, but the pinch of poverty is hard, and it has come.'

"'Shoot Faithful! Shoot old Faithful! Take him out into the forest and shoot him! Why, a man's last friends are his God, his mother, and his dog. Would you have me shoot old Faithful? How could I?'

"At the words 'Shoot old Faithful,' the great dog had started up as though he understood. He bent his large eyes on the old woman and whined, then wheeled around once and sank down at his master's feet.

"'He acts as though he understood what you were saying.'

"'No, he don't,' said the old woman. 'You set too much store by the dog, and imagine such things. He's too old to ever be of service to us any more, and he eats a deal. The storm will be over by morning. Hear the showers of the leaves! The fall wind is rending the forest. 'Tis seventy falls that we have seen, and we will not see many more. We must live while we do live, and the dog must be put out of the way. You must take Faithful out into the forest in the morning and kill him.'

"The dog started up again. 'Take Faithful and kill him!' He seemed to comprehend. He looked into his master's face and gave a piteous howl, and went to the door and pawed.

"'Let him go out,' said the old woman. 'What possesses him to go out to-night into the storm? But let him go, and

then I can talk easier about the matter. Did you see his eyes
—as if he knew? He haunts me! Let him go out.'

"The old man opened the door, and the dog disappeared in
the darkness, uttering another piteous howl.

"Then the old couple sat down and talked over the matter,
and Gragstein promised his wife that he would shoot the dog
in the morning.

" 'It is hard,' said the old woman, 'but Providence wills it,
and we must.'

"The wind lulled, and there was heard a wild, pitiful howl
far away in the forest.

" 'What is that?' asked the old woman, starting.

" 'It was Faithful.'

" 'So far away!'

" 'The poor dog acted strange. There it is again, farther
away.'

"The morning came, but the dog did not return. He had
never stayed away from the old hut before. The next day he
did not come, nor the next. The old couple missed him, and
the old man bitterly reproached his wife for what she had ad-
vised him to do.

"Winter came, with pitiless storms and cold, and the old
man would go forth to hunt alone, wishing Faithful was with
him.

" 'It is not safe for me to go alone,' said he. 'I wish that
the dog would come back.'

" 'He will never come back,' said the old woman. 'He is
dead. I can hear him howl nights, far away on the hill. He
haunts me. Every night, when I put out the light, I can hear

him howl out in the forest. 'Tis my tender heart that troubles me. 'Tis a troubled conscience that makes ghosts.'

" The old man tottered away with his gun. It was a cold morning after a snow. The old woman watched him from the frosty window as he disappeared, and muttered :

" ' It is hard to be old and poor. God pity us all ! '

" Night came, but the old man did not return. The old woman was in great distress, and knew not what to do. She set the candle in the window, and went to the door and called a hundred times, and listened, but no answer came. The silent stars filled the sky, and the moon rose over the snow, but no answer came.

" The next morning she alarmed the neighbors, and a company gathered to search for Gragstein. The men followed his tracks into the forests, over a cliff, and down to a stream of running water. They came to some thin ice, which had been weakened by the rush of the current, and there the tracks were lost.

" ' He attempted to cross,' said one, 'and fell in. We will find his body in the spring. I pity his poor old wife. What shall we tell her ?—What was that ? '

" There was heard a pitiful howl on the other side of the stream.

" ' Look ! ' said another.

" Just across the stream a great, lean shepherd dog came out of the snow tents of firs. His voice was weak, but he howled pitifully, as though calling the men.

" ' We must cross the stream ! ' said they all.

" The men made a bridge by pushing logs and fallen trees

across the ice. The dog met them joyfully, and they followed him.

"Under the tents of firs they found Gragstein, ready to perish with cold and hunger.

"'Take me home!' said he. 'I can not last long. Take me home, and call home the dog!'

"'What has happened?' asked the men.

"'I fell in. I called for help, and—the dog came—Faithful. He rescued me, but I was numb. He lay down on me and warmed me, and kept me alive. Faithful! Call home the dog!'

"The men took up the old man and rubbed him, and gave him food. Then they called the dog and gave him food, but he would not eat.

"They returned as fast as they could to the cottage. Frau Gragstein came out to meet them. The dog saw her and stopped and howled, dived into the forest, and disappeared.

"The old man died that night. They buried him in a few days. The old woman was left all alone. The night after the funeral, when she put out the light, she thought that she heard a feeble howl in the still air, and stopped and listened. But she never heard that sound again. The next morning she opened the door and looked out. There, under a bench where his master had often caressed him in the summer evenings of many years, lay the body of old Faithful, dead. He had never ceased to watch the house, and had died true. 'Tis the best thing that we can say of any living creature, man or dog, he was true-hearted.

"Remember the story. It will make you better. The storm is clearing."

The cloud had passed over, leaving behind the blue sky of spring.

"That was an awful good dog to have," said John Hanks. "There are human folks wouldn't 'a' done like that.'"

"I wouldn't," said one of the men. "But here, I declare, comes the old woman. Been out neighborin', and got caught in the storm, and gone back to Pigeon Creek. We won't have to tell that there story about her and the wig, and Johnnie Kongapod here. She'll tell it to you herself, elder—she'll tell it to you herself. She's a master-hand to go to meetin', and sing, and tell stories, she is.—Here, elder—this is Aunt Olive."

The same woman that Jasper had met on his way to Pigeon Creek came into the blacksmith's shop, and held her hands over the warm fire.

"Proper smart rain—spring tempest," said she. "Winter has broke, and we shall have steady weather.—Found your way, elder, didn't you? Well, I'm glad. It's a mighty poor sign for an elder to lose his way. You took my advice, didn't you? —turned to the right and kept straight ahead, and you got there. Well, that's what I tell 'em in conference-meetin's— turn to the right and keep straight ahead, and they'll get there; and then I sing out, and shout, 'I'm bound for the kingdom!' Come over and see me, elder. I'm good to everybody except lazy people.—Abraham Lincoln, what are you lazing around here for?—And Johnnie Kongapod! This ain't any place for men in the spring of the year! I've been neighborin'. I have to do it just to see if folks are doin' as they oughter. There are a great many people who don't do as they oughter in this world. Now I am goin' straight home between the drops."

The woman hurried away and disappeared under the trees.

The cloud broke in two dark, billowy masses, and red sunset, like a sea, spread over the prairie, the light heightening amid glimmerings of pearly rain.

Jasper went back to Pigeon Creek with Abraham.

"Isn't that woman a little queer?" he asked—"a little touched in mind, may be?"

"She does not like me," said the boy; "though most peopeople like me. I seem to have a bent for study, and father thinks that the time I spend in study is wasted, and Aunt Olive calls me lazy, and so do the Crawfords—I don't mean the master. Most people like me, but there are some here that don't think much of me. I am not lazy. I long for learning! I will have it. I learn everything I can from every one, and I do all I can for every one. She calls me lazy, though I have been good to her. They say I am a lively boy, and I like to be thought well of here, and when I hear such things as that it makes me feel down in the mouth. Do you ever feel down in the mouth? I do. I wonder what will become of me? Whatever happens, or folks may say, elder, I mean to make the best of life, and be true to the best that is in me. Something will come of it. Don't you think so, elder?"

They came to Thomas Lincoln's cabin, and the serene face of Mrs. Lincoln met them at the door. A beautiful evening followed the tempest gust, and the Lincolns and the old Tunker sat down to a humble meal.

The mild spring evening that followed drew together

another group of people to the lowly home of Thomas Lincoln. Among them came Aunt Olive, whose missionary work among her neighbors was as untiring as her tongue. And last among the callers there came stealing into the light of the pine fire, like a shadow, the tall, brown form of Johnnie Kongapod, or Konapod.

The pioneer story-telling here began again, and ended in an episode that left a strange, mysterious impression, like a prophecy, on nearly every mind.

" Let me tell you the story of my courtship," said Thomas Lincoln.

" Thomas ! " said a mild, firm voice.

" Oh, don't speak in that tone to me," said the backwoodsman to his wife, who had sought to check him.—" Sally don't like to hear that story, though I do think it is to her credit, if simple honesty is a thing to be respected. Sally is an honest woman. I don't believe that there is an honester creatur' in all these parts, unless it was that Injun that Johnnie Kongapod tells about."

A loud laugh arose, and the dusky figure of Johnnie Kongapod retreated silently back into a deep shadow near the open door. His feelings had been wounded. Young Abraham Lincoln saw the Indian's movement, and he went out and stood in the shadow in silent sympathy.

" Well, good folks, Sally and I used to know each other before I removed from Kentuck' to Indiany. After my first wife died of the milk-fever I was lonesome-like with two young children, and about as poor as I was lonesome, although I did have a little beforehand. Well, Sally was a widder, and used to imagine that she must be lonesome, too; and I thought at last, after that there view of the case had haunted me, that I would just go up to Kentucky and see. Souls kind o' draw each other a long way apart; it goes in the air. So I hitched up and went, and I found Sally at home, and all alone.

" ' Sally,' said I, ' do you remember me ? '

" ' Yes,' said she, ' I remember you well. You are Tommy Linken. What has brought you back to Kentuck' ? '

" ' Well, Sally,' said I, ' my wife is dead.'

" ' Is that so,' said she, all attention.

" ' Yes ; wife died more than a year ago, and a good wife she was ; and I've just come back to look for another.'

" She sat like a statue, Sally did, and never spoke a word. So I said :

" ' Do you like me, Sally Johnson ? '

" ' Yes, Tommy Linken.'

" ' You do ? '

" ' Yes, Tommy Linken, I like you well enough to marry you, but I could never think of such a thing—at least not now.'

" ' Why ? '

" ' Because I'm in debt, and I would never ask a man who had offered to marry me to pay my debts.'

" ' Let me hear all about it,' said I.

" She brought me her account-book from the cupboard. Well, good folks, how much do you suppose Sally owed? Twelve dollars ! It was a heap of money for a woman to owe in those days.

" Well, I put that account-book straight into my pocket and

run. When I came back, all of her debts were paid. I told her so.

"'Will you marry me now?' said I.

"'Yes,' said she.

"And, good folks all, the next morning at nine o'clock we were married, and we packed up all her things and started on our weddin' tour to Indiany, and here we be now. Now that is what I call an honest woman.—Johnnie Kongapod, can you beat that? Come, now, Johnnie Kongapod."

The Indian still stood in the shadow, with young Abraham beside him. He did not answer.

"Johnnie is great on telling stories of good Injuns," said Mr. Lincoln, "and we think that kind o' Injuns have about all gone up to the moonlit huntin'-grounds."

The tall form of the Indian moved into the light of the doorway. His eyes gleamed.

"Thomas Linken, that story that I told you was true."

"What! that an Injun up to Prairie du Chien was condemned to die, and that he asked to go home and see his family all alone, and promised to return on his honor?"

"Yes, Thomas Linken."

"And that they let him go home all alone, and that he spent his night with his family in weepin' and wailin', and returned the next mornin' to be shot?"

"Yes, Thomas Linken."

"And that they shot him?"

"Yes, Thomas Linken."

"Well, Johnnie, if I could believe that, I could believe anything."

"An Injun has honor as well as a white man, Thomas Linken."

"Who taught it to him?"

"His own heart—*here.* The Great Spirit's voice is in every man's heart; his will is born in all men ; his love and care are over us all. You may laugh at my poetry, but the Great Spirit will do by Johnnie Kongapod as he would have Johnnie Kongapod do by him if Johnnie Kongapod held the heavens. That story was true, and I know it to be true, and the Great Spirit knows it to be true. Johnnie Kongapod is an honest Injun."

"Then we have two honest folks here," said Aunt Olive. "Three, mebby—only Tom Linken owes me a dollar and a half. So, Jasper, you see that you have come to good parts. You'll see some strange things in your travels, way off to Rock River. Likely you'll see the Pictured Rocks on the Mississippi—dragons there. Who painted 'em? Or Starved Rock on the Illinois, where a whole tribe died with the water sparklin' under their eyes. But if you ever come across any of the family of that Indian that went home on his honor all alone to see his family, and came back to be shot or hung, you just let us know. I'd like to adopt one of his boys. That would be something to begin a Sunday-school with!"

The company burst into another loud laugh.

Johnnie Kongapod raised his long arm and stood silent. Aunt Olive stepped before him and looked him in the face. The Indian's red face glowed, and he said vehemently: "Woman, that story is true!"

Sally Lincoln arose and rested her hand on the Indian's

5

shoulder. "Johnny Kongapod, I can believe you—Abraham can."

There was a deep silence in the cabin, broken only by Aunt Olive, who arose indignantly and hurried away, and flung back on the mild air the sharp words " *I* don't ! "

The story of the Indian who held honor to be more than life, as related by Johnnie Kongapod, had often been told by the Indians at their camp-fires, and by traveling preachers and missionaries who had faith in Indian character. Among those settlers who held all Indians to be bad it was treated as a joke. Old Jasper asked Johnnie Kongapod many questions about it, and at last laid his hand on the dusky poet's shoulder, and said :

" My brother, I hope that it is true. I believe it, and I honor you for believing it. It is a good heart that believes what is best in life."

How strange all this new life.seemed to Jasper! How unlike the old castles and cottages of Germany, and the cities of the Rhine! And yet, for the tall boy by that cabin fire new America had an opportunity that Germany could offer to no peasant's son. Jasper little thought that that boy, so lively, so rude, so anxious to succeed, was an uncrowned king; yet so it was.

And the legend? A true story has a soul, and a peculiar atmosphere and influence. Jasper saw what the Indian's story was, though he had heard it only indirectly and in outline. It haunted him. He carried it with him into his dreams.

The Home of Abraham Lincoln when in his Tenth Year.

CHAPTER IV.

A BOY WITH A HEART.

PRING came early to the forests and prairies of southern Indiana. In March the maples began to burn, and the tops of the timber to change, and to take on new hues in the high sun and lengthening days. The birds were on the wing, and the banks of the streams were beginning to look like gardens, as indeed Nature's gardens they were.

The woodland ponds were full of turtles or terrapins, and these began to travel about in the warm spring air.

There was a great fireplace in Crawford's school, and, as fuel cost nothing, it was, as we have said, well fed with logs, and was kept almost continually glowing.

It was one of the cruel sports of the boys, at the noonings and recesses of the school, to put coals of fire on the backs of wandering terrapins, and to joke at the struggles of the poor creatures to get to their homes in the ponds.

Abraham Lincoln from a boy had a tender heart, a horror of cruelty and of everything that would cause any creature pain. He was merciful to every one but the unmerciful, and charitable to every one but the uncharitable, and kind to everyone but the unkind. But his nature made war at once on any one who sought to injure another, and he was especially severe on any one who was so mean and cowardly as to disregard the natural rights of a dumb animal or reptile. He had in this respect the sensitiveness of a Burns. All great natures, as biography everywhere attests, have fine instincts—this chivalrous sympathy for the brute creation.

Lincoln's nature was that of a champion for the right. He was a born knight, and, strangely enough, his first battles in life were in defense of the turtles or terrapins. He was a boy of powerful strength, and he used it roughly to maintain his cause. He is said to have once exclaimed that the turtles were his brothers.

The early days of spring in the old forests are full of life. The Sun seems to be calling forth his children. The ponds become margined with green, and new creatures everywhere stir the earth and the waters. Life and matter become, as it were, a new creation, and one can believe anything when he sees how many forms life and matter can assume under the mellowing rays of the sun. The clod becomes a flower; the egg a reptile, fish, or bird. The cunning woodchuck, that looks out of his hole on the awakening earth and blue sky, seems almost to have a sense of the miracle that has been wrought. The boy who throws a stone at him, to drive him back into the earth, seems less sensible of nature than he. It is a pleasing sight to see the little creature, as he stands on his haunches, wondering, and the brain of a young Webster would naturally seek to let such a groundling have all his right of birth.

One day, when the blue spring skies were beginning to glow, Abraham went out to play with his companions. It was one

of his favorite amusements to declaim from a stump. He
would sometimes in this way recite long selections from the
school Reader and Speaker.

He had written a composition at school on the defense of
the rights of dumb animals, and there was one piece in the
school Reader in which he must have found a sympathetic
chord, and which was probably one of those that he loved to
recite. It was written by the sad poet Cowper, and began thus:

> " I would not enter on my list of friends
> (Though graced with polished manners and fine sense,
> Yet wanting sensibility) the man
> Who needlessly sets foot upon a worm.
> An inadvertent step may crush the snail,
> That crawls at evening in the public path;
> But he that has humanity, forewarned,
> Will tread aside, and let the reptile live."

As Abraham and his companions were playing in the warm
sun, one said:

" Make a speech for us, Abe. Hip, hurrah! You've only to
nibble a pen to make poetry, and only to mount a stump to be
a speaker. Now, Abe, speak for the cause of the people, or
anybody's cause. Give it to us strong, and we will do the
cheering."

Abraham mounted a stump in the school-grounds, on
which he had often declaimed before. He felt something
stirring within him, half-fledged wings of his soul, that waited
a cause. He would imitate the few preachers and speakers
that he had heard—even an old Kentucky preacher named
Elkins, whom his own mother had loved, and whose teachings
the good woman had followed in her short and melancholy life.

He began his speech, throwing up his long arms, and lifting at proper periods his coon-skin cap. The scholars cheered as he waxed earnest. In the midst of the speech a turtle came creeping into the grounds.

"Hello!" said one of the boys, "here's another turtle come to school! He, too, has seen the need of learning."

The terrapin crawled along awkwardly toward the house, his head protruding from his shell, and his tail moving to and fro.

At this point young Abraham grew loud and dramatic. The boys raised a shout, and the girls waved their hoods.

In the midst of the enthusiasm, one of the boys seized the turtle. by the tail and slung it around his head, as an evidence of his delight at the ardor of the speaker.

"Throw it at him," said one of the scholars. "Johnson once threw a turtle at him, when he was preachin' to his sister, and it set him to runnin' on like a minister."

Abraham was accustomed to preach to the young members of his family. He would do the preaching, and his sister the weeping; and he sometimes became so much affected by his own discourses that he would weep with her, and they would have a very "moving service," as such a scene was called.

The boy swung the turtle over his head again, and at last let go of it in the air, so as to project it toward Abraham.

The poor reptile fell crushed at the foot of the stump and writhed in pain.

Abraham ceased to speak. He looked down on the pitiful sight of suffering, and his heart yearned over the helpless creature, and then his brain became fired, and his eyes flashed with rage.

" Who did that? " he exclaimed. " Brute! coward! wretch! "
He looked down again, and saw the reptile trying to move away
with its broken shell. His anger turned to pity. He began to
expostulate against all such heartlessness to the animal world
as the scene exhibited before him. The poor turtle again tried
to move away, his head just protruding, looking for some way
out of the world that would deny him his right to the sunshine
and the streams. The young orator saw it all; his lip curled
bitterly, and his words burned. He awakened such a sympathy
for the reptile, and such a feeling of resentment against the
hand which had ruined this little life, that the offender shrank
away from the scene, calling out defiantly :

" Come away, and let him talk. He's only chicken-hearted."

The scholars knew that there was no cowardice in the
heart of Lincoln. They felt the force of the scene. The boys
and girls of Andrew Crawford's school never forgot the pleas
that Abraham used to make for the animals and reptiles of
the woods and streams.

Nearly every youth exhibits his leading trait or characteristic in his school-days.

" The tenor of our whole lives," said an English poet, " is
what we make it in the first five years after we become our
masters "; and a wiser than he has said, " The thing that has
been is, and God requireth the past." Columbus on the quays
of Genoa; Zinzendorf forming among his little companions the
order of the " Grain of Mustard-Seed "; the poets who " lisped
in numbers "; the boy statesmanship of Cromwell; and the early
aspiration of nearly every great leader of mankind—all showed
the current of the life-stream, and it is the current alone that

knows and prophesies the future.   When Abraham Lincoln
fell, the world uncovered its head.   Thrones were sorrowful,
and humanity wept.   Yet his earliest rostrum was a stump,
and his cause the natural rights of the voiceless inhabitants
of the woods and streams.   The heart that throbbed for humanity, and that won the heart of the world, found its first
utterance in defense of the principles of the birds'-nest com-
mandment.   It was a beginning of self-education worthy of the
thought of a Pestalozzi.   It was a prophecy.

As the young advocate of the rights and feelings of the
dumb creation was ending his fiery discourse, the buttonless
Tunker, himself a disciple of Pestalozzi, came into the school-
grounds and read the meaning of the scene.   Jasper saw the
soul of things, and turned always from the outward expressions
of life to the inward motive.   He read the true character of the
boy in buckskin breeches, human heart, and fluent tongue.   He
sat down on the log step of the school-house in silence, and Mr.
Crawford presently came out with a quill pen behind his ear,
and sat down beside him.

"That boy has been teaching what you and I ought first to
teach," said Jasper.

"What is that?" asked Mr. Crawford.

"The heart!   What is head-learning worth, if the heart is
left uneducated?   As Pestalozzi used to say, The soul is the true
end of all education.   Religion itself is a failure, without right
character."

"But you wouldn't teach morals as a science, would you?"

"I would train the heart to feel, and the soul to love to be
just and do right, and make obedience to the moral sense the

habit of life. This can best be done at the school age, and I tell you that this is the highest education. A boy who can spell all the words in the spelling-book, and bound all the countries in the world, and repeat all the dates of history, and yet who could have the heart to crush a turtle, has not been properly educated."

"Then your view is that the end of education is to make a young person do right?"

"No, my good friend, pardon me if I speak plain. The end of education is not to *make* young people do right, but to train the young heart to love to do right; to make right doing the nature and habit of life."

"How would you begin?"

"As that boy has begun. He has made every heart on the ground feel for that broken-shelled turtle. That boy will one day become a leader among men. He has a heart. The head may make friends, but only the heart can hold them. It is the heart-power that serves and rules. The best thing that can be said of any one is, 'He is true-hearted.' I like that boy. He is true-hearted. His first client a turtle, it may not be his last. Train him well. He will honor you some day."

The boys took the turtle to the pond and left him on the bank. Jasper watched them. He then turned to the backwoods teacher, and said:

"That, sir, is the result of right education. First teach character; second, life; third, books. Let education begin in the heart, and everybody made to feel that right makes might."

CHAPTER V.

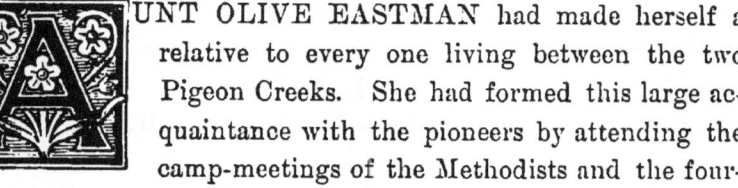UNT OLIVE EASTMAN had made herself a relative to every one living between the two Pigeon Creeks. She had formed this large acquaintance with the pioneers by attending the camp-meetings of the Methodists and the four-days' meetings of the Baptists in southern Indiana, and the school-house meetings everywhere. She was a widow, was full of rude energy and benevolence, had a sharp tongue, a kindly heart, and a measure of good sense. But she was "far from perfect," as she used to very humbly acknowledge in the many pioneer meetings that she attended.

"I make mistakes sometimes," she used to say, "and it is because I am a fallible creatur'."

She was an always busy woman, and the text of her life was "Work," and her practice was in harmony with her teaching.

"Work, work, my friends and brethren," she once said in the log school-house meeting. "Work while the day is passin'. We's all children of the clay. To-day we're here smart as pepper-grass, and to-morrer we're gone like the cucumbers of the ground. Up, and be doin'—up, and be doin'!"

One morning Jasper the Tunker appeared in the clear-

(62)

ing before her cabin. She stood in the door as he appeared,
shading her eyes with one hand and holding a birch broom
in the other. The sunset was flooding the swollen creek in the
distance, and shimmering in the tops of the ancient trees.
Jasper turned to the door.

"This is a lovely morning," said he. "The heavens are
blue above us. I hope that you are well."

"The top of the morning to you! You are a stranger that
I met the other day, I suppose. I've been hopin' you'd come
along and see me. Where do you hail from, anyway? Come
in and tell me all about it."

"I am a German," said Jasper, entering. "I came from
Germany to Pennsylvania, and went from there to Ohio, and
now I am here, as you see."

"How far are you goin'? Or are you just goin' to stop
with us here? Southern Injiany is a goodly country. 'Tis
all land around here, for *millions* of miles, and free as the air.
Perhaps you'll stop with us."

"I am going to Rock Island, on the Mississippi River,
across the prairie of the Illinois."

"Who are you now, may it please you? What's your callin'? Tell me all about it, now. I want to know."

"I am one of the Brethren, as I said. I preach and teach
and cobble. I came here now to ask you if you had any shoe-
making for me to do."

"One of the Tunkers—a Tunker, one o' them. Don't belong to no sect, nor nothin', but just preaches to everybody as
though everybody was alike, and wanders about everywhere, as
if you owned the whole world, like the air. I've seen several

Tunkers in my day. They are becomin' thick in these woods.
Well, I believe such as you mean well—let's be charitable; we
haven't long to live in this troublesome world. I'm fryin'
doughnuts; am just waitin' for the fat to heat. Hope you
didn't think that I was wastin' time, standin' there at the
door? I'll give you some doughnuts as soon as the fat is hot—
fresh ones and good ones, too. I make good doughnuts, just
such as Martha used to make in Jerusalem. I've fried doughnuts for a hundred ministers in my day, and they all say that
my doughnuts are good, whatever they may think of me.
Come in. I'm proper glad to see ye."

Jasper sat down in the kitchen of the cabin. The room
was large, and had a delightful atmosphere of order and neat-
ness. Over the fire swung an immense iron crane, and on the
crane were pot-hooks of various sizes, and on one of these hung
a kettle of bubbling fat.

The table was spread with a large dish of dough, a board
called a kneading-board, a rolling-pin, and a large sheet of
dough which had been rolled into its present form by the rolling-pin, which utensil was white with flour.

"I knew you were comin'," said Aunt Olive. "I dropped
my rollin'-pin this mornin'; it's a sure sign. You said that
you are goin' to Rock Island. The Injuns live there, don't
they? What are ye goin' there for?"

"Black Hawk has invited me. He has promised to let me
have an Indian guide, or runner, who can speak English and
interpret. I'm going to teach among the tribes, the Lord willing, and I want a guide and an interpreter."

"Black Hawk? He was born down in Kaskaskia, the old

Jesuit town, 'way back almost a century ago, wasn't he? Or was it in the Sac village? He was a Pottawattomie, I'm told, and then I've heard he wasn't. Now he's chief of the Sacs and Foxes. I saw him once at a camp-meetin'. His face is black as that pot and these hooks and trummels. How he did skeer me! Do you dare to trust him? Like enough he'll kill ye, some day. I don't trust no Injuns. Where did you stay last night?"

"At Mr. Lincoln's."

"Tom Linken's. Pretty poor accommodations you must have had. They're awful poor folks. Mrs. Linken is a nice woman, but Tom he is shiftless, and he's bringin' up that great tall boy Abe to be lazy, too. That boy is good to his mother, but he all runs to books and larnin', just as some turnips all run to tops. You've seen 'em so, haven't ye?"

"But the boy has got character, and character is everything in this world."

"Did you notice anything *peculiarsome* about him? His cousin, Dennis Hanks, says there's something peculiarsome about him. I never did."

"My good woman, do you believe in gifts?"

"No, I believe in works. I believe in people whose two fists are full of works. Mine are, like the Marthas of old."

Aunt Olive rolled up her sleeves, and began to cut the thin layer of dough with a knife into long strips, which she twisted.

"I'm goin' to make some twisted doughnuts," she said, "seein' you're a preacher and a teacher."

"I think that young lad Lincoln has some inborn gift, and that he will become a leader among men. It is he who is willing to serve that rules, and they who deny themselves the most receive the most from Heaven and men. He has sympathetic wisdom. I can see it. There is something peculiar about him. He is true."

"Oh, don't you talk that way. He's lazy, and he hain't got any calculation, 'n' he'll never amount to shucks, nor nothin'. He's like his father, his head in the air. Somethin' don't come of nothin' in this world; corn don't grow unless you plant it; and when you add nothin' to nothin' it just makes nothin'.

"Well, preacher, you've told me who you are, and now I'll tell ye who I am. But first, let me say, I'll have a pair of shoes. I have my own last. I'll get it for you, and then you can be peggin' away, so as not to lose any time. It is wicked to waste time. 'Work' is my motto. That's what time is made for."

Aunt Olive got her last. The fat was hot by this time— "all sizzlin'," as she said.

"There, preacher, this is the last, and there is the board on which husband used to sew shoes, wax and all. Now I will go to fryin' my doughnuts, and you and I can be workin' away at the same time, and I'll tell ye who I am. Work away—work away!

"I'm a widder. You married? A widower? Well, that ain't nothin' to me. Work away—work away!

"I came from old Hingham, near Boston. You've heard of Boston? That was before I was married. Our family came to Ohio first, then we heard that there was better land in Injiany, and we moved on down the Ohio River and came here. There was only one other family in these parts at that time. That was folks by the name of Eastman. They had a likely smart boy by the name of Polk—Polk Eastman. He grew up and became lonesome. I grew up and became lonesome, and so we concluded that we'd make a home together—here it is—and try to cheer each other. Listenin', be ye? Yes? Well, my doughnuts are fryin' splendid. Work away—work away!

"A curious time we had of it when we went to get married. There was a minister named Penney, who preached in a log church up in Kentuck, and we started one spring mornin', something like this, to get him to marry us. We had but one horse for the journey. I rode on a kind of a second saddle behind Polk, and we started off as happy as prairie plovers. A blue sky was over the timber, and the bushes were all alive with birds, and there were little flowers runnin' everywhere among the new grass and the moss. It seemed as though all the world was for us, and that the Lord was good. I've seen lots of trouble since then. My heart has grown heavy with sorrow. It was then as light as air. Work away!

"Well, the minister Penney lived across the Kentuck, and when we came to the river opposite his place the water was so deep that we couldn't ford it. There had been spring freshets. It was an evenin' in April. There was a large moon, and the weather was mild and beautiful. We could see the pine-knots burnin' in Parson Penney's cabin, so that we knew that he was there, but didn't see him.

"'What are we to do now?' Polk said he. 'We'll have to go home again,' banterin'-like."

"'Holler,' said I. 'Blow the horn!' We had taken a horn along with us. He gave a piercin' blast, and I shouted out, 'Elder Penney! Elder Penney!'

"The door of the cabin over the river opened, and the elder came out and stood there, mysterious-like, in the light of the fire.

"'Who be ye?' he called. 'Hallo! What is wanted?'

"'We're comin' to be married!' shouted Polk. 'Comin' to be married—*married!* How shall we get across the river?'

"'The ford's too deep. Can't be done. Who be ye?' shouted the elder.

"'I'm Polk Eastman—Polk Eastman!' shouted Polk.

"'I'm Olive Pratt—Olive Pratt—Olive!' shouted I.

"'Well, you just stay where you be, and I'll marry you there.'

"So he began shouting at the top of his voice:

"'Do you, Olive Pratt, take that there man, over there on the horse, to be your husband? Hey?'

"I shouted back, 'Yes, sir!'

"'Do you, Polk Eastman, take that there woman, over there on the horse, to be your wife?'

"Polk shouted back, 'Yes, elder, that is what I came for!'

"'Then,' shouted the minister, 'join your right hands.'

"Polk put up his hand over his shoulder, and I took it; and the horse, seein' his advantage, went to nibblin' young sprouts. The elder then shouted:

"'I pronounce you husband and wife. You can go home now, and I'll make a record of it, and my wife shall witness it. Good luck to you! Let us pray.'

"Polk hitched up the reins and the horse stood still. How solemn it seemed! The woods were still and shady. You could hear the water rushing in the timber. The full moon hung in the clear sky over the river, and seemed to lay on the water like a sparkling boat. I was happy then. On our journey home we were chased by a bear. I don't think that the bear would have hurt us, but the scent of him frightened the horse and made him run like a deer.

"Well, we portaged a stream at midnight, just as the moon was going down. We made our curtilage here, and here we lived happy until husband died of a fever. I'm a middlin' good woman. I go to all the meetin's round, and wake 'em up. I've got a powerful tongue, and there isn't a lazy bone in my whole body. Work away—work away! That's the way to get along in the world. Peg away!"

While Aunt Olive had been relating this odd story, John Hanks, a cousin of the Lincolns, had come quietly to the door, and entered and sat down beside the Tunker. He had come to Indiana from Kentucky when Abraham was fourteen years of age, and he made his home with the Lincolns for four years, when he went to Illinois, and was enthused by the wonders of prairie farming. It was Uncle John who gave to Abraham Lincoln the name of rail-splitter. He loved the boy Lincoln, and led his heart away to the rich prairies of Illinois a few years after the present scenes.

"He and I," he once said of Abraham, "worked barefooted, grubbed, plowed, mowed, and cradled together. When we returned from the field, he would snatch a piece of corn-bread, sit down on a chair, with his feet elevated, and read. He read constantly."

This man had heard Aunt Olive—Indiana, or "Injiany," he called her—relate her marriage experiences many times. He

6

was not interested in the old story, but he took a keen delight
in observing the curiosity and surprise that such a novel tale
awakened in the mind of the Tunker.

"This is very extraordinary," said the Tunker, "very extraordinary. We do not have in Germany any stories like that.
I hardly know what my people would say to such a story as
that. This is a very extraordinary country — very extraordinary."

"I can tell you a wedding story worth two o' that," said
Uncle John Hanks. "Why, that ain't nowhere to it.—Now,
Aunt Injiany, you wait, and set still. I'm goin' to tell the
elder about the 'TWO TURKEY-CALLS.'"

The Tunker only said, "This is all very extraordinary."
Uncle John crossed his legs and bent forward his long whisk-
ers, stretched out one arm, and was about to begin, when Aunt
Olive said :

"You wait, John Hanks—you wait. I'm goin' to tell the
elder that there story myself."

John Hanks never disputed with Aunt Olive.

"Well, tell it," said he, and the backwoods woman began :

"'Tis a master-place to get married out here. There's a
great many more men than women in the timber, and the men
get lonesome-like, and no man is a whole man without a wife.
Men ought not to live alone anywhere. They can not out here.
Well, well, the timber is full of wild turkeys, especially in the
fall of the year, but they are hard to shoot. The best way to
get a shot at a turkey is by a turkey-call. You never heard
one, did you? You are not to blame for bein' ignorant. It is
like this—"

Aunt Indiana put her hands to her mouth like a shell, and blew a low, mysterious whistle.

" Well, there came a young settler from Kentucky and took up a claim on Pigeon Creek; and there came a widow from Ohio and took a claim about three miles this side of him, and neither had seen the other. Well, well, one shiny autumn mornin' each of them took in to their heads to go out turkey-huntin', and curiously enough each started along the creek toward each other. The girl's name was Nancy, and the man's name was Albert. Nancy started down the creek, and Albert up the creek, and each had a right good rifle.

" Nancy stood still as soon as she found a hollow place in the timber, put up her hand—*so*—and made a turkey-call—*so*—and listened.

" Albert heard the call in the hollow timber, though he was almost a mile away, and he put up his hands—*so*—and answered—*so*.

" ' A turkey,' said Nancy, said she. ' I wish I had a turkey to cook.'

" ' A turkey,' said Albert, said he. ' I wish I had some one at home to cook a turkey.'

" Then each stole along slowly toward the other, through the hollow timber.

" It was just a lovely mornin'. Jays were callin', and nuts were fallin', and the trees were all yellow and red, and the air put life into you, and made you feel as though you would live forever.

" Well, they both of them stopped again, Nancy and Albert. Nancy she called—*so*—and Albert—*so*.

" ' A turkey, sure,' said Nancy.

" ' A turkey, sure,' said Albert.

" Then each went forward a little, and stopped and called again.

" They were so near each other now that each began to hide behind the thicket, so that neither might scare the turkey.

" Well, each was scootin' along with head bowed—*so*—gun in hand—*so*—one wishin' for a husband and one for a wife, and each for a good fat turkey, when what should each hear but a voice in a tree! It was a very solemn voice, and it said :

" ' Quit ! '

" Each thought there was a scared turkey somewhere, and each became more stealthy and cautious, and there was a long silence.

" At last Nancy she called again—*so*—and Albert he answered her—*so*—and each thought there was a turkey within shootin' distance, and each crept along a little nearer each other.

" At last Nancy saw the bushes stir a few rods in front of her, and raised her gun into position, still hiding in the tangle. Albert discovered a movement in front of him, and he took the same position.

" Nancy was sure she could see something dark before her, and that it must be the turkey in the tangle. She put her finger on the lock of the gun, when a voice in the air said:

" ' Quit ! '

" ' It's a turkey in the tops of the timber,' thought she, ' and he is watchin' me, and warnin' the other turkey.'

" Albert, too, was preparin' to shoot in the tangle when the command from the tree-top came. Each thought it would be well to reconnoiter a little, so as to get a better shot.

"Nancy kneeled down on the moss among the red-berry bushes, and peeked cautiously through an openin' in the tangle. What was that?

"A hat? Yes, it was a hat!

"Albert he peeked through another openin', and his heart sunk like a stone within him. What was that? A bonnet? Yes, it was a bonnet!

"Was ever such a thing as that seen before in the timber? Bears had been seen, and catamounts, and prairie wolves, but a bonnet! He drew back his gun. Just then there came another command from the tree-top:

"'Quit!'

"Now, would you believe it? Well, two guns were discharged at that turkey in the tree, and it came tumblin' down, a twenty-pounder, dead as a stone.

"Nancy run toward it. Albert run towards it.

"'It's yourn,' said Nancy.

"'It's yourn,' said Albert.

"Each looked at the other.

"Nancy looked real pink and pretty, and Albert he looked real noble and handsome-like.

"'I'm thinkin',' said Albert, 'it kind o' belongs to both of us.'

"So I think, too,' said Nancy, said she. 'Come over to my cabin and I'll cook it for ye. I'm an honest girl, I am.'

"The two went along as chipper as two squirrels. The creek looked really pretty to 'em, and the prairie was all a-glitter with frost, and the sky was all pleasant-like, and you know the rest. There, now. They're livin' there yet. Just like poetry—wasn't it, now?"

"Very extraordinary," said the Tunker, "very! I never read a novel like that. Very extraordinary!"

A tall, lank, wiry boy came up to the door.

"Abe, I do declare!" said Aunt Olive. "Come in. I'm makin' doughnuts, and you sha'n't have one of them. I make Scriptur' doughnuts, and the Scriptur' says if a man spends his time porin' over books, of which there is no end, neither shall he eat, or somethin' like that—now don't it, elder?—But seein' it's you, Abe, and you are a pretty good boy, after all, when people are in trouble, and sick and such, I'll make you an elephant. There ain't any elephants in Injiany."

Aunt Olive cut a piece of doughnut dough in the shape of a picture-book elephant and tossed it into the fat. It swelled up to enormous proportions, and when she scooped it out with a ladle it was, for a doughnut, an elephant indeed.

"Now, Abe, there's your elephant.—And, elder, here's a whole pan full of twisted doughnuts. You said that you were goin' to meet Black Hawk. Where does he live? Tell us all about him."

"I will do so, my good woman," said Jasper. "I want you to be interested in my Indian missions. When I come this way again, I shall be likely to bring with me an Indian guide, an uncommon boy, I am told. You shall hear my story."

CHAPTER VI.

JASPER GIVES AN ACCOUNT OF HIS VISIT TO BLACK HAWK.—AUNT INDIANA'S WIG.

UNT INDIANA, Jasper, John Hanks, and young Abraham Lincoln sat between the dying logs in the great fireplace and the open door. The company was after a little time increased for Thomas Lincoln came slowly into the clearing, and saying, "How-dy?" and "The top of the day to ye all," sat down in the sunshine on the log step; and soon after came Dennis Hanks and dropped down on a puncheon.

"I think that you are misled," said Jasper, "when you say that Black Hawk was born at Kaskaskia. If I remember rightly, he said to me: 'I was born in this Sac village. Here I spent my youth; my fathers' graves are here, and the graves of my children, and here where I was born I wish to die.' Rock Island, as the northern islands, rapids, and bluffs of the Mississippi are called, is a very beautiful place. Black Hawk clings to the spot as to his life. 'I love to look down,' he said, 'upon the big rivers, shady groves, and green prairies from the graves of my fathers,' and I do not wonder at this feeling. His blood is the same and his rights are the same as any other king, and he loves Nature and has a heart.

"It is my calling to teach and preach among the Indians

and new towns of Illinois. This call came to me in Pennsylvania. God willed it, and I had no will but to obey. I heard
the Voice within, just as I heard it in Germany on the Rhine.
There it said, ' Go to America.' In Pennsylvania it said, ' Go
to the Illinois.'

"I went. I have walked all the way, teaching and preaching in the log school-houses. I sowed the good seed, and left
the harvest to the heavens. Why should I be anxious in regard
to the result? I walk by faith, and I know what the result will
be in God's good time, without seeking for it. Why should I
stop to number the people? I know.

"I wanted an Indian guide and interpreter, and the inward
Voice told me to go to Black Hawk and secure one from the
chief himself. So I went to the bluffs of the Mississippi, and
told Black Hawk all my heart, and he let me preach in his
lodges, and I made some strong winter shoes for him, and tried
to teach the children by signs. So I was fed by the ravens of
the air. He had no interpreter or runner such as he would
trust to go with me; but he told me if I would return in the
May moon, he would provide me one. He said that it would be
a boy by the name of Waubeno, whose father was a noble
warrior and had had a strange and mysterious history. The
boy was then traveling with an old uncle by the name of Main-
Pogue. These names sound strange to German ears: Waubeno
and Main-Pogue! I promised to return in May. I am on my
way.

"If I get the boy Waubeno—and the Voice within tells
me that I will—I intend to travel a circuit, round and round,
round and round, teaching and preaching. I can see my circuit

now in my mind. This is the map of it: From Rock Island to
Fort Dearborn (Chicago); from Fort Dearborn to the Ohio,
which will bring me here again; and from the Ohio to the
Mississippi, and back to Rock Island, and so round and round,
round and round. Do you see?"

The homely travels of Thomas Lincoln and the limited
geography of Andrew Crawford had not prepared Jasper's
audience to see even this small circuit very distinctly. Thomas
Lincoln, like the dwellers in the Scandinavian valleys, doubt-
less believed that there "are people beyond the mountains,
also," but he knew little of the world outside of Kentucky and
Illinois. Mrs. Eastman was quite intelligent in regard to New
England and the Middle States, but the West to her mind was
simply land—"oceans of it," as she expressed herself—"where
every one was at liberty to choose without infringin' upon
anybody."

"Don't you ever stop to build up churches?" said Mrs.
Eastman to Jasper.

"No."

"You just baptize 'em, and let 'em run. That's what I can't
understand. I can't get at it. What are you really doin'?
Now, say?"

"I am the Voice in the wilderness, preparing the way."

"No family name?"

"No. What have I to do with a name?"

"No money?"

"Only what I earn."

"That's queerer yet. Well, you are just the man to preach
to the uninhabited places of the earth. Tell us more about

Black Hawk. I want to hear of him, although we all are wastin' a pile of time when we all ought to be to work. Tell us about Black Hawk, and then we'll all up and be doin'. My fire is goin' out now."

"He's a revengeful critter, that Black Hawk," said Thomas Lincoln, "and you had better be pretty wary of him. You don't know Indians. He's a flint full of fire, so people say that come to the smithy. You look out."

"He has had his wrongs," said Jasper, "and he has been led by his animal nature to try to avenge them. Had he listened to the higher teachings of the soul, it might have been different. We should teach him."

"What was it that set him against white folks?" asked Mrs. Eastman.

"He told me the whole story," said Jasper, "and it made my heart bleed for him. He's a child of Nature, and has a great soul, but it needs a teacher. The Indians need teachers. I am sent to teach in the wilderness, and to be fed by the birds of the air. I am sent from over the sea. But listen to the tale of Black Hawk. You complain of your wrongs, don't you? Why should not he?

"Years ago Black Hawk had an old friend whom he dearly loved, for the friendships of Indians are ardent and noble. That friend had a boy, and Black Hawk loved this boy and adopted him as his own, and became as a father to him, and taught him to hunt and to go to war. When Black Hawk joined the British he wished to take this boy with him to Canada; but his own father said that he needed him to care for him in his old age, to fish and to hunt for him. He said, moreover, that he did not like his boy to fight against the Americans, who had always treated him kindly. So Black Hawk left the boy with his old father.

"On his return to Rock River and the bluffs of the Mississippi, after the war on the lakes, and as he was approaching his own town in the sunset, he chanced to notice a column of white smoke curling from a hollow in one of the bluffs. He stepped aside to see what was there. As he looked over the bluff he saw a fire, and an aged Indian sitting alone on a prayer-mat before it, as though humbling himself before the Great Spirit. He went down to the place and found that the man was his old friend.

"'How came you here?' asked Black Hawk. But, although the old Indian's lip moved, he received no answer.

"'What has happened?' asked Black Hawk.

"There was a pitiful look in the old man's eyes, but this was his only reply. The old Indian seemed scarcely alive. Black Hawk brought some water to him. It revived him. His consciousness and memory seemed to return. He looked up. With staring eyes he said, suddenly:

"'Thou art Black Hawk! O Black Hawk, Black Hawk, my old friend, he is gone!'

"'Who has gone?'

"'The life of my heart is gone, he whom you used to love. Gone, like a maple-leaf. Gone! Listen, O Black Hawk, listen.

"'After you went away to fight for the British, I came down the river at the request of the pale-faces to winter there. When I arrived I found that the white people had built a fort

there. I went to the fort with my son to tell the people that
we were friendly."

" ' The white war-chief received me kindly, and told us that
we might hunt on this side of the Mississippi, and that he
would protect us. So we made our camp there. We lived
happy, and we loved to talk of you, O Black Hawk !

" ' We were there two moons, when my boy went to hunt
one day, unsuspicious of any danger. We thought the white
man spoke true. Night came, and he did not return. I could
not sleep that night. In the morning I sent out the old woman
to the near lodges to give an alarm, and say that my boy must
be sought.

" ' There was a band formed to hunt for him. Snow was
on the ground, and they found his tracks—my boy's tracks.
They followed them, and saw that he had been pursuing a deer
to the river. They came upon the deer, which he had killed
and left hanging on the branch of a tree. It was as he had
left it.

" ' But here they found the tracks of the white man. The
pale-faces had been there, and had taken our boy prisoner.
They followed the tracks and they found him. O Black Hawk !
he was dead—my boy ! The white men had murdered him for
killing the deer near the fort; and the land was ours. His
face was all shot to pieces. His body was stabbed through and
through, and they had torn the hair from his head. They had
tied his hands behind him before they murdered him. Black
Hawk, my heart is dead. What do the hawks in the sky say ? '

" The old Indian fell into a stupor, from which he soon ex-
pired. Black Hawk watched over his body during the night,

and the next day he buried it upon the bluff. It was at that
grave that Black Hawk listened to the hawks in the sky, and
vowed vengeance against the white people forever, and summoned his warriors for slaughter."

"He's a hard Indian," said Thomas Lincoln. "Don't you
trust Black Hawk. You don't know him."

"Hard? Yes, but did not your brother Mordecai make the
same vow and follow the same course after the murder of your
father by the Indians? A slayer of man is a slayer of man
whoever and wherever he may be. May the gospel bring the
day when the shedding of human blood will cease! But the
times are still evil. The world waits still for the manifestation
of the sons of God; as of old it waits. I have given all I am to
the teaching of the gospel of peace. The Indians need it; *you*
need it, all of you. You do the same things that the savages
do."

"Just hear him!" said Aunt Indiana.—"Who are you
preachin' to, elder? Callin' us savages! I'm an exhorter myself, I'd like to have you know. I could exhort *you*. Savages?
We know Indians here better than you do. You wait."

"Let me tell you a story now," said Thomas Lincoln.

"Of course you will," said Aunt Indiana. "Thomas Lincoln never heard a story told without telling another one to
match it; and Abe, here, is just like him. The thing that has
been, is, as the Scriptur' says."

AN ASTONISHED INDIAN.

"Well," said Thomas Lincoln, "I hain't no faith at all, elder,
in Injuns. I once knew of a woman in Kentuck, in my father's

day, who knew enough for 'em, and the way that she cleared 'em out showed an amazin' amount of spirit. Women was women in Daniel Boone's time, in old Kentuck. The Injuns found 'em up and doin', and they learned to sidle away pretty rapid-like when they met a sun-bonnet.

"Well, as I was sayin', this was in my father's time. The Injuns were prowlin' about pretty plenty then, and one day one of 'em came, all feathers and paint, and whoops and prancin's, to a house owned by a Mr. Daviess, and found that the man of the house was gone.

"But the wimmin-folks were at home—Mrs. Daviess and the children. Well, the Injun came on like a champion, swingin' his tommyhawk and liftin' his heels high. The only weapon that the good woman had was a bottle of whisky.

"Well, whisky is a good weapon sometimes—there's many a man that has found it a slow gunpowder. Well, this woman, as I was sayin', had her wits about her. What do you think that she did?

"Well, she just brought out the whisky-bottle, and held it up before him—*so*. It made his eyes sparkle, you may be sure of that!

"'Fire-water,' said she, 'mighty temptin'.

"'Ugh!' said the Indian, all humps and antics and eyes.

"Ugh! Did you ever hear an Injun say that—'Ugh?'

"'Have some?' said she.

"Have some? Of course he did.

"She got a glass and put it on the table, and then she uncorked the bottle and *handed* it to him to pour out the whisky. He lost his wits at once.

" He set down his gun to pour out a dram, all giddy, when Mrs. Daviess seized the shooter and lifted it up quick as a flash and pointed to his head.

" ' Set that down, or I'll fire! Set that bottle down ! '

" The poor Injun's jaw dropped. He set down the bottle, looked wild, and begged for his life.

" ' Set still,' said she; and he looked at the whisky-bottle and then slunk all up in a heap and remained silent as a dead man until Mr. Daviess came home, when he was allowed to crawl away into the forest. He gave one parting look at the bottle, but he never wanted to see a white woman again, I'll be bound."

" You ridicule the Indian for his love of whisky," said the Tunker, " but who taught him to love it? Woe unto the world because of offenses."

" Hello!" said John Hanks, starting up. " Here comes Johnnie Kongapod again, from the Illinois. I like to see any one from Illinois, even if he is an Indian. I'm goin' there myself some day. I've a great opinion of that there prairie country—hain't you, elder?"

" Yes, it is a garden of wild flowers that seems as wide as the sky. It can all be turned into green, and it will be some day."

Aunt Indiana greeted the Indian civilly, and the Tunker held out his hand to him.

" Elder," said Aunt Indiana, " I must tell you one of my own experiences, now that Johnnie Kongapod has come—the one that they bantered me about over to the smithy. Johnnie and I are old friends. I used to be a kind of travelin' preacher myself; I am now—I go to camp-meetin's, and I always do my duty.

"Well, a few years ago, durin' the Injun troubles, there was goin' to be a camp-meetin' on the Illinois side, and I wanted to go. Now, Johnnie Kongapod is a good Injun, and I arranged with him that he should go with me.

"You didn't know that I wore a wig, did ye, elder? No? Well, most people don't. I have had to wear a wig ever since I had the scarlet fever, when I was a girl. I'm kind o' ashamed to tell of it, I've so much nateral pride, but have to speak of it when I tell this story.

"Johnnie Kongapod never saw a wig before I showed him mine, and I never showed it to him until I had to.

"Well, he came over from Illinois, and we started off together to the camp-meetin'. It was a lovely time on the prairies. The grass was all ripe and wavin', and the creeks were all alive with ducks, and there were prairie chickens everywhere. I felt very brisk and chipper.

"We had two smart horses, and we cantered along. I sang hymns, and sort o' preached to Johnnie, when all at once we saw a shadow on the prairie like a cloud, and who should come ridin' up but three Injuns! I was terribly frightened. I could see that they were hostile Injuns—Sacs, from Black Hawk. One of them swung his tommyhawk in the air, and made signs that he was goin' to scalp me. Johnnie began to beg for me, and I thought that my last hour had come.

"The Injun wheeled his pony, rode away, then turned and came dashin' towards me, with tommyhawk lifted.

"'Me scalp!' said he, as he dashed by me. Then he turned his horse and came plungin' towards me again.

"Elder, what do you think I did? I snatched off my bonnet and threw it upon the ground. Then I grabbed my wig, held it up in the air, and when the Injun came rushin' by I held it out to him.

"'There it is,' said I.

"Well—would you believe it?—that Injun gave one glance at it, and put spurs to his horse, and he never stopped runnin' till he was out of sight. The two other Injuns took one look at my wig as I held it out in my hand.

"'Scalped herself!' said one.

"'Took her head off!' said the other. 'She conjur's!'

"They spurred their horses and flew over the prairie like the wind. And—and—must I say it?—Johnnie Kongapod— he ran too; and so I put on my wig, picked up my sun-bonnet, and turned and came home again.

"There are some doughnuts, Johnnie Kongapod, if you did desert me.

"Elder, this is a strange country. And don't you believe any stories about honest Injuns that the law condemns, and that go home to see their families overnight and return again; you will travel a long way, elder, before you find any people of that kind, Injuns or white folks. I know. I haven't lived fifty years in this troublesome world for nothin'. People who live up in the air, as you do, elder, have to come down. I'm sorry. You mean well!"

Johnnie Kongapod arose, lifted his brown arm silently, and, bending his earnest face on Jasper, said:

7

" *That* story is true.   You will know.   Time tells the truth.
Wait!"

"Return in the morning to be shot!" said Aunt Olive.
"Injuns don't do that way here.   When I started for Injiany
I was told of a mother-in-law who was so good that all her
daughters' husbands asked her to come and live with them.
They said she moved to Injiany.   Now, I have traveled about
this State to all the camp-meetin's, and I never found her
anywhere.   Stands to reason that no such story as that is true.
You'll have to travel a long way, elder, before you find any
people of that kind in these parts."

Whom was Jasper to believe—the confident Indian or the
pioneers?

CHAPTER VII.

THE EXAMINATION AT CRAWFORD'S SCHOOL.

XAMINATION-DAY is an important time in country schools, and it excited more interest seventy years ago than now. Andrew Crawford was always ambitious that this day should do credit to his faithful work, and his pupils caught his inspiration.

There were great preparations for the examination at Crawford's this spring. The appearance of the German schoolmaster in the place who could read Latin was an event. Years after, when the pure gold of fame was no longer a glimmering vision or a current of fate, but a wonderful fact, Abraham Lincoln wrote of such visits as Jasper's in the settlement a curious sentence in an odd hand in an autobiography, which we reproduce here:

If a stranger supposed to understand latin, happened to sojourn in the neighborhood, he was looked upon as a wizzard—

With such a "wizard" as Jasper in the settlement, who would certainly attend the examination, it is no wonder that this special event excited the greatest interest in all the cabins between the two Pigeon Creeks of southern Indiana.

"May we decorate the school-house?" asked a girl of Mr. Crawford, before the appointed day. "May we decorate the school-house out of the woods?"

"I am chiefly desirous that you should decorate your minds out of the spelling-book," said Mr. Crawford; "but it is a commendable thing to have an eye to beauty, and to desire to present a good appearance. Yes, you may decorate the house out of the woods."

The timber was green in places with a vine called creeping Jenney, and laurels whose leaves were almost as green and waxy as those of the Southern magnolia. The creeping Jenney could be entwined with the laurel-leaves in such a way as to form long festoons. The boys and girls spent the mornings and recesses for several days in gathering Jenney, and in twining the vines with the laurel and making decorative festoons.

They hung these festoons about the wooden walls of the low building and over the door. Out of the tufts of boxberry leaves and plums they made the word "Welcome," which they hung over the door. They covered the rude chimney with pine-boughs, and in so doing filled the room with a resinous odor. They also covered the roof with boughs of evergreen.

The spelling-book was not neglected in the preparations of the eventful week. There was to be a spelling-match on the day, and, although it was already felt that Abraham Lincoln would easily win, there was hard study on the part of all.

One afternoon, after school, in the midst of these heroic

preparations, a party of the scholars were passing along the path in the timber. A dispute arose between two boys in regard to the spelling of a word.

" I spelled it just as Crawford did," said one.

" No, you didn't. Crawford spelled it with a *i*."

" He spelled it with a *y*, and that is just the way I spelled it."

" He didn't, now, I know! I heard Crawford spell it himself."

" He did!"

" Do you mean to tell me that I lie?"

" You do—it don't need telling."

" I won't be called a liar by anybody. I'll make you ache for that!"

" We'll see about that. You may ache yourself before this thing is settled. I've got fists as well as you, and I will not take such words as that from anybody. Come on!"

The two backwoods knights rushed toward each other with a wounded sense of honor in their hearts and with uplifted arms.

Suddenly a form like a giant passed between them. It took one boy under one of its arms and the other under the other, and strode down the timber.

" He called me a liar," said one of the boys. " I won't stand that from any *man*."

" He *sassed* me," said the other, " and I won't stand any sassin', not while my fists are alive."

" *You* wouldn't be called a liar," said the first.

" Nor take any sassin'," said the second.

The tall form in blue-jean shirt and leather breeches strode on, with the two boys under its arms.

"I beg!" at last said one of the boys.

"I beg!" said the other.

"Then I'll let you go, and we'll all be friends again!"

"Yes, Abraham, I'll give in, if he will."

"I will. Let me go."

The tall form dropped the two boys, and soon all was peace in the April-like air.

"Abraham Lincoln will never allow any quarrels in our school," said another boy. "Where he is there has to be peace. It wouldn't be fair for him to use his strength so, only he's always right; and when strength is right it is all for the best."

The boy had a rather clear perception of the true principles of human government. A will to do right and the power to enforce it, make nations great as well as character powerful.

The eventful day came, with bluebirds in the glimmering timber, and a blue sky over all. People came from a distance to attend the examination, and were surprised to find the school-house changed into a green bower.

The afternoon session had been assigned to receiving company, and the pupils awaited the guests with trembling expectation. It was a warm day, and the oiled paper that served for panes of glass in the windows had been pushed aside to admit the air and make an outlook, and the door had been left open. The first to arrive was Jasper. The school saw him coming; but he looked so kindly, benevolent, and patriarchal, that the boys and girls did not stand greatly in awe of him. They seemed to feel instinctively that he was their friend and was

ABRAHAM AS A PEACE-MAKER.

with them. But a different feeling came over them when 'Squire Gentry, of Gentryville, came cantering on a horse that looked like a war-charger. 'Squire Gentry was a great man in those parts, and filled a continental space in their young minds. The faces of all the scholars were turned silently and deferently to their books when the 'Squire banged with his whip-handle on the door. Aunt Olive was next seen coming down the timber. She was dressed in a manner to cause solicitude and trepidation. She wore knit mits, had a lofty poke bonnet, and a "checkered" gown gay enough for a valance, and, although it was yet very early spring, she carried a parasol over her head. There was deep interest in the books as her form also darkened the festooned door.

Then the pupils breathed freer. But only for a moment. Sarah Lincoln, Abraham's sister, looked out of the window, and beheld a sight which she was not slow to communicate.

"Abe," she whispered, "look there!"

"Blue-nose Crawford," whispered the tall boy, "as I live!"

In a few moments the school was all eyes and mouths. Blue-nose Crawford bore the reputation of being a very hard taskmaster, and of holding to the view that severe discipline was one of the virtues that wisdom ought to visit upon the youth. He once lent to Abraham Lincoln Weems's "Life of Washington." The boy read it with absorbing interest, but there came a driving storm, and the rain ran in the night through the walls of the log-cabin and wet and warped the cover of the book. Blue-nose Crawford charged young Lincoln seventy-five cents for the damage done to the book. "Abe," as he was called, worked three days, at twenty-five cents a day, pulling fodder, to pay the fine. He said, long after this hard incident, that he did his work well, and that, although his feelings were injured, he did not leave so much as a strip of fodder in the field.

"The class in reading may take their places," said Andrew Crawford.

It was a tall class, and it was provided with leather-covered English Readers. One of the best readers in the class was a Miss Roby, a girl of some fifteen years of age, whom young Lincoln greatly liked, and whom he had once helped at a spelling match, by putting his finger on his eye (i) when she had spelled *defied* with a y. This girl read a selection with real pathos.

"That gal reads well," said Blue-nose Crawford, or Josiah Crawford, as he should be called. "She ought to keep school. We're goin' to need teachers in Indiana. People are comin' fast."

Miss Roby colored. She had indeed won a triumph of which every pupil of Spencer County might be proud.

"Now, Nathaniel, let's hear you read. You're a strappin' feller, and you ought not to be outread by a gal."

Nathaniel raised his book so as to hide his face, like one near-sighted. He spread his legs apart, and stood like a drum-major awaiting a word of command.

"You may read Section V in poetry," said Mr. Crawford, the teacher. "Verses supposed to be written by Alexander Selkirk. Speak up loud, and mind your pauses."

He did.

"I am monarch of all I survey," he began, in a tone of

vocal thunder. Then he made a pause, a very long one. Josiah Crawford turned around in great surprise; and Aunt Olive planted the chair in which she had been sitting at a different angle, so that she could scrutinize the reader.

The monarch of all he surveyed, which in the case of the boy was only one page of the English Reader, was diligently spelling out the next line, which he proceeded to pronounce like one long word with surprising velocity:

" My-right-there-is-none-to-dispute."

There was another pause.

" Hold down your book," said the master.

" Yes, hold down your book," said Josiah Crawford. " What do ye cover yer face for? There's nuthin' to be ashamed of. Now try again."

Nathaniel lowered the book and revealed the singular struggle that was going on in his mind. He had to spell out the words to himself, and in doing so his face was full of the most distressing grimaces. He unconsciously lifted his eyebrows, squinted his eyes, and drew his mouth hither and thither.

" From the cen-t-e-r, center; center, all round *to* the sea,

I am lord of the f-o-w-l *and*-the-brute."

The last line came to a sudden conclusion, and was followed by a very long pause.

" Go on," said Andrew Crawford, the master.

" Yes, go on," said Josiah. " At the rate you're goin' now you won't get through by candle-light."

Nathaniel lifted his eyebrows and uttered a curiously exciting—

" O."—

"That boy'll have a fit," said Aunt Olive. "Don't let him read any more, for massy sake!"

"O— What's that word, master? S-o-l-i-t-u-d-e, so-li-tu-de. O—So-li-tu-de."

"O Solitude, where are the charms?" read Mr. Andrew Crawford,

"That sages have seen in thy face?
Better dwell in the midst of alarms
Than reign in this horrible place."

Nathaniel followed the master like a race-horse. He went on smoothly until he came to "this horrible place," when his face assumed a startled expression, like one who had met with an apparition. He began to spell out *horrible*, h-o-r-, hor— there's your hor, *hor*; r-i-b-, there's your *rib*, horrib—"

"Don't let that boy read any more," said Aunt Olive.

Nathaniel dropped his book by his side, and cast a far-away glance into the timber.

"I guess I ain't much of a reader," he remarked, dryly.

"Stop, sir!" said the master.

Poor Nathaniel! Once, in attempting to read a Bible story, he read, "And he smote the Hittite that he died"—"And he-smote him Hi-ti-ti-ty, that he *did*," with great emphasis and brief self-congratulation.

In wonderful contrast to Nathaniel's efforts was the reading in concert by the whole class. Here was shown fine preparation for a forest school. The reading of verses, in which "sound corresponded to the signification," was smoothly, musically, and admirably done, and we give some of these curious exercises here:

Felling trees in a wood.

Loud sounds the axe, redoubling strokes on strokes;
On all sides round the forest hurls her oaks
Headlong. Deep echoing groan the thickets brown,
Then rustling, crackling, crashing, thunder down.

Sounds of a bow-string.

The string let fly
Twanged short and sharp, like the shrill swallow's cry.

The pheasant.

See! from the brake the whirring pheasant springs,
And mounts exulting on triumphant wings.

Scylla and Charybdis.

Dire Scylla there a scene of horror forms,
And here Charybdis fills the deep with storms.
When the tide rushes from her rumbling caves,
The rough rock roars; tumultuous boil the waves.

Boisterous and gentle sounds.

Two craggy rocks projecting to the main,
The roaring winds' tempestuous rage restrain:
Within, the waves in softer murmurs glide,
And ships secure without their hawsers ride.

Laborious and impetuous motion.

With many a weary step, and many a groan,
Up the high hill he heaves a huge round stone:
The huge round stone resulting with a bound,
Thunders impetuous down, and smokes along the ground.

Regular and slow movement.

First march the heavy mules securely slow;
O'er hills, o'er dales, o'er crags, o'er rocks they go.

Motion slow and difficult.

A needless Alexandrine ends the song,
That, like a wounded snake, drags its slow length along.

A rock torn from the brow of a mountain.

Still gath'ring force, it smokes. and urged amain,
Whirls, leaps, and thunders down impetuous to the plain.

Extent and violence of the waves.

The waves behind impel the waves before,
Wide-rolling, foaming high, and tumbling to the shore.

Pensive numbers.

In these deep solitudes and awful cells,
Where heav'nly pensive contemplation dwells,
And ever-musing melancholy reigns.

Battle.

Arms on armor clashing brayed
Horrible discord ; and the madding wheels
Of brazen fury raged.

Sound imitating reluctance.

For who, to dumb forgetfulness a prey,
This pleasing anxious being e'er resigned ;
Left the warm precincts of the cheerful day,
Nor cast one longing, ling'ring look behind?

A spelling exercise followed, in which the pupils spelled for
places, or for the head. Abraham Lincoln stood at the head
of the class. He was regarded as the best speller in Spencer
County. He is noted to have soon exhausted all that the three
teachers whom he found there could teach him. Once, in after
years, when he was asked how he came to know so much, he

answered, " By a willingness to learn of every one who could teach me anything."

" Abraham," said Master Crawford, " you have maintained your place at the head of the class during the winter. You may take your place now at the foot of the class, and try again."

The spelling for turns, or for the head, followed the method of the old Webster's " Speller," that was once so popular in country schools :

ail, to be in trouble.	al-tar, a place for offerings.
ale, malt liquor.	al-ter, to change.
air, the atmosphere.	ant, a little insect.
heir, one who inherits.	aunt, a sister to a parent.
all, the whole.	ark, a vessel.
awl, an instrument.	arc, part of a circle.*

All went correctly and smoothly, to the delight and satisfaction of Josiah Crawford and Aunt Olive, until the word *drachm* was reached, when all the class failed except Abraham Lincoln, who easily passed up to the head again.

The writing-books, or copy-books, were next shown to the visitors. The writing had been done on puncheon-desks with home made ink. Abraham Lincoln's copy-book showed the same characteristic hand that signed the Emancipation Proclamation. In one corner of a certain page he had written an odd bit of verse in which one may read a common experience in the struggles of life after what is better and higher. Emerson said, " A high aim is curative." Poor backwoods Abe seemed to have the same impression, but he did not write it down in an Emersonian way, but in this odd rhyme :

"Abraham Lincoln,
    His hand and pen,
    He will be good,
    But God knows when."

The exercises ended with a grand dialogue translated from
Fénelon between Dionysius, Pythias, and Damon, in which
fidelity in friendship was commended. After this, each of the
visitors, Aunt Olive included, was asked to make a "few remarks." Aunt Olive's remarks were "few," but to the point:

"Children, you have read well, and spelled well, and are good
arithme*tickers*, but you ain't sot still. There!"

Josiah Crawford thought the progress of the school had
been excellent, but that more of the rod had been needed.

(Where had all the green bushes gone in the clearing, but
to purposes of discipline?)

Then good Brother Jasper was asked to speak. The
"wizard" who could speak Latin arose. The pupils could see
his great heart under his face. It shone through. His fine
German culture did not lead him away from the solid merits
of the forest school.

"There are purposes in life that we can not see," he began,
"but the secret comes to those who listen to the beating of the
human heart, and at the doors of heaven. Spirits whisper, as
it were. The soul, a great right intention, is here; and there is
a conscience here which is power; and here, for aught we can
say, may be some young Servius Tullius of this wide republic."

Servius Tullius? Would any one but he have dreamed that
the citizens of Rome would one day delight to honor an
ungainly pupil of that forest school?

One day there came to Washington a present to the Liberator of the American Republic. It looked as follows, and bore the following inscription :

" To Abraham Lincoln, President, for the second time, of the American Republic, citizens of Rome present this stone, from the wall of Servius Tullius, by which the memory of each of those brave assertors of liberty may be associated.   Anno 1865."

It is said that the modest President shrank from receiving such a compliment as that.   It was too much.   He hid away the stone in a storeroom of the capital, in the basement of the White House.   It now constitutes a part of his monument, being one of the most impressive relics in the Memorial Hall of that structure.   It is twenty-four hundred years old, and it traveled across the world to the prairies of Illinois, a tribute from the first advocate of the rights of the people to the latest defender of all that is sacred to the human soul.

CHAPTER VIII.

THE PARABLE PREACHES IN THE WILDERNESS.

HE house in which young Abraham Lincoln attended church was simple and curious, as were the old forest Baptist preachers who conducted the services there. It was called simply the "meeting-house." It stood in the timber, whose columns and aisles opened around it like a vast cathedral, where the rocks were altars and the birds were choirs. It was built of rude logs, and had hard benches, but the plain people had done more skillful work on this forest sanctuary than on the school-house. The log meeting-house stood near the log school-house, and both revealed the heart of the people who built them. It was the Prussian school-master, trained in the moral education of Pestalozzi, that made the German army victorious over France in the late war. And it was the New England school-master that built the great West, and made Plymouth Rock the crown-stone of our own nation. The world owes to humble Pestalozzi what it never could have secured from a Napoleon. It is right ideas that march to the conquest, that lift mankind, and live.

It had been announced in the school-house that Jasper the Parable would preach in the log church on Sunday. The

school-master called the wandering teacher "Jasper the Parable," but the visitor became commonly known as the "Old
Tunker" in the community. The news flew for miles that "an
old Tunker" was to preach. No event had awakened a greater
interest since Elder Elkins, from Kentucky, had come to the
settlement to preach Nancy Lincoln's funeral sermon under
the great trees. On that occasion all the people gathered
from the forest homes of the vast region. Every one now
was eager to visit the same place in the beautiful spring
weather, and to "hear what the old Tunker would have to
say."

Among the preachers who used to speak in the log meeting-
house and in Thomas Lincoln's cabin were one Jeremiah Cash,
and John Richardson, and young Lamar. The two latter
preachers lived some ten miles distant from the church; but ten
miles was not regarded as a long Sabbath-day journey in those
days in Indiana. When the log meeting-house was found too
small to hold the people, such preachers would exhort under
the trees. There used to be held religious meetings in the
cabins, after the manner of the present English cottage prayer-
meetings. These used to be appointed to take place at "early
candle-lighting," and many of the women who attended used
to bring tallow dips with them, and were looked upon as the
"wise virgins" who took oil in their lamps.

It was a lovely Sunday in April. The warm sunlight filled
the air and bird-songs the trees. The notes of the lark, the
sparrow, and the prairie plover were bells—

> "To call me to duty, while birds in the air
>   Sang anthems of praise as I went forth to prayer,"

8

as one of the old hymns used to run. The buds on the trees were swelling. There was an odor of walnut and "sassafrax" in the tides of the sunny air. Cowslips and violets margined the streams, and the sky over all was serene and blue, and bright with the promise of the summer days.

The people began to gather about the meeting-house at an early hour. The women came first, in corn-field bonnets which were scoop-shaped and flaring in front, and that ran out like horns behind. On these funnel-shaped, cornucopia-like head-gears there might now and then be seen the vanity of a ribbon. The girls carried their shoes in their hands until they came in sight of the meeting-house, when they would sit down on some mossy plat under an old tree, "bein' careful of the snakes," and put them on. All wore linsey-woolsey dresses, of which four or five yards of cloth were an ample pattern for a single garment, as they had no use for any superfluous polonaises in those times.

Long before the time for the service the log meeting-house was full of women, and the yard full of men and horses. Some of the people had come from twenty miles away. Those who came from the longest distances were the first to arrive—as is usual, for in all matters in life promptness is proportioned to exertion.

When the Parable came, Thomas Lincoln met him.

"You can't preach here," said he. "Half the people couldn't hear you. You have a small voice. You don't holler and pound like the rest of 'em, I take it. Suppose you preach out under the trees, where all the people can hear ye. It looks mighty pleasant there. With our old sing-song preachers it don't make so much difference. We could hear one of them if you were to shut him up in jail. But with you it is different. You have been brought up different among those big churches over there. What do you say, preacher?"

"I would rather preach under the trees. I love the trees. They are the meeting-house of God."

"Say, preacher, would you mind goin' over and preachin' at Nancy's grave? Elder Elkins preached there, and the other travelin' ministers. Seems kind o' holy over there. Nancy was a good woman, and all the people liked her. She was Abraham's mother. The trees around her grave are beautiful."

"I would like to preach there, by that lonely grave in the wilderness."

"The Tunker will preach at Nancy's grave," said Thomas Lincoln in a loud voice. He led the way to the great cathedral of giant trees, which were clouded with swelling buds and old moss, and a long procession of people followed him there.

Among them was Aunt Olive, with a corn-field bonnet of immense proportions, and her hymn-book. She was a lively worshiper. At all the meetings she sang, and at the Methodist meetings she shouted; and after all religious occasions she "tarried behind," to discuss the sermon with the minister. She usually led the singing. Her favorite hymns were, "Am I a soldier of the Cross," "Come, thou Fount of every blessing," and "My Bible leads to glory." The last hymn and tune suited her emotional nature, and she would pitch it upon a high key, and make the woods ring with the curious musical exhortation of the chorus :

> " Sing on, pray on,
> Ye followers of Emmanuel."

At the early candle-meetings at Thomas Lincoln's cabin
and other cabins, she sang hymns of a more persuasive character.   These were oddly appropriate to the hard-working, weary,
yet hopeful community.   One of these began thus :

> "Come, my brethren, let us try,
> For a little season,
> Every burden to lay by—
> Come, and let us reason.
> What is this that casts you down ?
> What is this that grieves you ?
> Speak, and let the worst be known—
> Speaking may *relieve* you."

The music was weird and in a minor key.   It was sung
often with a peculiar motion of the body, a forward-and-back-
ward movement, with clasped hands and closed eyes.   Another
of the pioneer hymns began :

> " Brethren, we have met for worship,
> And to adore the Lord our God :
> Will you pray with all your power,
> While we wait upon the Lord ?
> All is vain unless the Spirit
> Of the Holy One comes down ;
> Brethren, pray, and heavenly manna
> Will be showered all around.
>
> " Sisters, will you join and help us ?
> Moses' sister help-ed him," etc.

The full glory of a spring day in Indiana shone over the
vast forests, as the Tunker rose to speak under the great trees.
It was like an Easter, and, indeed, the hymn sung at the open-

ing of the service was much like an Easter hymn. It related
how—

> " On this lovely morning my Saviour was rising,
> The chains of mortality fully despising ;
> His sufferings are over, he's done agonizing—
> This morning my Saviour will think upon *me*."

The individuality of the last line seemed especially comfort-
ing to many of the toiling people, and caused Aunt Olive to
uplift her voice in a great shout.

"Come with me," said Jasper; "come with me this morning, and we will walk beside the Sea of Galilee together. Galilee! I love to think of Galilee—far, far away. The words
spoken on the shores of Galilee, and on the mountains over-
looking Galilee, are the hope of the world. They are the final
words of our all-loving Father to his children. Times may
change, but these words will never be exceeded or superseded ;
nothing can ever go beyond these teachings of the brotherhood
of man, and the way that the heart may find God, and become
conscious of the presence of God, and know its immortality,
and the everlasting truth. What did the great Teacher say on
Galilee?" .

The Parable began to repeat from memory the Sermon on
the Mount and the Galilean teachings. The birds came and
sang in the trees during the long recitations, and the people
sank down on the grass. Once or twice Aunt Olive's corn-field
bonnet rose up, and out of it came a shout of "Glory!" One
enthusiastic brother shouted, at one point of the quotations:
"That's right, elder; pitch into 'em, and give it 'em—they
need it. We're all sinners here; a good field to improve upon!
Go on!"

It was past high noon when Jasper finished his quotations from the Gospels. He then paused, and said:

"Do you want to know who I am, and why I am here, and what has sent me forth among the speckled birds of the forest? I will tell you. A true life has no secrets—it needs none; it is open to all like the revelations of the skies, and the sea, and the heart of Nature—what is concealed in the heart is what should not be.

"I had a teacher. He is living now—an old, broken man— a name that will sound strange to your ears. He gave up his life to teach the orphans made by the war. He studied with them, learned with them, ate with them; he saw with their eyes and felt with their hearts. He taught after the school of Nature; as Nature teaches the child within, so he taught, using outward objects.

"He once said to me:

"'For thirty years my life has been a struggle against poverty. For thirty years I have had to forego many of the barest necessities of life, and have had to shun the society of my fellow-men for want of decent clothes. Many and many times I have gone without a dinner, and eaten in bitterness a dry crust of bread on the road, at a time when even the poorest were seated around a table. All this I have suffered, and am suffering still to-day, and with no other object than to realize my plan for helping the poor.'

"When I heard him say that, I loved him. It made me ashamed of my selfish life. Then I heard the Dunkards preach, and tell of America over the sea. I began to study the words of the Teacher of Galilee. I, too, longed to teach. My

wife died, and my two children. Then I said : 'I will live for
the soul. That is all that has any lasting worth. I will give
up everything for the good of others, and go over the sea, and
teach the children of the forest.' I am now on my way to see
Black Hawk, who has promised to send out with me an interpreter and guide. I have given up my will, my property, and
my name, and I am happy. Good-by, my friends. I have
nothing, and am happy."

At this point Aunt Olive's corn-field bonnet rose up, and
her voice rang out on the air :

> " My brother, I wish you well !
> My brother, I wish you well !
> When my Lord calls, I hope I shall
> Be *mentioned* in the promised land.

> " My sister, I wish you well !" etc.

> " Poor sinners, I wish you well !" etc.

Galilee ! There was one merry, fun-making boy in that
sacred place, to whom, according to tradition, that word had a
charm. He used to love to mimic the old backwoods preachers, and he became very skeptical in matters of Christian faith
and doctrine, but he never forgot the teachings of the Teacher
of Galilee. In the terrible duties that fell to his lot the principles of the Galilean teachings came home to his heart, and
he came to know in experience what he had not accepted from
the mouths of men. He is said to have said, just before his
death, which bowed the nation : " When the cares of state are
over, I want to go to Galilee," or words of like meaning. The
legend is so beautiful that we could wish it to be true.

CHAPTER IX.

AUNT INDIANA'S PROPHECIES.

ASPER heard the local stories at the smithy and at Aunt Indiana's with intense interest. To him they furnished a study of the character of the people. They were not like stories of beautiful spiritual meaning that he had been accustomed to hear at Marienthal, at Weimar, and on the Rhine. The tales of Richter, Haupt, Hoffman, and Baron Fouqué could never have been created here. These new settlements called for the incident or joke that represented a practical fact, and not the soul-growth of imagination. The one question of education was. "Can you cipher to the rule of three?" and of religion, "Have you found the Lord?" The favorite tales were of Indians, bears, and ghosts, and the rough hardships that overcome life. Jasper heard these tales with a sympathetic heart.

The true German story is a parable, a word with a soul. Jasper loved them, for the tales of a people are the heart of a people, and express the progress of culture and opinion.

One day, as Jasper was cobbling at Aunt Olive's, he sought to teach her a lesson of contentment by a German household story. Johnnie Kongapod had come in, and the woman was complaining of her hard and restricted life.

(108)

" Aunt Indiana," said Jasper, " do you have fairies here ? "

" Never have seen any. We don't spin air here in America."

" We have fairies in Germany. All the children there pass through fairy-land. There once came a fairy to an old couple who were complaining, like you."

" Like me ? I'm the contentedest woman in these parts. 'Tis no harm to wish for what you haven't got."

" There came a fairy to them, and said :

" ' You may have three wishes. Wish.'

" The old couple thought :

" ' We must be very wise,' said the woman, ' and not make any mistake, since we can only wish three times. I wish I had a pudding.'

" Immediately there came a pudding upon the table. The poor woman was greatly surprised.

" ' There, you see what you have done by your foolish wishing !' said the man.

" ' One of our opportunities has gone,' said the woman. ' We have but two chances left. We must be *wiser*.'

" They sat and looked into the fire. The fairy had disappeared from the hearth, and there were only embers and ashes there.

" The man grew angry that his wife had lost one of their opportunities.

" ' Nothin' but a pudding !' said he. ' I wish that that miserable pudding were hung to your nose !'

" The pudding leaped from the table and hung at the end of the old woman's nose.

" ' There ! ' said she, ' now you see what you have done by *your* foolish wishing.'

" The old man sighed. ' We have but one wish left. We must now be the wisest people in all the world.'

" They watched the dying embers, and thought. As they did so, the pudding grew heavy at the end of the old woman's nose. At last she could endure it no longer.

" ' Oh ! ' she said, ' how I wish that pudding was off again ! '

" The pudding disappeared, and the fairy was gone."

" Tain't true," said Aunt Indiana.

" Yes," said Jasper, " what is true to life is true. Stories are the alphabet of life."

Johnnie Kongapod had listened to the tale with delight. Aunt Indiana knew that no fairy would ever appear on her hearth, but Johnnie was not so sure.

" I've seen 'em," said he.

" You—what? What have you seen? I'd like to know," said Aunt Indiana.

" Fairies—"

" Where ? "

" When I've been asleep."

" There never was any fairies in my dreams," said Aunt Indiana.

No, there were not. The German Tunker and the prairie Indian might see fairies, but the hard-working Yankee pioneer had no faculties for creative fancy. Her fairy was the plow that breaks the ground, or the axe that fells the timber. Yet the German soul-tale seemed to haunt her, and she at last said :

" I wish that we had more such stories as that.' It is

pleasant talk. Abe Lincoln tells such things out of the Pilgrim's Progress. He's all imagination, just like you and the Indians. People who don't have much to do run to such things. I suppose that he has read that Pilgrim's Progress over a dozen times."

"I have observed that the boy had ideals," said Jasper.

"What's them?" said Aunt Indiana.

"People build life out of ideals," said Jasper. "A cathedral is an ideal before it is a form. So is a house, a glass— everything. He has the creative imagination."

"Yes—that's what I said : always going around with a book in his hand, as though he was walking on the air."

"His step-mother says that he's one of the best of boys. He does everything that he can for her, and he has never given her an unkind word. He loves his step-mother like an own mother, and he forgets himself for others. These are good signs."

"Signs—signs! Stop your cobblin', elder, and let me prophesy! That boy just takes after his father, and he will never amount to anything in this world or any other. His mother what is dead was a good woman—an awful good woman; but she was sort o' visionary. They say that she used to see things at camp-meetin's, and lose her strength, and have far-away visions. She might have seen fairies. But she was an awful good woman—good to everybody, and everybody loved her; and we were all sorry when she died, and we all love her grave yet. It is queer, but we all seem to love her grave. A sermon goes better when it is preached there under the great trees. Some folks had rather hear a sermon preached there than at the meetin'-house. Some people leave a kind o' influence; *Miss* Linken did. The boy means well—his heart is all right, like his poor dead mother's was—but he hasn't got any head on 'im, like as I have. He hasn't got any calculation. And now, elder, I'm goin' to say it, though I'm sorry to: he'll never amount to shucks! There, now! Josiah Crawford says so, too."

"There is one very strong point about Abraham," said Jasper. "He has a keen sense of what is right, and he is always governed by it. He has faith that right is might. Didn't you ever notice it?"

"Yes, I'll do him justice. I never knew him to do a thing that he thought wrong—never. He couldn't. He takes after his mother's folks, and they say that there is Quaker blood in the Linkens."

"But, my good woman, a fool would be wise if he always did right, wouldn't he? There is no higher wisdom than to always do right. And a boy that has a heart to feel for every one, and a conscience that is true to a sense of right, and that loves learning more than anything else, and studies continually, is likely to find a place in the world.

"Now, I am going to prophesy. This country is going to need men to lead them, and Abraham Lincoln will one day become a leader among men. He leads now. His heart leads; his mind leads. I can see it. The world here is going to need men of knowledge, and it will select the man of the most learning who has the most heart, the most sympathy with the people. It will select him. I have a spiritual eye, and I can see."

"A leader of the people—Abe Lincoln! You have said it

now. I would as soon think of Johnnie Kongapod! A leader of the people! Are you daft? When the prairies leap into corn-fields and the settlements into banks of gold, and men can travel a mile a minute, and clodhoppers become merchants and Congressers, and as rich as Spanish grandees, then Abraham Lincoln may become a leader of the people, but not till then! No, elder, you are no Samuel, that has come down here among the sons of Jesse to find a shepherd-boy for a king. You ain't no Samuel, and he ain't no shepherd-boy. He all runs to books and legs, and I tell you he ain't got no calculation. Now, I've prophesied and you've prophesied."

"Time tells the truth about all things," said Jasper. "We shall meet, if I make my circuits, and we will talk of our prophecies in other years, should Providence permit. My soul has set its mark on that boy : wait, and we will see if the voice within me speaks true. It has always spoken true until now."·

At the close of this prophetic dialogue the subject of it appeared at the door. He was a tall boy, with a dark face, homely, ungainly, awkward. He wore a raccoon-skin cap, a linsey-woolsey shirt, and leather breeches, and was barefooted, although the weather was yet cool. He did not look like one who would ever cause the thrones of the world to lean and listen, or who would find in .the Emperor of all the Russias the heart of a brother.

"Abe," said Aunt Indiana, "the Tunker here has been speakin' well of you, though you don't deserve it. He just says as how you are goin' to be somebody, and make somethin' in the world. I hope you will, though you're a shaky tree to hang hopes on. I ain't got nothin' ag'in ye. He says that

you'll become a leader among men. What do you think o'
that, Abe? Don't stand there gawkin'. Come in and sit
down."

"It helps one to have some one believe in him," said the
tall boy. "One tries to fulfill the good prophecies made about
him. I wish I was good.—Thank ye, elder, for your good
opinion. I wonder if I will ever make anything? I sometimes
think I will. I look over toward mother's grave there, and
think I will; but you can't tell. Crawford the schoolmaster
he thinks good of me, but the other Crawford—Josiah—he's
ag'in me. But if we do right, we'll all come out right."

"Yes, my boy," said Jasper, "have faith that right is might.
This is what the Voice and the Being within tells me to preach
and to teach. Let us have faith that right is might, and do
our duty, and the Spirit of God will give us a new nature, and
make us new creatures, and the rebirth of the spiritual life into
the eternal kingdom."

The prairie winds breathed through the trees. A robin
came and sang in the timber.

The four sat thoughtful—the Tunker, the Indian, the
pioneer woman, and the merry, sad-faced boy. It was a com-
mon-place scene in the Indiana timber, and that one lonely
grave is all that is left to recall such scenes to-day—the grave
of the pioneer mother.

CHAPTER X.

THE INDIAN RUNNER.

HE young May moon was hanging over the Mississippi on the evening when Jasper came to the village of the Sacs and Foxes. This royal town, the head residence of the two tribes, and the ancient burying-ground of the Indian race, was very beautifully situated at the junction of the Rock River with the Mississippi. The Father of Waters, which is in many places turbid and uninteresting, here becomes a clear and impetuous stream, flowing over beds of rock and gravel, amid high and wooded shores. The rapids—the water-ponies of the Indians—here come leaping down, surging and foaming, and are checked by monumental islands. The land rises from the river in slopes, like terraces, crowned with hills and patriarchal trees. From these hills the sight is glorious. On one hand rolls the mighty river, and on the other stretch vast prairies, flower-carpeted, sun-flooded, a sea of vegetation, the home of the prairie plover and countless nesters of the bright, warm air. It is a park, whose extent is bounded by hundreds of miles.

Water-swept and beautiful lies Rock Island, where on a parapet of rock was built Fort Armstrong in the days of the later Indian troubles.

The royal town and burying-ground was a place of remarkable fertility. The grape-vine tangled the near woods, the wild honeysuckle perfumed the air, and wild plums blossomed white in May and purpled with fruit in summer. If ever an Indian race loved a town, it was this. The Indian mind is poetic. Nature is the book of poetry to his instinct, and here Nature was poetic in all her moods.

The Indians venerated the graves of their ancestors. Here they kept the graves beautiful, and often carried food to them and left it for the dead.

The chant at these graves was tender, and shows that the human heart everywhere is the same. It was like this:

> " Where are you, my father ?
> Oh, where are you now ?
> I'm longing to see thee ;
> I'm wailing for thee.
>   (Wail.)

> " Are you happy, my father ?
> Are you happy now ?
> I'm longing to see thee ;
> I'm wailing for thee.
>   (Wail.)

> " Spring comes to the river.
> But where, then, art thou ?
> I'm longing to see thee ;
> I'm wailing for thee.
>   (Wail.)

> " The flowers come forever ;
> I'll meet thee again ;
> I'm longing to see thee—
> Time bears me to thee ! "
>   (Wail.)

As Jasper ascended the high bluffs of the lodge where Black Hawk dwelt, he was followed by a number of Indians who came out of their houses of poles and bark, and greeted him in a kindly way. The dark chief met him at the door of the lodge.

"You are welcome, my father. The new moon has bent her bow over the waters, and you have come back. You have kept your promise. I have kept mine. There is the boy."

An Indian boy of lithe and graceful form came out of the lodge, followed by an old man, who was his uncle. The boy's name was Waubeno, and his uncle's was Main-Pogue. The latter had been an Indian runner in Canada, and an interpreter to the English there. He spoke English well. The boy Waubeno had been his companion in his long journeys, and, now that the interpreter was growing old, remained true to him. The three stood there, looking down on the long mirror of the Mississippi—Black Hawk, Main-Pogue, and Waubeno—and waiting for Jasper to speak.

"I have come to bring you peace," said Jasper—"not the silence of the hawk or the bow-string, but peace here."

He laid his hand on his breast, and all the Indians did the same.

"I am a man of peace," continued Jasper. "If any one should seek to slay me, I would not do him any harm. I would forgive him, and pray that his blindness might go from his soul, and that he might see a better life. You welcome me, you are true to me, and, whatever may happen, I will be true to your race."

The black chief bowed, Main-Pogue, and the boy Waubeno.
9

"I believe you," said Black Hawk. "Your face says 'yes' to your words. The Indian's heart is always true to a friend. Sit down ; eat, smoke the peace-pipe, and let us talk. Sit down. The sky is clear, and the night-bird cries for joy on her wing. Let us all sit down and talk. The river rolls on forever by the graves of the braves of old. Let us sit down."

The squaws brought Jasper some cakes and fish, and Black Hawk lighted some long pipes and gave them to Main-Pogue and Waubeno.

"I have brought the boy here for you," said Black Hawk. "He comes of the blood of the brave. Let me tell you his story. It will shame the pale-face, but let me tell you the story. You will say that the Indian can be great, like the pale-face, when I tell you his story. It will smite your heart. Listen."

A silence followed, during which a few puffs of smoke curled into the air from the black chief's pipe. He broke his narrative by such silences, designed to be impressive, and to offer an opportunity for thought on what had been said.

Strange as it may seem to the reader, the story that follows is substantially true, and yet nothing in classic history or modern heroism can surpass in moral grandeur the tale that Black Hawk was always proud to tell :

"Father, that is the boy. He knows all the ways from the Great Lakes to the long river, from the great hills to Kaskaskia. You can trust him ; he knows the ways. Main-Pogue knows all the ways. Main-Pogue was a runner for the pale-face. He has taught him the ways. Their hearts are like one heart, Main-Pogue's and Waubeno's.

BLACK HAWK TELLS THE STORY OF WAUBENO.

" His father is dead, Waubeno's. Main-Pogue has been a father to him. They would die for each other. Main-Pogue says that Waubeno may run with you, if I say that he may run. I say so. Main-Pogue and Waubeno are true to me.

" The boy's father is dead, I said. Who was the father of that boy?—Waubeno, stand up."

The boy arose, like a tall shadow. There was a silence, and Black Hawk puffed his pipe, then laid it beside his blanket.

" Who was the father of Waubeno? He was a brave, a warrior. He wore the gray plume, and honor to him was more than life. He would not lie, and they put him to death. He was true as the stars, and they killed him."

There followed another silence.

" Father, you teach. You teach the head; you teach the heart: to live a true life, is the thing to teach—the thing you call conscience, soul, those are the right things to teach. What are books to the head, if the soul is not taught to be true?

" Father, the father of Waubeno could teach the pale-face. In the head? No, in the heart? No, in the soul, which is the true book of the Great Spirit that you call God. You came to us to teach us God. It is good. You are a brother, but God came to us before. He has written the law of right in the soul of every man. The right will find the light. You teach the way—you bring the Word of him who died for mankind. It is good. I've got you a runner to run with you. It is good. You help the right to find the light.

" Father, listen. I am about to speak. Before the great war with the British brother (1812) that boy's father struck down to the earth a pale-face who had done him wrong. The white man died. He who wrongs another does not deserve the sun. He died, and his soul went to the shadows. The British took the red warrior prisoner for killing this man who had wronged him. Waubeno was a little one then, when they took his father prisoner.

"The British told the old warrior that they had condemned him to die.

"'I am not afraid to die,' said the warrior. 'Let me go to the Ouisconsin (Wisconsin) and see my family once more, and whisper my last wish in the ear of my boy, and I will return to you and die. I will return at the sunrise.'

"'You would never return,' said the commander of the stockade.

"The warrior strode before him.

"'Can a true man lie?'

"The commander looked into his face, and saw his soul.

"'Well, go,' said he. 'I would like to see an Indian who would come back to die.'

"The warrior went home, under the stars. He told his squaw all. He had six little children, and he hugged them all. Waubeno was the oldest boy. He told him all, and pressed him to his heart. He whispered in his ear.—What was it he said, Waubeno?"

The shadowy form of the boy swayed in the dim light, as he answered. He said:

"'Avenge my death! Honor my memory. The Great Spirit will teach you how.' That is what my father said to me, and I felt the beating of his heart."

There was a deep silence. Then Black Hawk said:

"The warrior looked down on the Ouisconsin under the stars. He looked up to heaven, and cried, 'Lead thou my boy!' Then he set his face toward the stockades of Prairie du Chien.

"He strode across the prairie as the sun was rising; he arrived in time, and— Father, listen!"

There was another silence, so deep that one might almost hear the puffing smoke as it rose on the air.

"*They shot him!* That is his boy, Waubeno."

Jasper stood silent; he thought of Johnnie Kongapod's story, and the night-scene at Pigeon Creek.

"I shall teach him a better way," said Jasper, at last. "I will lead him to honor the memory of his great father in a way that he does not now know. The Great Spirit will guide us both. His father was a great man. I will lead him to become a greater."

"Father," said the boy, coming forward, "I will always be true to you, but I have sworn by the stars."

Jasper stood like one in a dream. Could such a tale as this be true among savages? Honor like this only needed the gospel teaching to do great deeds. Jasper saw his opportunity, and his love of mankind never glowed before as it did then. He folded his hands, closed his eyes, and his silent thoughts winged upward to the skies.

CHAPTER XI.

THE CABIN NEAR CHICAGO.

ASPER and Waubeno crossed the prairies to Lake Michigan. It was June, the high tide of the year. The long days poured their sunlight over the seas of flowers. The prairie winds were cool, and the new vegetation was alive with insects and birds.

The first influence that Jasper tried to exert on Waubeno was to induce him to forego the fixed resolution to avenge his father's death.

"The first thing in education," he used to say, "is conscience, the second is the heart, and the third is the head."

He had planned to teach Waubeno while the Indian boy should be teaching him, and he wished to follow his own theory that a new pupil should first learn to be governed by his moral sense.

"Waubeno," he said, in their long walk over the prairie, "I wish to teach you and make you wise, but before I can do you justice you must make a promise. Will you, Waubeno?"

"I will. You would not ask me to do what is wrong."

"It may be a hard thing, but, Waubeno, I wish you to

promise me that you will never seek to avenge your father. Will you, Waubeno?"

"Parable, I will promise you any right thing but that. I have made another promise about that thing—it must hold."

"Waubeno, I can not teach you as I would while you carry malice in your heart. The soul does not see clearly that is dark with evil. Do you see? I wish it for your good."

"The white man punishes his enemies, does he not? Why should not I avenge a wrong? The white fathers at Malden" (the trade-post on Lake Erie) "avenge every wrong that is done them by the Indians, do they not?"

"Christ died for his enemies. He forgave them, dying. You have heard."

"Then why do his followers not do the same?"

"They do."

"I have never seen one who did."

"Not one?"

"No, not one."

"Then they are false to the cross. Waubeno, I love you. I am seeking your good. Trust me. I would make you any promise that I could. Make me this promise, and then we will be brothers. Your vow rises between us like a cloud."

"Parable, listen. I will promise, on one condition."

"What, Waubeno?"

"You say that right is might, Parable?"

"Yes."

"When I find a single white man who defends an Indian to his own hurt because it is right, I will promise. I have known many white men who defended the Indian because they thought that it was good for them to do it—good for their pockets, good for their church, good for their souls in another world—but never one to his own harm, because it was right; listen, Parable—never one to his own harm because it was right. When I meet one—such a one—I will promise you what you ask. Parable, my folks did right because it was right."

" Waubeno, I once knew a boy who defended a turtle to his own harm, because it was right. The boys laughed at him, but his soul was true to the turtle."

" I would like to meet that boy," Waubeno said. " He and I would be brothers. But I have never seen such a boy, Parable. I have never seen any man who had the worth of my own father, and, till I do, I shall hold to my vow to him! God heard that vow, and he shall see that I prove true to a man who died for the truth ! "

The two came in sight of blue Lake Michigan, where the old Jesuit explorer had had a vision of a great city ; and where Point au Sable, the San Domingo negro, for a time settled, hoping to be made an Indian king. Here he found the hospitable roofs of John Kinzie, the pioneer of Chicago, the Romulus of the great mid-continent city, where storehouses abounded with peltries and furs.

John Kinzie (the father of the famous John II. Kinzie) was a grand pioneer, like the Pilgrim Fathers of the elder day. He dealt honestly with the Indians, and won the hearts of the several tribes. He settled in Chicago in 1804, at which time a block-house was built by the Government as a frontier house or garrison. This frontier house stood near the present Rush Street Bridge. Mr. Kinzie's house stood on the north side of the Chicago River, opposite the fort. The storm-beaten block-house was to be seen in Chicago as late as 1857, and the place of Mr. Kinzie's home will ever be held as sacred ground. The frontier house was known as Fort Dearborn. A little settle-ment grew around the fort and the hospitable doors of Mr. Kinzie, until in 1830 it numbered twelve houses. Twelve houses in Chicago in 1830! Pass the bridge of sixty years, and lo! the rival city of the Western world, with its more than a million people—more than fulfilling the old missionary's dream!

For twenty years John Kinzie was the only white man not connected with the garrison and trading-post who lived in northern Illinois. He was a witness of the Indian massacre of the troops in 1812, when he himself was driven from his home by the lake.

He saw another and different scene in August, 1821—a scene worthy of a poet or painter—the Great Treaty, in which the Indian chiefs gave up most of their empire east of the Mis-sissippi. There came to this decisive convocation the plumes of the Ottawas, Chippewas, and Pottawattamies. General Cass was there, and the old Indian agents. The chiefs brought with them their great warriors, their wives and children. There the prairie Indians made their last stand but one against the march of emigration to the Mississippi.

Me-te-nay, the young orator of the Pottawattamies, was there, to make a poetic appeal for his race. But the counsels of the white chiefs were too persuasive and powerful. A treaty was concluded, which virtually gave up the Indian empire east of the Mississippi.

Then the chiefs and the warriors departed, their red plumes

disappearing over the prairie in the sunset light. Before them rolled the Mississippi. Behind them lay the blue seas of the lakes. It was a sorrowful procession that slowly faded away. Some twelve years after, in August, 1835, another treaty was concluded with the remaining tribes, and there occurred the last dance of the Pottawattamies on the grounds where the city of Chicago now stands.

Five thousand Indians were present, and nearly one thousand joined in the dance. The latter assembled at the council-house, on the place where now is the northeast corner of North Water and Rush Streets, and where the Lake House stands. Their faces were painted in black and vermilion; their hair was gathered in scalp-locks on the tops of their heads, and was decorated with Indian plumes. They were led by drums and rattles. They marched in a dancing movement along the river, and stopped before each house to perform the grotesque figures of their ancient traditions.

They seemed to be aware that this was their last gathering on the lake. The thought fired them. Says one who saw them :

" Their eyes were wild and bloodshot. Their muscles stood out in great, hard knots, as if wrought to a tension that must burst them. Their tomahawks and clubs were thrown and brandished in every direction."

The dance was carried on in a procession through the peaceful streets, and was concluded at Fort Dearborn in presence of the officers and soldiers of the garrison. It was the last great Indian gathering on the lake.

A new civilization began in the vast empire of the inland

seas with the signing of the Treaty of Chicago and these con-
cluding rites. Around the home of pastoral John Kinzie were
to gather the new emigrations of the nations of the world, and
the Queen City of the Lakes was to rise, and Progress to make
the seat of her empire here. Never in the history of mankind
did a city leap into life like this, which is now setting on her
brow the crown of the Columbus domes.

On the arrival of Jasper and Waubeno at Fort Dearborn,
an incident occurred which affords a picture of the vanished
days of the prairie chiefs and kings. There came riding up to
the trading-houses a middle-aged chief named Shaubena.

This chief may be said to have been the guardian spirit of
the infant city of Chicago. He hovered around her for her
good for a half-century, and was faithful to her interests from
the first to the end of his long life. If ever an Indian merited
a statue or an imperishable memorial in a great city, it is
Shaubena.

He was born about the year 1775, on the Kankakee River.
His home was on a prairie island, as a growth of timber surrounded by a prairie used to be called. It was near the head-
waters of Big Indian Creek, now in De Kalb County. This
grove, or prairie island, still bears his name.

Here were his corn-fields, his sugar-camps, his lodges, and
his happy people. In his youth he had been employed by two
Ottawa priests, or prophets, to instruct the people in the
principles of their religion, and so he had traveled extensively
in the land of the lakes, and spoke English well. The old
Methodist circuit-riders used to visit him on his prairie island,
and his family was brought under their influence and accepted

their faith. When, in 1812, Indian runners from Tecumseh visited the tribal towns of the Illinois River to tell the warriors that war had been declared between the United States and England, and to counsel them to unite with the English, Shaubena endeavored to restrain his people from such a course, and to prevent a union of the tribes against the American settlers. When he found that the Indians were marching against Chicago, he followed them on his pony.

He arrived too late. A scene of blood met his eyes. Along the lake, where the blue waves rolled in the sun, lay forty-two dead bodies, the remains of white soldiers, women, and children. These bodies lay on the prairie for four years, until the rebuilding of Fort Dearborn in 1816, with the exception of the mutilated remains of Captain Wells, which Black Partridge buried.

John Kinzie and his family had been saved, largely by the influence of Shaubena. Black Partridge summoned his warriors to protect the house. Shaubena rushed up to the porch-steps and set his rifle across the doorway. The rooms were occupied by Mrs. Kinzie, her children, and Mrs. Helm A party of excited Indians rushed upon the place and forced their way into the house, to kill the women. The intended massacre was delayed by the friendly Indians.

In the mean time a half-breed girl, who had been employed by good John Kinzie, and who was devoted to his family, had stolen across the prairie to Sauganash, or Billy Caldwell, the friendly chief. This warrior seized his canoe and came paddling down the waters, plumed with eagle-feathers, with a rifle in his hand. He rose up in his canoe, in the dark, as he came to the shore.

"Who are you?" asked Black Partridge.

"I am Sauganash."

"Then save your white friends. You only can save them."
The chief came to the house.

"Go!" he said to the Indians. "I am Sauganash!"

John Kinzie was not only ever after grateful to Sauganash and the half-breed girl for what they had done to save him and his family, but he saw that he had found a faithful heart in Shaubena. So when, to-day, Shaubena came riding up to his door from his prairie island on his little pony, he said, heartily:

"Shaubena, thou art welcome!"

Jasper and Waubeno joined John Kinzie and the prairie chief.

"Thou, too art welcome," said John Kinzie. "Whence do you come?"

Jasper told again his simple story: how that he was a Tunker, traveling to preach to every one, and to hold schools among the Indians; how that he had been to Black Hawk for an interpreter and guide, and how Black Hawk had sent out Waubeno as his companion.

Jasper and Waubeno built a cabin of logs, bark, and bushes, in view of the lake, a little distance above the fort. They spent several days on the rude structure.

"There are many Indian children who come to the trading-post," said Jasper, "and I may be able to begin here my first Indian school. You will do all you can for me, will you not, Waubeno?"

"Parable, listen! You love my people, and I will do all

that this arm, this heart, and this head can do for you. Whatever may happen, I will be true to you. If it costs my life, I will be true to you ! You may have my life. Do you not believe Waubeno?"

"Yes, I believe you, Waubeno. You hold honor dearer than life. You say that I love your people. You know that I would do right by your people, to my own harm. Then why will you not make to me the promise I sought from you on the prairie?"

"I have not seen you tried. We know not any one until he is tried. My father was tried. He was true. I would talk with the boy that was laughed at for defending the turtle. He was tried. He did right because it was right. We will know each other better by and by. But Waubeno will always be true to you while you are true to Waubeno."

The school opened in the new cabin about the time that the troops were withdrawn from the fort and the place left in the charge of the Indian agent. Waubeno was the teacher, and Jasper his only pupil. After a time Jasper secured a few pupils from the post-trading Indians. But these remained but for a short time. They did not like the confinement of instruction.

One day a striking event occurred. The Indian agent came to visit the school. He was interested in the Indian boys, and especially in the progress of Waubeno, who was quick to learn. Before leaving, he said :

"I have a medal in my hand. It was given to me by the general of Michigan. On one side of it is the Father of his Country—see him with his sword—Washington, the immortal Washington."

He held up the medal and paused.

"On the other side is an Indian chief. He is burying his hatchet. I was given the medal as a reward, and I will give it at the end of three weeks to the boy in this school who best learns his lessons Jasper shall decide who it shall be."

"I am glad you have said that," said Jasper. "That is the education of good-will. I am glad."

The Indian boys studied well, but Waubeno excelled them all. At the end of three weeks the Indian agent again appeared, and Jasper hoped to gain the heart of Waubeno by the award of the medal.

"To whom shall I give the medal?" asked the agent, at the end of the visit.

Jasper looked at his boy.

"It has been won by Waubeno," said Jasper. "I would be unjust not to say that all have been faithful, but Waubeno has been the most faithful of all."

Waubeno sat like a statue. He did not lift his eyes.

"Waubeno," said the agent, "you have heard what your teacher has said. The medal is yours. Here it is. You have reason to be proud of it. Waubeno, arise."

Waubeno arose. The agent held out the medal to him.

"Will you let me look at the medal?" said the boy.

The medal was handed to him. He examined it. He did not smile, or show any emotion. His look was indifferent and stoical. What was passing in his mind?

"The Indian chief is burying his hatchet, in the picture on this side of the medal," he said, slowly.

"Yes," said the Indian agent, "he is a good chief."

"The picture on this side represents Washington, you say?"

" Yes—Washington, the Father of his Country."

" He has a sword by his side, general, has he not? See."

" Yes, Waubeno, he has a sword by his side."

" He is a good chief, too?"

" Yes, Waubeno."

" Then why does he not bury his sword? I do not want the medal. What is good for the red chief should be as good for the white chief. I would be unlike my father to take a mean thing like that."

He stood like a statue, with curled lip and a fiery eye. The agent looked queerly at Jasper. He had nothing more to say. He took back the medal and went away. When he had gone, Waubeno said to Jasper:

" Pardon, brother; *he* is not *the* man—my promise to my father holds. They teach well, but they do not do well: it is the doing that speaks to the heart. The chief that buried his hatchet is a plumb fool, else the white chief would do so too. I have spoken!"

He sat down in silence and looked out upon the lake, on which the waves were breaking into foam in the purple distances. His face had an injured look, and his eyes glowed.

He arose at last and raised his hand, and said:

" I will pay them all some day!—"

Then he turned to Jasper and marked his disappointed face, and added:

" I will be true to you. Waubeno will be true to you."

CHAPTER XII.

THE WHITE INDIAN OF CHICAGO.

NE morning, as Jasper threw aside the curtain of skins that answered for a door to his cabin, a strange sight met his eyes. In the clearing between the cabin and the lake stood the tall form of an Indian. It was the most noble and beautiful form that he had ever seen, and the Indian's face and hands were white.

Jasper stood silent. The white Indian bent his eyes upon him, and the two looked in surprise at each other.

The Indian's eyes were dark, and like the eyes of the native races; but his nose was Roman, and his skin English, with a slight brown tinge. His hair was long and curly, and tinged with brown.

"Waubeno," said Jasper, "who is that?"

Waubeno came to the entrance of the cabin, and said:

"The white Indian. *They* bring good. Speak to him. It is a good sign."

"They?" said Jasper. "I never knew that there were white Indians, Waubeno. Where do they live? Where do they come from?"

"From the Great River. They come and go, and come and

10 (133)

go, and they are unlike other Indians. They know things that other Indians do not know. They have a book that talks to them. It came from heaven."

Jasper stepped out on to the clearing, and Waubeno followed him. The white Indian awaited their approach.

" Welcome, stranger," said Jasper. " Where are you journeying from ? "

" From the Great River (Mississippi) to the land of the lakes. They are coming, coming, my brothers from over the sea, as the prophet said. I have not seen you here before. I am glad that you have come."

" Where do you live ? " asked Jasper.

" My tribe is few, and they wander. They wander till the brothers come. We are not like other people here, though all the tribes treat us well and give us food and shelter. We are wanderers. We have lived in the country many years, and we have often visited Kaskaskia. You will hear of us there. When the French came, we thought they were brothers. Then the English came, and we felt that they were brothers. The white people are our brothers."

" Come in," said Jasper, " and breakfast with us. You are strange to me. I never heard of you. You seem like a visitant from another world. Tell me, my brother, how came you to be white ? "

" I beg your pardon, stranger, but I ask you the same question, How came you to be white ? The same Power that made your face like the cloud and the snow, made mine the same. There is kindred blood in our veins, but I know not how it is —we do not know. Our ancestors had a book that told us of

God, but it was lost when the French raised the cross at Kas-kaskia. We had a legend of the cross, and of armies marching under the cross, and when the bell began to ring over the praise house there, we found that we, too, had ancient tales of the bell. More I can not tell. All the tribes welcome us, and we belong to all the tribes, and we have wandered for years and years. Our fathers wandered."

"This is all very strange," said Jasper. "Tell us more."

"I expected your coming," said the white Indian. "I was not surprised to see you here. I expected you. I knew it. There are more white brothers to come—many. Let me tell you about it all.

"We had a prophet once. He said that we came from over the sea, and that we would never return, but that we must wander and wander, and that one day our white brothers would come from over the sea to us. They are coming; their white wagons are crossing the plains. Every day they are coming. I love to see them come and pass. The prophet spoke true.

"The French say that we came from a far-away land called Wales. The French say that a voyager, whose name was Modoc, set sail for the West eight hundred years ago, and was never heard of again in his own land; that his ships drifted West, and brought our fathers here. That is what the French say. I do not know, but I think that you and I are brothers. I feel it in my heart. You have treated me like a brother, and I kiss you in my heart. I love the English. They are my friends. I am going to Malden. There will be more white faces here when I come again."

He took breakfast in the cabin, and went away. Jasper

hardly comprehended the visit. He sought the Indian agent, and described to him the appearance of the wandering stranger, and related the story that the man had told.

"There are white crows, white blackbirds, white squirrels, and white Indians," said the agent, "strange as it may seem. I know nothing about the origin of any of them—only that they do exist. Ever since the French and Indians came to the lakes white Indians have been seen. So have white crows and black-birds. The French claim that these white Indians are of Welsh origin, and are the descendants of a body of mariners who were driven to our shores in the twelfth century by some accident of navigation or of weather. If so, the Welsh are the second dis-coverers of America, following the Northmen. But I put no faith in these traditions. I only know that from time to time a white-faced Indian is seen in the Mississippi Valley. There are many tales and traditions of them. It is simply a mystery that will never be solved."

"But what am I to think of the white Indian's story?"

"Simply that he had been taught by the French romancers, and that he believed it himself. Black faces have strangely appeared among white peoples, and Nature alone, could she speak, could explain her laws in these cases. The Indians have various traditions of the white Indian's appearance in the regions about Chicago; they regard him as a medicine-man, or a prophet, or a kind of good ghost. It is thought to be good fortune to meet him."

"Why does he come here?" said Jasper.

"To see the white people. He believes that the white people are his kindred, and that they are coming, 'coming,' and one day that they will flock here in multitudes. The French have told him this. He is a mythical character. Somehow he has white blood in his veins. I can not tell how. The Welsh tradition may be true, but it is hardly probable."

Years passed. The white Indian appeared again. The fort had become a town. The Indian races were disappearing. He saw the white wagons crossing the prairies, and the reluctant Pottawattomies making their way toward the Great River and the lands of the sunset. He went away, solitary as when he came, and was never seen again.

Who may have been these mysterious persons whose white faces for generations haunted the lakes and the plains? They appeared at Kaskaskia, their canoes glided mysteriously along the Mississippi, and they were often seen at the hunting-camps of the North. They sought the French and the English as soon as these races began to make settlements, and they seemed to be strangely familiar with English tones, sounds, and words.

Jasper loved to look out from his cabin on the blue lake, and to dream of the old scenes of the Prussian war, of Körner, Von Weber, of Pestalozzi, and his friend Froebel, and contrast them with the rude new life around him. The past was there, but the future was here, and here was his work for the future. It is not what a man has that makes him happy, but what he is; not his present state, but the horizon of the future around him that imparts glow to life, and Jasper was at peace with himself in the sense of doing his duty. Heaven to him was bright with the smile of God, and he longed no more for the rose-gardens of Marienthal or the castles of the Rhine.

The appearance of the white Indian filled the mind of Waubeno with pride and hope.

"We will be happy now," he said. "You will be happy now; nothing happens to them who see the white Indian; all goes well. I know that you are good within, else he would not come; only they whose beings within are good see the white Indian, and he brings bright suns and moons and calumets of peace, and so the days go on forever. I now know that you speak true. And Waubeno has seen him; he will do well; he has seen the white crow among the black crows, and he will do well. Happy moons await Waubeno."

The lake was glorious in these midsummer days. The prairie roses hung from the old trees in the groves, and the air rang with the joyful notes of the lark and plover. Indians came to the fort and went away. Pottawattomies encamped near the place and visited the agency, and white traders occasionally appeared here from Malden and Fort Wayne.

But these were uneventful days of Fort Dearborn. The stories of Mrs. John Kinzie are among the most interesting memories of these days of general silence and monotony. The old Kinzie house was situated where is now the junction of Pine and North Water Streets. The grounds sloped toward the banks of the river. It had a broad piazza looking south, and before it lay a green lawn shaded by Lombardy poplars and a cottonwood tree. Across the river rose Fort Dearborn, amid groves of locust trees, the national flag blooming, as it were, above it.

The cottonwood tree in the yard was planted by John Kinzie, and lived until Chicago became a great city, in Long John Wentworth's day.

The old residents of Chicago will ever recall the beauty of the outlook from the south piazza. At the dull period of the agency, only an Indian canoe, perhaps from Mackinaw, disturbed the peace of the river.

It was on this piazza that on a June morning was heard the chorus of Moore's Canadian Boat Song on the Chicago River, and here General Lewis Cass presently appeared. The great men of the New West often gathered here after that. Here the best stories of the lake used to be told by voyagers, and Mark Beaubien, we may well suppose, often played his violin.

The scene of the lake and river from the place was changed by moonlight into romance.

Amid such scenes the old Chief Shaubena related the legends of the tribes, and Mrs. Kinzie the thrilling episodes of the massacre of 1812. Jasper, we may imagine, joined the company, with the beautiful spiritual tales of the Rhine, and Waubeno added his delightful wonder-tale of the white Indian, whose feet brought good fortune. No one then dreamed that John Kinzie's home stood for two millions of people who would come there before the century should close, or that the cool cottonwood tree would throw its shade over some of the grandest scenes in the march of the world.

CHAPTER XIII.

LAFAYETTE AT KASKASKIA—THE STATELY MINUET.

JASPER made the best use of the story-telling method of influence in his school in the little cabin on the lake near Chicago River. He sought to impart moral ideas by the old Roman fables and German folk-lore stories. He often told the tale of the poor girl who went out for a few drops of water for her dying mother, in the water famine, and how her dipper was changed into silver, gold, and diamonds, as she shared the water with the sufferers on her return. But neither Æsop nor fairy lore so influenced the Indian boys as his story of the Indiana boy who defended the turtles and pitied the turtle with the broken shell.

"I would like to meet him," said Waubeno, one day when the story had been told. "What is his name, Parable? What do you call him by?"

"Lincoln," said Jasper, "Abraham Lincoln."

"Where does he live, Parable?"

"On Pigeon Creek, in Indiana."

"Is the place far away?"

"Yes, very far away by water, and a hard journey by land. Pigeon Creek is far away, near the Ohio River; south, Waubeno—far away to the south."

" Will you ever go there again ? "

" Yes—I hope to go there again, and to take you along with me," said Jasper. " I have planned to go down the Illinois in the spring, in a canoe, to the Mississippi, and down the Mississippi to the Ohio, and visit Kaskaskia, and thence along the Ohio to the Wabash, and to the home where the boy lives who defended the turtles. It will be a long journey, and I expect to stop at many places, and preach and teach and form schools. I want you to go with me and guide my canoe. All these rivers are beautiful in summer. They are shaded by trees, and run through prairies of flowers. The waters are calm, and the skies are bright, and the birds sing continually. O Waubeno, this is a beautiful world to those who use it rightly—a beautiful, beautiful world ! "

" Me will go," said Waubeno. " Me would see that boy. I want to see a story boy, as you say."

The attempt to establish an Indian school on the Chicago was not wholly successful. The pupils did not remain long enough to receive the intended influence. They came from encampments that were never stable. The Indian village was there one season, and gone the next. The Indians who came in canoes to the agency soon went away again. Jasper, in the spring of 1825, resolved to carry out the journey that he had described to Waubeno, and with the first warm winds he and the Indian boy set out for Kaskaskia by the way of the Illinois to the Mississippi, and by the Mississippi to the Kaskaskia.

It was a long journey. Jasper stopped often at the Indian encampments and the new settlements. Waubeno was a faithful friend, and he came to love him for true-heartedness, sympathy, and native worth of soul. He often tried to teach him by stories, but as often as he said, " Now, Waubeno, we will talk," he would say, " Tell me the one with broken shell " —meaning the story. There was some meaning behind this story of the turtle with the broken shell that had completely won the heart of Waubeno. The boy Abraham Lincoln was his hero. Again and again, after he had listened to the simple narrative, he asked :

" Is the story boy alive ? "

" Yes, Waubeno."

" And we will meet him ? "

" Yes."

" That is good. I feel for him here," and he would lay his hand on his heart. " I love the story boy."

They traveled slowly. After a long journey down the Illinois, the Mississippi rolled before them in the full tides of early spring. They passed St. Louis, and one late April evening found them before the once royal town of Kaskaskia.

The bell was ringing as they landed, the bell that had been cast in fair Rochelle, and that was the first bell to ring between the Alleghanies and the Mississippi. Most of the black-robed missionaries were gone, as had the high-born French officers, with their horses, sabers, and banner-plumes, who once sought treasure and fame in this grand town of the Mississippi Valley. The Bourbon lilies had fallen from old Fort Chartres a generation ago, and the British cross had come down, and to-day all the houses, new and old, were decked with the stars and stripes. It was not a holiday. What did it mean ?

Jasper and Waubeno entered the old French town, and gazed at the brick buildings, the antique roofs, the high dormer windows, and the faded houses of by-gone priest and nun. The tavern was covered with flags, French and American, as were the grand house of William Morrison and the beautiful Edgar mansion. The house once occupied by the French commandant was wrapped in the national colors. It had been the first State House of Illinois. A hundred years before—just one hundred years—Kaskaskia Commons had received its grand name from his most Christian Majesty Louis XV, and it then seemed likely to become the capital of the French midcontinent empire in the New World. The Jesuits flocked here, zealous for the conversion of the Indian races. Here came men of rank and military glory, and Fort Chartres rose near it, grand and powerful as if to awe the world. But there was a foe in the fort of the French heart, and the boundless empire faded, and the old French town went to the American pioneer, and the fort became a ruin, like Louisburg at Cape Breton.

As Jasper and Waubeno passed along the broad streets they noticed that the town was filled with country people, and that there were Indians among them.

One of these Indians approached Waubeno, and said:

" She—yonder—see—Mary Panisciowa—daughter of the Great Chief—Mary Panisciowa."

Waubeno followed with his eye' the daughter of the Chief of the Six Nations. He went forward with the crowd and came to the house that she was making her home, and asked to meet her. Jasper had followed him.

They turned aside from the street, which was full of excited people—excited Jasper knew not why. The door of the house where Mary Panisciowa was visiting stood open, and they were asked to enter.

She looked a queen, yet she had the graces of the English and French people. She was a most accomplished woman. She spoke both English and French readily, her education having been conducted by an American agent to whom she had been commended by her father.

"This is good news," she said.

"What?" said Jasper. "Good news comes from God. Yet all events are news from heaven. The people seem greatly exercised. What has happened?"

"Lafayette, the great Lafayette—have you not heard?—the marquis—he is on his way to Kaskaskia, and that is why I am here. My father fought under him, and the general sent him a letter thanking him for his services in the American cause. It was written forty years ago. I have brought it. I hope to meet him. Would you like to see it?—a letter from the great Lafayette."

Mary Panisciowa took from her bosom a faded letter, and said :

"My father fought for the new people, and I have taken up their religion and customs. I suppose that you have done the same," she said to Waubeno.

"No ; that can not be, for me."

"Why? I supposed that you were a Christian, as you travel with the Tunker."

" Mary Panisciowa knows how my father died. I am his son. I swore to be true to his name. The Tunker says that I must forswear myself to become a Christian. That I shall never do. I respect the teachings of your new religion, and I love the Tunker and shall always be true to him, but I shall be true to the memory of my father. Mary Panisciowa, think how he died, and of the men who killed him. They claimed to be Christians. Think of that! I am not a Christian. Mary Panisciowa, there is a spot that burns in my heart. I do not dissemble. I do not deceive. But that fire will burn there till I have kept my vow, and I shall do it."

" Waubeno," said the woman, " listen to better counsels. Revenge only spreads the fires of evil. Forgiveness quenches them.—That is a noble letter," she said to Jasper.

" Yes, a noble letter, and the marquis is an apostle of human liberty, a friend of all men everywhere. What brings him here ? "

" The old French and new English families. His visit is unexpected. The people can not receive him as they ought to, but he is to dine at the tavern, and there are to be two grand receptions at the great houses, one at Mr. Edgar's. I wish I could see him and show him this letter. I shall try. But they have not invited me. They are proud people, and they will not invite me; but I shall try to see him. It would be the happiest hour of my life if I could take the hand of the great Lafayette."

Mary Panisciowa was thrilled with her desire to meet General Lafayette.

Cannons boomed, drums and fifes played, and all the people hurried toward the landing. The marquis came in the steamer Natchez from St. Louis. When Mary Panisciowa heard the old bell ringing she knew that the marquis was coming, and she hid the faded old letter in her bosom and wept. She sent a messenger to the tavern, who asked Lafayette if he would meet the daughter of Panisciowa, and receive a message from her.

Just at night she looked out of the door, and saw an officer in uniform and a party of her own people coming toward the house. The officer appeared before the door, touched his head and bowed, and said:

" Mary Panisciowa, I am told."

" My father was Panisciowa."

" He fought under General Lafayette ? "

" Yes, he fought under Lafayette, and I have a letter from the general here, written to him more than forty years ago. Will you read it? "

The officer took the letter, read it, and said:

" You should meet the general."

" You are very kind, sir." I want to meet him; but how ? There is to be a reception at the Morrisons, but I am not invited. The Governor is to be there. But they would not invite me."

" Come to the reception at the Morrisons. I will be responsible. The marquis will welcome you. He is a gentleman. To say that a man is a gentleman, is to cover all right conduct. Bring your letter, and he will receive you. I will speak to Governor Coles about you. You will come? "

"May my friend Waubeno come with me? I am the daughter of a chief, and he is the son of a warrior. It would be befitting that we should come together. I wish that he might see the great Lafayette."

"As you like," said the officer, hurrying away with uncovered head.

Mary Panisciowa prepared to go to the grand reception. Early in the evening she and Waubeno, followed by Jasper, came up to the Morrison mansion, where a kind of court reception was to be held.

The streets were full of people. The houses were everywhere illuminated, and people were hurrying to and fro, or listening to the music in the hall.

Lafayette was now nearly threescore and ten years of age, the beloved hero of France and America, and the leader of human liberty in all lands. He had left Havre on July 12th, 1824, and had arrived in New York on the 15th of August. He was accompanied by his son, George Washington Lafayette, and his private secretary, M. Levasseur. His passage through the country had been a triumphal procession, under continuous arches of flags, evergreens, and flowers, bearing the words, "Welcome, Lafayette." Forty years had passed since he was last in America. The thirteen States had become twenty-four. He had visited Joseph Bonaparte, the grave of Washington, and the battle-field of Yorktown. His reception in the South had been an outpouring of hearts. And now he had turned aside from the great Mississippi to see Kaskaskia, the romantic town of the vanished French empire of the Mississippi.

Mary and Waubeno waited outside of the door. The Indian woman listened for a time to the gay music, and watched the bright uniforms as they passed to and fro under the glittering astrals. At last an American officer came down the steps, lifted his hat, and said to the two Indians and to Jasper:

"Follow me."

Lafayette had already received the public men of the place. Airy music arose, and the officials and their wives and guests were going through the form of the old court minuet.

The music of Mozart's Don Giovanni minuet has been heard in a thousand halls of state and at the festivals of many lands. We may imagine the charm that such music had here, in this oaken room of the forest and prairie. At the head of the plumed ladies and men in glittering uniforms stood the Marquis of France, whom the world delighted to honor, and led the stately obeisances to the picturesque movement of the music under the flags and astrals. A remnant of the old romantic French families were there, soldiers of the Revolution, the leaders of the new order of American life, Governor Coles and his officers, and rich traders of St. Louis. As the music swayed these stately forms backward and forward with the fascinating poetry of motion that can hardly be called a dance, the two Indian faces caught the spirit of the scene. Waubeno had never heard the music of the minuet before, and the strains entranced him as they rose and fell.

Minuet from Don Giovanni.

BY MOZART.　ARR. BY CARL ERICH.

Published by the permission of Arthur P. Schmidt.

After the minuet, Lafayette and Governor Coles received the towns-people, and among the first to be presented to the marquis was Mary Panisciowa.

She bowed modestly, and told him her simple tale. The marquis listened at first with courtly interest, then with profound emotion. She drew from her bosom the letter that he had written to her father, the chief. His own writing brought before him the scenes of almost a half-century gone, the struggle for liberty in the new land to which he had given his young soul. He remembered the old chief, and the forest scenes of those heroic years; Washington, and the generals he had loved, most of whom were gone, arose again. His heart filled with emotion, and he said:

"Nothing in my visit here has affected me so much as

this. I thank you for seeking me. I welcome you with all my heart. Let me spend as much time as I may in your company. Your father was a hero, and your presence fills my heart with no common pleasure and delight. Stay with me."

The marquis welcomed Waubeno cordially, and expressed his pleasure at meeting him here. At the romantic festival no people were more warmly met than the chief's daughter and her escort.

"The French have always been true to the Indians," said Waubeno, on leaving the general, "and the Indians have been as true to the French."

"Never did rulers have better subjects," said the general.

"Never did subjects have better rulers," said Waubeno, almost repeating the scene of Dick Whittington, thrice Lord Mayor of London, by virtue of his wonderful cat, to King Henry.

The Indians withdrew amid the gay strains of national music, the stately minuet haunting Waubeno and ringing in his ears.

He tried to hum the rhythms of the beautiful air of the courts. Jasper saw how the music had affected him, and that he was happy and susceptible, and said :

"Waubeno, you have met a man to-night who would forget his own position and pleasure to do honor to the Indian girl."

"Yes, I am sure of that."

"You are your best self to-night—in your best mood; the

music has awakened your better soul. You remember your promise?"

"Yes, but, Brother Jasper—"

"What, Waubeno?"

"Lafayette is a *Frenchman*, and—a gentleman. The Indians and French do not spill each other's blood. Why?"

CHAPTER XIV.

WAUBENO AND YOUNG LINCOLN.

NE leafy afternoon in May, Jasper and Waubeno came to Aunt Olive's, at Pigeon Creek. Southern Indiana is a glory of sunshine and flowers at this season of the year, and their journey had been a very pleasant one.

They had met emigrants on the Ohio, and had seen the white sail of the prairie schooner in all of the forest ways.

"The world seems moving to the west," said Jasper, "as in the white Indian's dream. There is need of my work more and more. Every child that I can teach to read will make better this new empire that is being sifted out of the lands. Every school that I can found is likely to become a college, and I am glad to be a wanderer in the wilderness for the sake of my fellow-men."

In the open door, under the leafing vines, stood Aunt Indiana, in cap, wig, and spectacles. She arched her elbow over all to shade her eyes.

"The old Tunker, as I live, come again, and brought his Indian boy with him!" said she. "Well, you are welcome to Pigeon Creek. You left a sight of good thoughts here when you were here before. You're a good pitcher, if you are a little

cracked, with the handle all one side.   Come in, and welcome.
Take a chair and sit down—

> ''Tis a long time since I see you.
> How does your wife and children do?'

as the poet sings."

"I am well, and am glad to be toiling for the bread that
does not fail in the wilderness.   How are the people of
Pigeon Creek—how are my good friends the Lincolns?"

"The Linkens?   Well, Tom Linken makes out to hold together after a fashion—all dreams and expectations.   'The
thing that hath been is,' the Scriptur' says, and Thomas Linken *is*—just as he always was, and always will be to the end
of the chapter.   He's got to the p'int after which there is no
more to be told, long ago.   The life of such as he repeats
itself over and over, like a buzzin' spinnin'-wheel.   And *Miss*
Linken, she is as patient as ever; 'tis her mission just to be
patient with old Tom."

"And Abraham?"

"That boy Abe—the one that we prophesied about!   Well,
elder, I do hate to say, 'cause it makes you out to be no
prophet, and you mean well, goin' about tryin' to get a little
larnin' into the skulls of the people in this new country; but
that boy promises pretty slim, though I ain't nothin' to say
agin' him.   In the first place, he's grown up to be a giant,
all legs and ears, mouth and eyes.   Why, he is the tallest
young man in this part of Indiana!

"Then, his head's off.   He goes about readin' books, just
as he did when you were here last—this book, and that book,
and the other book; and then he all runs to talk, which

some folks takes for wisdom. He tells stories that makes everybody laugh, and he seems very chipper and happy, but they do say that he has melancholy spells, and is all down in the mouth at times. But he's good-hearted, and speaks the truth, and helps poor folks, and there's many a wuss one than Abraham Linken now. They didn't invite him to the great weddin' of the Grigsbys, cos he's so homely, and hadn't anythin' to wear but leather breeches, and they only come down a little below his knees. Queer-lookin' he'd 'a' been to a weddin'!

"He felt orful bad at not bein' invited, and made some poetry about 'em. When I feel poetic I talk prose, and give people as good as they send. I don't write no poetry.

"You are welcome to stay here, elder. You needn't go to the Linkens'. I have a prophet's chamber in my house—though you ain't a prophet—and you can always sleep there, and your Indian boy can lay down in the kitchen; and I can cook, elder—now you know that—and I won't ask ye to cobble; your time is too valuable for that."

Jasper, who was not greatly influenced by Aunt Indiana's unfavorable views of her poor neighbor, went to see Thomas Lincoln. Waubeno went with him. Here the young Indian met with a hearty greeting from both Mr. and Mrs. Lincoln.

"I am glad that you have come again," said poor Mrs. Lincoln to Jasper. "You comforted me and encouraged me when you were here last. I want to talk with you. Abe has all grown up, and wants to make a new start in life; and I wish to see him started right. There's so much in gettin' started right; a right start is all the way, sometimes. We don't travel twice over the same years. I want you to talk with him. You have seen this world, and we haven't, but you kind o' brought the world to us when you were here last. Elder, you don't know how much good you are doin'."

"Where is Abraham?" asked Jasper.

"He's gone to the store for the evenin'. He's been keepin' store for Jones, in Gentryville, and he spends his evenin's there. There ain't many places to go to around here, and Abe he's turned the store into a kind of debatin' club. He speaks pieces there. There's goin' to be a debate there to-night. He's great on debatin'. I do hope you'll go. The subject of the debate to-night is, 'Which has the greater cause for complaint, the negro or the Indian?'"

"I'm goin' over to the store to-night myself, elder," said Thomas Lincoln. "You must go along with me and hear Abraham talk, and then come back and spend the night here. The old woman has been hopin' that you would come. It pleased her mightily, what you said good about Abraham when you was here last. She sets her eyes by Abraham, and he does by her. Abraham and I don't get along none too well. The fact is, he all runs to books, and is kind o' queer. He takes after his mother's folks—they all had houses in the air, and lived in 'em. Abe might make somethin'; there's somethin' in him, if larnin' don't spile him. I have to warn him against larnin' all the time, but it all goes agin the grain, and I declare sometimes I do get all out of patience, and clean discouraged. Why, elder, he even takes a book out when he goes to shuck corn, and he composes poetry on the wooden shovel, and planes it out with my plane, and wears the shovel all up. There, now, look there!—could you stand it?"

Thomas Lincoln took up a large wooden fire-shovel, and held it before the eyes of the Tunker. On the great bowl of the shovel were penned some lines in coal.

"What does that read, elder?—I can't tell. I ain't got no larnin' to spare. What does it read, elder?"

Jasper scanned the writing on the surface of the back of the shovel. The writing was clear and plain. Mrs. Lincoln came and looked over his shoulder.

"Writ it himself, likely as not," said she. "Abe writes poetry; he can't help it sometimes—it's a gift. Read it, elder."

Jasper read slowly:

> "'Time! what an empty vapor 'tis!
>   And days, how swift they are!
> Swift as an arrow speed our lives,
>   Swift as the shooting star.
> The present moment—'"

"He didn't finish it, did he, elder? I think it is real pooty—don't you?"

Mrs. Lincoln turned her broad, earnest face toward the Tunker.

"Real pooty, ain't it?"

"Yes," said Jasper. "He'll be likely to do some great work in life, and leave it unfinished. It comes to me so."

"Don't say so, elder. His father don't praise him much, but he's real good to me, and I hope no evil will ever happen to him. I set lots of store by Abe. I don't know any differ-

A QUEER PLACE TO WRITE POETRY.

ence between him and my own son. His poor, dead mother, that lies out there all alone under the trees, knows that I have done by him as if he were my own. You know, the guardian angels of children see the face of the Father, and I kind o' think that she is his guardian; and if she is, now, I hain't anything to reflect upon."

"Only you're spilin' him — that's all," said Mr. Lincoln. "Some women are so good that they are not good for anything, and between me and Sarah and his poor, dead mother, Abraham has never had the discipline that he ought to have had. But Andrew Crawford, the schoolmaster, and Josiah Crawford, the farmer, did their duty by him. Come, elder, let us go up to Jones's store, and talk politics a while. Jones, he's a Jackson man. He sets great store by Abe, and thinks, like you and Sarah, that the boy will make somethin' some day. Well, I hope he will—can't tell."

Mr. Jones's store was the popular resort of Gentryville. Says one of the old pioneers, Dougherty: "Lincoln drove a team, and sold goods for Jones. Jones told me that Lincoln read all of his books, and I remember the History of the United States as one. Jones afterward said to me that Lincoln would make a great man one of these days—had said so long before to other people, and so as far back as 1828 and 1829."

The store was full of men and boys when Thomas Lincoln and Jasper and Waubeno arrived. Dennis Hanks was there, and the Grigsbys. Josiah Crawford, who had made Abraham pull fodder for three days for allowing a book that he had lent him to get wet one rainy night, was seated on a barrel. His nose was very long, and he had a high forehead, and wide look

across the forehead.   He looked very wise and thought himself
a Solomon.

The men and boys all seemed to be glad to see the Tunker,
and they greeted Waubeno kindly, though curiously, and plied
him with civil questions about Black Hawk.

There was to be a debate that evening, and Mr. Jones
called the men to order, and each one mounted a barrel and lit
his pipe—or all except Abraham and Waubeno, who did not
smoke, but who stood near each other, almost side by side.

"Abraham," said Thomas Lincoln, "you'll have to argue
the p'int for the Indian well to-night, or—there he is!"—
pointing to Waubeno—"he'll answer ye."

The debate went slowly at first, then grew exciting.   When
Abraham Lincoln's turn came to speak, all the store grew still.
The subject of the debate was, as Thomas Lincoln had said:
"Which has the greater cause for complaint, the Indian or
the negro?"

Abraham Lincoln claimed the Indian was more wronged
than the negro, and his homely face glowed as with a strange
fire as he pictured the red man's wrongs.   He towered above
the men like a giant, and moved his arms as though they
possessed some invisible power.

Waubeno fixed his eyes on him, and felt the force and
thrust of his every word.

"If I were a negro," said Lincoln, "I would hope that
some redeemer and deliverer would arise, like Moses of old.
But if I were an Indian, what would I have to hope for, if I
fell under the avarice of the white man?   Let the past answer
that."

"Let the heavens answer that," said Waubeno, "or let their gates be ever closed."

Thomas Lincoln started.

"Waubeno, you have come from Black Hawk. He slays men, and we know him. An Indian killed my father."

"An Indian killed your father—and what did you do?"

"My brother Mordecai avenged his death, and caused many Indians to bite the dust."

"White brother," said Waubeno, "a white man killed my father. What ought I to do?"

The men held their pipes in silence.

"My father was an innocent man," said the pioneer.

"My father was an honorable warrior," said Waubeno, "and defended his own rights—rights as dear to him as your father's, or your's, or mine. What ought I to do?" He turned to young Lincoln. "What would you do?"

"I hold that in all things right is might, and I defend the right of an Indian as I would the rights of a white man, but I never would shed any man's blood for avarice or malice. Waubeno, I would defend you in a cause of right against the world. I would rather have the approval of Heaven than the praise of all mankind."

"Brother," said Waubeno, "I believe that you speak true, but I do not know. If I only knew that you spoke true, I would not do as Mordecai did. I would forgive the white man."

The candles smoked, and the men talked long into the night. At last Thomas Lincoln and Jasper and Waubeno went home, where Mrs. Lincoln was awaiting them. They expected Abraham to follow them. They sat up that night late, and talked about the prairie country, and the prospects of the emigrants to Illinois.

"Now you had better go to rest," said Sarah Lincoln. "I will sit up until Abe comes. I do not see why he is so late to-night, when the Tunker is here, too, and the Indian boy."

"He's with the Grigsbys, I guess," said Mr. Lincoln.

The two men went to their beds, and Waubeno laid down on a mat on the floor. Hour after hour passed, and Mrs. Lincoln went again and again to the door and listened, but Abraham did not return. It was midnight when she laid down, but even then it was to listen, and not to sleep.

In the morning Abraham returned. His eyes were sunken and his cheeks were white.

"Get me some coffee, mother," he said. "I have not slept a wink to-night."

"Why, where have you been, Abraham?"

"Watchin'—watchin' with a frozen drunken man. I found him on the road, and carried him to Dennis's on my back. He seemed to be dead, but I rubbed him all night long, and he breathed again."

"Why did you not get some one to help you?"

"The boys all left me. They said that old Holmes was not worth revivin', even if he had any life left in him; that it would be better for himself and everybody if he were left to perish."

"Holmes! Did you carry that man on your back, Abraham?"

"Yes. I could not leave him by the road. He is a human

being, and I did by him as I would have him do by me if I lost my moral senses. They told me to leave him to his fate, but I couldn't, mother. I couldn't."

Waubeno gazed on the young giant as he drank his coffee, and sank into a deep slumber on a mat in the room. He watched him as he slept.

When he woke, Jasper said to him :

"Abraham, I wish you to know this Indian boy. I think there is a native nobility in him. Do you remember Johnnie Kongapod's story, at which the people all used to laugh ?"

"Yes, elder."

"Abraham Lincoln, I can believe that story was true. I have faith in men. You do. Your faith will make you great."

CHAPTER XV.

THE DEBATING SCHOOL.

HERE were some queer people in every town and community of the new West, and these were usually active at the winter debating school. These schools of the people for the discussion of life, politics, literature, were, on the whole, excellent influences; they developed what was original in the thought and character of a place, and stimulated reading and study. If a man was a theorist, he could here find a voice for his opinions; and if he were a genius, he could here uncage his gifts and find recognition. Nearly all of the early clergymen, lawyers, congressmen, and leaders of the people of early Indiana and Illinois were somehow developed and educated in these so-called debating schools.

Among the odd people sure to be found in such rural assemblies were the man with visionary schemes for railroads, canals, and internal improvements, the sanguine inventor, the noisy free-thinker, the benevolent Tunker, the man who could preach without notes by "direct inspiration," the man who thought that the world was about to come to an end, and the patriot who pictured the American eagle as a bird of fate and divinity. The early pioneer preacher learned to talk in public in the debating school. The young lawyer here made his first pleas.

The frequent debates in Jones's store led to the formation of a debating school in Gentryville and Pigeon Creek. In this society young Abraham Lincoln was the leader, and his cousin Dennis Hanks and his uncle John were prominent disputants. The story-telling blacksmith furnished much of the humor, and Josiah Crawford, or "Blue-Nose Crawford," as he was called, was regarded as the man of hard sense on such occasions as require a Solomon, or a Daniel, or a Portia, and he was very proud to be so regarded.

There was a revival of interest in the cause of temperance in the country at this time, and the noble conduct of Abraham Lincoln, in carrying to his cousin Dennis's the poor drunkard whom he had found in the highway on the chilly night after the debate at Jones's store, may have led to a plan for a great debate on the subject of the pledge, which was appointed to take place in the log school-house at Pigeon Creek. The plan was no more than spoken of at the store than it began to excite general attention.

"We must debate this subject of the temperance pledge," said Thomas Lincoln, "and get the public sense. New times are at hand. On general principles, I'm a temperance man ; and if nobody drank once, then nobody would drink twice, and the world would all go dry. But there's the corn-huskin's, and the hoe-down, and the mowin' times, and the hog-killin's, and the barn-raisin's. It is only natural that men should wet their whistles at such times as these. In the old Scriptur' times people who wanted to get great spiritual power abstained from strong drink; but you can't expect no such people as those down here at Pigeon Creek."

" But Abe is a temperancer, and I want the debate to come off in good shape, so that all you uns can hear what he has to say."

It was decided by the leading debaters that the subject for the debate should be, " Ought temperance people to sign the temperance pledge? " and that Abraham Lincoln should sustain the affirmative view of the question.

The success of young Lincoln as a debater had greatly troubled Aunt Indiana.

" It's all like the rattlin' of a pea-pod in the blasts o' ortum," she said. " It don't signify anything. He just rains words upon ye, and makes ye laugh, and the first thing ye know he's got ye. Beware—beware! his words are just like stool-pigeons, what brings you down to get shot. It's amazin' what a curi'us gift of talk that boy has! "

When she heard of the plan of the debate, and the part assigned to young Lincoln, she said:

" 'Twill be a great night for Abe, unless I hinder it. I'm agin the temperance pledge. Stands to reason that a man's no right to sign away his liberty. And I'm agin Abe Linkern, because he's too smart for anythin', and lives up in the air like a kite; and outthinks other people, because he sits round readin' and turkey-dreamin' when he ought to be at work. I shall work agin him."

And she did. She first consulted upon the subject with Josiah Crawford—" the Esquire," as she called him—and he promised to give the negative of the question all the weight of his ability.

There was a young man in Gentryville named John Short, who thought that he had had a call to preach, and who often came to Aunt Indiana for theological instruction.

"Don't run round the fields readin' books, like Abraham Linkern," she warned him. "He'll never amount to a hill o' beans. The true way to become a preacher is to go into the desk, and open the Bible, and put yer fingers on the first passage that you come to, and then open yer mouth, and the Lord will fill it. I do not believe in edicated ministers. They trust in chariots and horses. Go right from the plow to the pulpit, and the heavens will help ye."

John Short thought Aunt Indiana's advice sound, and he resolved to follow it. He once made an appointment to preach after this unprepared manner in the school-house. He could not read very well. He had once read at school, "And he smote the Hittite that he died" "And he smote the Hi-ti-ti-ty, that he did," and he opened the Bible at random for a Scripture lesson on this trying occasion. His eye fell upon the hard chapters in Chronicles beginning "Adam, Sheth, Enoch." He succeeded very well in the reading until he came to the generations of Japheth and the sons of Gomer, which were mountains too difficult to pass. He lifted his eyes and said, "And so it goes on to the end of the chapter, without regard to particulars."

"That chapter was given me to try me," he said, as a kind of commentary, "and, my friends, I have been equal to it. And now you shall hear me preach, and after that we'll take up a contribution for the new meetin'-house."

The sermon was a short one, and began amid much mental

confusion. "A certain man," he began, "went down from
Jerusalem to Jericho and fell among thieves; and the thieves
sprang up and choked him; and he said, 'Who is my neighbor?' You all know who your neighbors are, O my friends."
Here followed a long pause. He added:

"Always be good to your neighbors. And now we will pass
around the contribution-box, and after that we'll *all* talk."

This beginning of his work as a speaker did not look promising, but he had conducted "a meetin'," and that fact made
John Short a shining light in Aunt Indiana's eyes. To this
young man the good woman went for a champion of her ideas
in the great debate.

But, notwithstanding her theory, she proceeded to instruct
him as to what he should say on the occasion.

"Say to 'em, John, that he who comes to ye with a temperance pledge insults yer character. It is like askin' ye to
promise not to become a jackass; and what would ye think of
a man who would ask ye to sign a paper like that? or to sign
the Ten Commandments? or to promise that ye'd never lie any
more? It's one's duty to maintain one's dignity of character,
and, John, I want ye to open yer mouth in defense of the
rights of liberty on the occasion; and do yer duty, and bring
down the Philistine with a pebble-stun, and 'twill be a glorious night for Pigeon Creek."

The views of Aunt Olive Eastman on preaching without
preparation and on temperance were common at this time in
Indiana and Illinois. By not understanding a special direction
of our Lord to his disciples as to what they should do in times
of persecution, many of the pioneer exhorters used to speak from

the text on which their eyes first rested on opening the Bible. They seemed to think that this mental field needed no planting or culture—no training like Paul's in the desert of Arabia, and that the pulpit stood outside of the universal law. The moral education of the pledge of Father Matthew was just beginning to excite attention. Strange as it may seem, the thoughts and plans of the Irish apostle of temperance and founder of the Order of St. Vincent de Paul seemed to have come to Abraham Lincoln in his early days much as original inspiration. His first public speech was on this subject. It was made in Springfield, Illinois, in 1842, and advocated the plan which Father Matthew was then originating in Ireland, the education of the public conscience by the moral force of the temperance pledge.

It was a lengthening autumn evening when the debate took place in the school-house in the timber. The full moon rose like a disk of gold as the sun sank in clouds of crimson fire, and the light of the day became a mellowed splendor during half of the night. The corn-fields in the clearings rose like armies, bearing food on every hand. Flocks of birds darkened the sunset air, and little animals of the woods ran to and fro amid the crisp and fallen leaves. The air was vital with the coolness that brings the frost and causes the trees to unclasp their countless shells, barks, and burrs, and let the ripe nuts fall.

The school-room filled with earnest faces early in the evening. The people came over from Gentryville, among them Mr. Gentry himself and Mr. Jones the store-keeper. Women brought tallow dips for lights, and curious candlesticks and snuffers.

Aunt Indiana and Josiah Crawford came together, an imposing-looking couple, who brought with them the air of special sense and wisdom. Aunt Indiana wore a bonnet of enormous proportions, which distinguished her from the other women, who wore hoods. She brought in her hand a brass candlestick, which the children somehow associated with the ancient Scripture figures, and which looked as though it might have belonged to the temples of old. She was tall and stately, and the low room was too short for her soaring bonnet, but she bent her head, and sat down near Josiah Crawford, and set the candle in the shining candlestick, and cast a glance of conscious superiority over the motley company.

The moderator rapped for order and stated the question for debate, and made some inspiring remarks about " parliamentary " rules. John Short opened the debate with a plea for independence of character, and self-respect and personal liberty.

" What would you think," he asked, "of a man who would come to you *in the night* and ask you to sign a paper not to lie any more? What? You would think that he thought you had been lying. Would you sign that paper? No! You would call out the dogs of retribution, and take down your father's sword, and you would uplift your foot into the indignant air, and protect your family name and honor. Who would be called a liar, in a cowardly way like that? And who would be called a drunkard, by being asked to sign the paper of a tee-totaler? Who? "

Here John Short paused. He presently said :

" Hoo ? "— which sounded in the breathless silence like

the inquiries of an owl. But his ideas had all taken wings again and left him, as on the occasion when he attempted to preach without notes or preparation.

Aunt Indiana looked distressed. She leaned over toward Josiah Crawford, and said :

"Say somethin'."

But Josiah hesitated. Then, to the great amusement of all, Aunt Indiana rose to the ceiling, bent her generously bonneted head, stretched forth her arm, and said :

"He is quite right—quite right, Josiah. Is he not, Josiah?"

"Quite right," said Josiah.

"People do not talk about what is continuous—what goes right along. Am I not right, Josiah?"

"Quite right! quite right!"

"If a man tells me he is honest, he is not honest. If he tells me that he is pure, he isn't pure. If he were honest or pure he says nothing about it. Am I not right, Josiah?"

"Quite right! quite right!"

"Nobody tells about his stomach unless it is out of order; and no one puts cotton into keyholes unless he himself is peeking through keyholes. Am I not right, Josiah?"

"Quite right! quite right!"

"And no one asks ye to sign a temperance pledge unless he's been a drunkard himself, or thinks ye are one, or likely to be. Ain't I right, Josiah?"

"Quite right!"

"The best way to support temperance is to live temperately and say nothin' about it. There, now! If I had held my peace, the stones would have cried out. Olive Eastman has spoken, and Josiah says that I am right, and I'm agin the temperance pledge, and there's nothin' more to be said about it."

Aunt Indiana sat down amid much applause. Then Jasper rose, and showed that intemperance was a great evil, and that public sentiment should be educated against it.

."This education should begin in childhood," he said, "in habits of self-respect and self-restraint. The child should be first instructed to say "No" to himself."

He proceeded to argue for the temperance pledge from his point of view.

"The world is educated by pledges," he said. "The patriot is kept in his line of march by the pledge; the business man makes a pledge when he signs a note; and the Christian takes pledges when he joins the Church. We should be willing to take any pledge that will make life better. If eating meat cause my brother to stumble and offend, then I will not eat meat. I will sacrifice myself always to that which will help the world and honor God. I am sorry to differ from the good woman who has spoken, but I am for the use of the pledge. I never drank strong drink, and this hand shall sign any pledge that will help a poor tempted brother by my example."

Tall Abraham Lincoln arose.

"There! he's goin' to speak—I know he'd been preparin'," whispered Aunt Indiana to Josiah Crawford. "Wonder what he'll have to say. *You'll* have to answer him. He's just a regular Philistine, and goes stalkin' through the land, and turns people's heads; and he's just Tom Linkern's son, who is shiftless and poor, and I'm goin' agin him."

The tall young man stood silent. The people were silent.

Aunt Indiana gave her puncheon seat a push to break the force of that silence, and whispered to Josiah:

"There! they are all ears. I told ye 'twould be so. You must answer him."

Young Lincoln spoke slowly, and after this manner:

"My friends: When you pledge yourself to enforce a principle, you identify yourself with that principle, and give it power."

There was a silence. Then the people filled the little room with applause. He continued most impressively in the words of grand oration: *

"The universal sense of mankind on any subject is an argument, or at least an influence, not easily overcome. The success of the argument in favor of the existence of an over-ruling Providence mainly depends upon that sense; and men ought not, in justice, to be denounced for yielding to it in any case, or giving it up slowly, especially when they are backed by interest, fixed habits, or burning appetites.

"If it be true that those who have suffered by intemperance personally and have reformed are the most powerful and efficient instruments to push the reformation to ultimate success, it does not follow that those who have not suffered have no part left them to perform. Whether or not the world would be vastly benefited by a total and final banishment from it of all intoxicating drinks seems to me not now an open question. Three fourths of mankind confess the affirmative with their tongues; and, I believe, all the rest acknowledge it in their hearts.

---

* We use here some of the exact sentences which young Lincoln employed on a similar occasion at Springfield.

"But it is said by some, that men will think and act for themselves; that none will disuse spirits or anything else because his neighbors do; and that moral influence is not that powerful engine contended for. Let us examine this. Let me ask the man who could maintain this position most stiffly, what compensation he will accept to go to church some Sunday and sit during the sermon with his wife's bonnet upon his head? Not a trifle, I'll venture. And why not? There would be nothing irreligious in it, nothing immoral, nothing uncomfortable—then why not? Is it not because there would be something egregiously unfashionable in it? Then, it is the influence of fashion. And what is the influence of fashion but the influence that other people's actions have on our own actions—the strong inclination each of us feels to do as we see all our neighbors do? Nor is the influence of fashion confined to any particular thing or class of things. It is just as strong on one subject as another. Let us make it as unfashionable to withhold our names from the temperance pledge as for husbands to wear their wives' bonnets to church, and instances will be just as rare in the one case as in the other."

The people saw the moral point clearly. They felt the force of what the young orator had said. No one was willing to follow him.

"Have you anything to say, Mr. Crawford?" said the moderator.

Josiah merely shook his head.

"He don't care to put on his wife's bonnet agin public opinion," said the blacksmith.

CHAPTER XVI.

THE SCHOOL THAT MADE LINCOLN PRESIDENT.

HILE teaching and preaching in Decatur, Jasper heard of the new village of Salem, Illinois, on the Sangamon. He thought that the little town might offer him a chance to exert a new influence, and he resolved to visit it, and to preach and to teach there for a time should the people receive him kindly.

The village was a small one, consisting of a community store, a school-house, a tavern, and a few houses; and Jasper knew of only one friend there at the time, a certain Mr. Duncan, who lived some two miles from the main street and the store.

One afternoon, after a long journey over prairie land, Jasper came to Mrs. Duncan's door, and was met cordially by the good woman, and invited by her to make his home there for a time.

The family gathered around the story-telling missionary after supper, and listened to his tales of the Rhine, all of which had some soul-lesson in his view, and enabled him to preach by parables. No stories better served this peculiar mission than Baron Fouqué's, and this night he related Thiodolf, the Icelander.

There came a rap at the door.

"Who can that be?" said Mrs. Duncan in alarm.

She opened the door, and a tall, dark-faced young man stood before her.

"Why, Abe," said Mrs. Duncan, "what has brought you here at this late hour? I hope that nothing has happened!"

"That bill of yours. You paid me two dollars and six cents, did you not? It was not right."

"Isn't it? Well, I paid you all that you asked me, like an honest woman, so I am not to blame for any mistake. How much more do you want? If it isn't too much I'll pay it, for I think that you mean well."

"More! That isn't it, Mrs. Duncan; you paid me six cents too much—you overpaid me. It was my fault."

"Your fault!—and honest Abe Lincoln, you have walked two miles out of your way to pay me that six cents! Why didn't you wait until to-morrow?"

"I couldn't."

"Why, what is going to happen?"

"I can't sleep with a thing like that on my conscience. Now I feel light and free again."

"Come in, if it is late. We've got company—a Tunker—teaches, preaches, and works. May be you have met him before. He's been traveling down in Indiana and middle Illinois."

Abraham came in, and Jasper rose to receive him.

"Lincoln," said the wandering school-master, "it does my heart good to see you. I see that you have grown in body and in soul. What brought you here? I have been telling stories for hours. Sit down, and tell us about what has happened to you since we met last."

The tall young man sat down.

" He's clark down to Orfutt's store now," said Mrs. Duncan, " and his word is as good as gold, and his weights are as true as the scales of the Judgment Day. Why, one day he made a wrong weight of half a pound, and as soon as he found it out he shut up the shop and went shivering through the village with that half-pound of tea as though the powers of the air were after him. He's schooled his conscience so that he couldn't be dishonest if he were to try. I do believe a dishonorable act would wither him and drive him crazy."

" Character, which is the habit of obedience to the universal law of right, is the highest school of life," said Jasper. " That is what I try to teach everywhere. But Abraham has heard me say that before. Where have you been since I saw you last? Tell me, what has been your school of life?"

" I have been to New Orleans in a flat-boat. I went for Mr. Orfutt, who now keeps the store in this place. When I came back he gave me a place in his store here. I have been here ever since."

" What did you see in New Orleans?"

" Slavery—men sold in the market like cattle. Jasper, it made me long to have power—to control men and congresses and armies. If I only had the power, I would strike that institution hard. I said that to John Hanks, and he thought that slavery wasn't in any danger from anything that I would be likely to do. It don't look so, does it, elder? I have one

vote, and I shall always cast that against wrong as long as I
live. That is my right to do.

"Elder, listen. I want to tell you what I saw there one
day, in a slave-pen. I saw a handsome young girl, with white
blood in her, brought forward by a slave-driver and handled
and struck with a whip like a horse. I had heard of such
things before, but it did not seem possible that they could be
true. Then I saw the same girl sold at auction, and purchased
by a man who carried the face of a brute. When she saw
who had purchased her, she wrung her hands and cried, but
she was helpless and hopeless; and I turned my face toward the
sky and vowed to give my soul against a system like that.
I'm a Free-Soiler in my heart, and I have faith that right
is might, and that the right in this matter will one day prevail."

Jasper remained with Mrs. Duncan for some days, and then
formed a small school in the neighborhood, on the road to the
town of Springfield, Illinois.

While teaching here he could not but notice the growth of
Orfutt's clerk in the confidence of all the people. In all the
games, he was chosen umpire or referee; in most cases of
dispute he was consulted, and his judgment was followed.
Long before he became a lawyer, people were accustomed to
say, in a matter of casuistry:

"Take the case to Lincoln. He will give an opinion that
will be fair."

Amid this growing reputation for character, a test happened which showed how far this moral education and discipline had gone.

A certain Henry McHenry, a popular man, had planned a horse-race, and applied to young Lincoln to go upon the racing stand as judge.

"The people have confidence in you," he said to Lincoln.

"I must not, and I will not do it," said Lincoln. "This custom of racing is wrong."

The man showed him that he was under a certain obligation to act as judge on this occasion.

"I will do it," he said; "but be it known to all that I will never appear at a horse-race again; and were I to become a lawyer, I would never accept a case into which I could not take an honest conscience, no matter what the inducements might be."

There was a school-master in New Salem who knew more than the honest clerk had been able to learn. This man, whose name was Graham, could teach grammar.

Abraham went to him one day, and said:

"I have a notion to study grammar."

"If you ever expect to enter public life, you should do so," said Mr. Graham. "Why not begin now and recite to me?"

"Where shall I secure a book?" asked the student of this hard college of the wood.

"There is a man named Vaner, who lives six miles from here, who has a grammar that I think he will be willing to sell."

"If it be possible, I will secure it," said Lincoln.

He made a long walk and purchased the book, and so made a grammar-school, a class of one, of his leisure moments in Orfutt's store.

13

While he thus was studying grammar, the men whom he thirty or more years afterward made Cabinet ministers, generals, and diplomats were enjoying the easy experiences of schools, military academies, and colleges. Not one of them ever dreamed of such an experience of soul-building and mind-building as this; and some of them, had they met him then, would have felt that they could not have invited him to their homes. Orfutt's store and that one grammar were not the elms of Yale, or the campus of Harvard, or the great libraries or bowery streets of English Oxford or Cambridge. Yet here grew and developed a soul which was to tower above the age, and hold hands with the master spirits not only of the time but the ages.

Years passed, and one day that sad-faced boy, who was always seeking to make others cheerful amid the clouds of his own gloom, stood before a grim council of war. He had determined to call into the field of arms five hundred thousand men.

"If you do that thing," said a leader of the council, "you can not expect to be elected again President of the United States."

The dark form rose to the height of a giant and poured forth his soul, and he said :

"It is not necessary for me to be re-elected President of the United States, but it is necessary for the soldiers at the front to be re-enforced by five hundred thousand men, and I shall call for them; and if I go down under the act, I will go down like the Cumberland, with my colors flying."

It required a high school of experience to train a soul to

an utterance like that; and that fateful declaration began in those moral syllables that defended the rights of the animals of the woods, that said " No " to a horse-race, that refused from the first to accept an unjust case at law, and that from the first declared that right is might.

CHAPTER XVII.

THOMAS LINCOLN MOVES.

ASPER taught school for a time in Boonesville, Indiana, and preached in the new settlements along the Wabash. While at Boonesville, he chanced to meet young Lincoln at the court house, under circumstances that filled his heart with pity.

It was at a trial for murder that greatly excited the people. The lawyer for the defense was John Breckinridge, a man of great reputation and ability.

Jasper saw young Lincoln among the people who had come to hear the great lawyer's plea, and said to him :

"You have traveled a long distance to be here to-day."

"Yes," said the tall young man. "There is nothing that leads one to seek information of the most intelligent people like a debating society. We, who used to meet to discuss questions at Jones's store, have formed a debating society, and I want to learn all I can of law for the sake of justice, and I owed it to myself and the society not to let this great occasion pass. I have walked fifteen miles to be here to-day. Did you know that father was thinking of moving to Illinois ?"

"No. Will you go with him ?"

" Yes, I shall go with him and see him well settled, and then I shall strike out for myself in the world. Father hasn't the faculty that mother has, you know. I can do some things better than he, and it is the duty of one member of the family to make up when he can for what another member lacks. We all have our own gifts, and should share them with others. I can split rails faster than father can, and do better work at house-building than he, and I am going with him and do for him the best I can at the start. I shall seek first for a roof for him, and then a place for myself."

The great lawyer arrived. The doors of the court-house were open, and the people filled the court-room.

The plea was a masterly one, eloquent and dramatic, and it thrilled the young soul of Lincoln. Full of the subject, the young debater sought Mr. Breckinridge after the court adjourned, and extended his long arm and hand to him.

The orator was a proud man of an aristocratic family, and thought it the proper thing to maintain his dignity on all occasions. He looked at the boy haughtily, and refused to take his hand.

" I thank you," said Lincoln. " I wish to express my gratitude."

" Sir ! "

With a contemptuous look Breckinridge passed by, and the slight filled the heart of the young man with disappointment and mortification. The two met again in Washington in 1862. The backwoods boy whose hand the orator had refused to take had become President of the United States. He extended his hand, and it was accepted.

"Sir," said the President, "that plea of yours in Boones-ville, Indiana, was one of the best that I ever heard."

"In Boonesville, Indiana?"

How like a dream to the haughty lawyer the recollection must have been! Such things as this hurt Lincoln to the quick. He was so low-spirited at times in his early manhood that he did not dare to carry with him a pocket-knife, lest he should be overcome in some dark and evil moment to end his own life. There were times when his tendencies were so alarming that he had to be watched by his friends. But these dark periods were followed by a great flow of spirits and the buoyancy of hope.

In the spring of 1830, Jasper and Waubeno came to Gentry-ville, and there met James Gentry, the leading man of the place.

"Are the Linkens still living in Spencer County?" he asked.

"Yes," said Mr. Gentry, "but it has been a hard winter here, and they are about to move. The milk sickness has been here again and has carried off the cattle, and the people have become discouraged, and look upon the place as unhealthy. I have bought Thomas Linken's property. The man was here this morning. You will find him getting ready to go away from Indiana for good and all."

"Where is he going?" asked Jasper.

"Off to Illinois."

"So I thought," said Jasper. "I must go to see him. How is that bright boy of his?"

"Abe?"

"Yes. I like that boy. I am drawn toward him. There is something about him that doesn't belong to many people —a spiritual graft that won't bear any common fruit. I can see it with my spiritual eye, in the open vision, as it were. You don't understand those things—I see you don't. I must see him. There are not many like him in soul, if he is ungainly in body. I believe that he is born to some higher destiny than other men. I see that you do not understand me. Time will make it plain."

"I'm a trader, and no prophet, and I don't know much about such matters as these. But Abe Linken, he's grown up now, and *up* it is, more than six feet tall. He's a giant, a great, ungainly, awkward, clever, honest fellow, full of jokes and stories, though down at times, and he wouldn't do a wrong thing if it were for his right hand, and couldn't do an unkind one. He comes up to the store here often and tells stories, and sometimes stays until almost midnight, just as he used to do at Jones's. Everybody likes him here, and we shall all miss him when he goes away."

Jasper and Waubeno left the little Indiana town, and went toward the cabin of the Lincolns. On the way Jasper turned aside to pay a short visit to Aunt Olive.

The busy woman saw the preacher from her door, and came out to welcome him.

"I knew it was you," was her salutation, "and I am right glad that you have come. It has been distressin' times in these parts. Folks have died, and cattle have died, and we're all poor enough now, ye may depend. Where are ye goin'?"

"To see the Lincolns."

"Sho'! goin' to see them again. Well, ye're none too soon. They're gettin' ready to move to Illinois. Thomas Linken's always movin.' Moved four times or more already, and I 'magine he'll just keep movin' till he moves into his grave, and stops for good. He just lives up in the air, that man does. He always is imaginin' that it rains gold in the *next* State or county, but it never rains anythin' but rain where he is; and if it rained puddin' and sugar-cane, his dish would be bottom upward, sure. Elder, what does make ye take such an interest in that there family?"

"Mrs. Lincoln is a very good woman, an uncommon one; and Abraham—"

"Yes, elder, I knew ye were goin' to say somethin' good of Abraham. Yer heart is just set on that boy. I could see it when ye were here. I remember all that ye prophesied about him. I ain't forgot it. Well, I am a very plain-spoken woman. Ye ain't much of a prophet, in my opinion. He hain't got anywhere yet—now, has he? He's just a great, tall, black, jokin' boy; awful lazy, always readin' and talkin'; tellin' stories and makin' people laugh, with his own mind as blue as my indigo-bag behind it all. That is just what he is, elder, and he'll never amount to anythin' in this world or any other. It's all just as I told ye it would be. There, now, elder, that's as true as preachin', and the plain facts of the case. You wait and see. Time tells the truth."

"His opportunity is yet to come; and when it does, he will have the heart and mind to fill it," said Jasper. "A soul that is true to what is best in life, becomes a power among men at last—it is spiritual gravitation. 'Tis current leads the river. You do not see."

"No, I do not understand any such things as those; but when you've been over to see the Linkens, you come back here, and I'll make ye some more doughnuts. Come back, won't ye, and bring yer Indian boy? I'm a plain woman, and live all alone, and I do love to hear ye talk. It gives me somethin' to think about after ye're gone; and there ain't many preachers that visit these parts."

Jasper moved on under the great trees, and came to the simple Lincoln cabin.

"You have come back, elder," said Thomas Lincoln. "Travelin' with your Indian boy? I'm glad to see you, though we are very poor now. We're goin' to move away—we and some other families. We're all off to Illinois. You've traveled over that kentry, preacher?"

"Yes, I've been there."

"Well, what do you think of the kentry?"

"It is a wonderful country, Mr. Lincoln. It can produce grain enough to feed the world. The earth grows gold. It will some day uplift cities—it will be rich and happy. I like the prairie country well."

"There! let me tell my wife.—Mother, here's the preacher. What do you think he says about the prairie kentry? Says the earth grows gold."

Poor Mrs. Lincoln looked sad and doubtful. She had heard such things before. But she welcomed Jasper heartily, and the three, with Waubeno, sat down to a meal of plain Indian pudding and milk, and talked of the sorrowful winter that had passed and the prospects of a better life amid the flowery prairies of Illinois.

A little dog played around them while they were thus eating and talking.

"It is not our dog," said Mrs. Lincoln, "but he has taken a great liking to Abraham. The boy is away now, but he will be back by sundown. The dog belongs to one of the family, and is always restless when Abraham has gone away. Abraham wants to take him along with us, but it seems to me that we've got enough mouths to feed without him. We are all so poor! and I don't see what good he would do. But if Abraham says so, he will have to go."

"How is Abraham?" asked Jasper.

"Oh, he is well, and as good to me as ever, and he studies hard, just as he used to do."

"And is as lazy as ever," said Thomas Lincoln. "At the lazy folks' fair he'd take the premium."

"You shouldn't say that," said Mrs. Lincoln. "Just think how good he was to everybody during the sickness! He never thought of himself, but just worked night and day. His own mother died of the same sickness years ago, and he's had a feelin' heart for the sufferers in this calamity. I tell you, elder, that he's good to everybody, and if he does not take hold to work in the way that father does, his head and heart are never idle. I am sorry that he and father do not see more alike. The boy is goin' to do well in the world. He begins right."

When Abraham returned, there was one heart that was indeed glad to see him. It was the little dog. The animal bounded heels over head as soon as he heard the boy's step, and almost leaped upon his tall shoulder as he met him.

"Humph!" said Mr. Lincoln.

"Animals know who are good to them," said Mrs. Lincoln. "Abraham, here is the preacher."

How tall, and dark, and droll, and yet how sad, the boy looked! He was full grown now, uncouth and ungainly. Who but Jasper would have seen behind the features of that young, sinewy backwoodsman the soul of the leader and liberator?

It was a busy time with the Lincolns. Their goods were loaded upon a rude and very heavy ox-wagon, and the oxen were given into the charge of young Abraham to drive.

The young man's voice might have been heard a mile as he swung his whip and called out to the oxen on starting. They passed by the grave under the great trees where his poor mother's body lay. and left it there, never to be visited again. There were some thirteen persons in the emigrant party.

Emigrant wagons were passing toward Illinois, the "prairie country," as it was called, over all the roads of Indiana. The "schooners," as these wagons were called, were everywhere to be seen on the great prairie sea. • It was the time of the great emigration. Jasper had never dreamed of a life like this before. He looked into one prairie wagon, whose young driver had gone for water. He turned to Waubeno, and said:

"What do you think I saw?"

"Guns to destroy the Indians; trinkets and trifles to cheat us out of our lands; whisky for tent-making."

"No, Waubeno. There was an old grandmother there, a sick woman, and a little coffin. This is a sad world sometimes.

I pity everybody, and I would that all men were brothers. Go, look into the wagon, Waubeno."

The Indian went, and soon returned.

"Do you pity them, Waubeno?"

"Yes; but—"

"What, Waubeno?"

"I pity the Indian mother too. Your people drove her from her corn-fields at Rock Island, and she left the graves of her children behind her."

There was a shadow of sadness in the hearts of the Lincoln family as they turned away forever from the grave of Nancy Lincoln under the trees. The poor woman who rested there in the spot soon to be obliterated, little thought on her dying bed that the little boy she was leaving to poverty and adventure would be one day ranked with great men of the ages—with Servius Tullius, Pericles, Cincinnatus, Cromwell, Hampden, Washington, and Bolivar; that he would sit in the seat of a long line of illustrious Presidents, call a million men to arms, or that his rude family features would find a place among the grand statues of every liberated country on earth.

Poor Nancy Hanks! Every one who knew her had felt the warmth of her kindness and marked her sadness. She was an intellectual woman, was deeply religious, and is believed to have been a very emotional character in the old Methodist camp-meetings. Her family, the Hankses, were among the best singers and loudest shouters at the camp-meetings, and she was in sympathy with them.

Her heart lived on in Abraham. When she fell sick of the epidemic fever, Abraham, then a boy of ten years of age, waited upon her and nursed her. There was no doctor within twenty-five miles. She was so slender, and had been so ill-sustained that the fever-fires did their work in a week. Finding her end near, she called Abraham and his little sister to her, and said :

" Be good to one another."

Her face looked into Abraham's for the last time.

" Live," she said, " as I have taught you. Love your kindred, and worship God."

She faded away, and her husband made her coffin with a whip-saw out of green wood, and on a changing October day they laid her away under the trees. They were leaving her grave now, the humblest of all places then, but a shrine to-day, for her son's character has glorified it.

He must have always remembered the hymns that she used to sing. Some of them were curious compositions. In the better class of them were ; " Am I a soldier of the cross," "Alas ! and did my Saviour bleed," and " How tedious and tasteless the hour." The camp-meeting melodies were simple, mere movements, like the negro songs.

Abraham swung his whip lustily over the oxen's heads on that long spring journey, and directed the way. The wheels of the cart were great rollers, and they creaked along. Here and there the roads were muddy, but the sky was blue above, and the buds were swelling, and the birds were singing, and the little dog that belonged to the party kept close to his heels, and the poor people journeyed on under the giant timber, and out of it at times along the ocean-like prairies of the Illinois. The world was before them—an expanse of forest and prairie that in fifty years were to be changed by the axe and plowshare into prosperous farms and homesteads, and settled by the restless nations of the world.

The journey was long. There were spells of wintry weather, for the spring advanced by degrees even here. Streams overflowing their banks lay across their way, and these had to be forded.

One morning the party came to a stream covered with thin ice. The oxen and horses hesitated, but were forced into the cold water. After a dreary effort the hardy pilgrims passed over and mounted the western bank. A sharp cry was heard on the opposite side.

"You have left the dog, Abe," said one. "Good riddance to him! I am glad that we are quit of him at last."

The dog's pitiable cry rang out on the crisp, cool air. He was barking *to* Abraham, and the teamster's heart recognized that the animal's call was to him.

"See him run, and howl!" said another. "Whip up, Abe, and we will soon be out of sight."

Young Lincoln looked behind. The little animal would go down to the water, and try to swim across, but the broken ice drove him back. Then he set up a cry, as much as to say:

"Abe, Abe, you will not leave me!"

"Drive on," said one of the men. "He'll take care of himself. He'd no business to lag behind. What do we want of the dog, anyway?"

The animal cried more and more piteously and lustily.

"Whoa!" said Lincoln.

"What are you going to do, Abe?"

"To do as I would be done by. I can't stand that."

Lincoln plunged into the frozen water and waded across. The dog, overjoyed, leaped into his arms. Lincoln returned, having borne the little dog in his arms across the stream. He was cold and dripping, and was censured for causing a needless delay. But he had a happy face and heart.

Referring to this episode of the journey a long time afterward, Lincoln said to a friend:

" I could not endure the idea of abandoning even a dog. Pulling off shoes and socks, I waded across the stream, and triumphantly returned with the shivering animal under my arms. His frantic leaps of joy, and other evidences of gratitude, repaid me for all the exposure I had undergone."

CHAPTER XVIII.

MAIN-POGUE.

ASPER taught for a time near New Salem, then made again his usual circuit, after which he made his home for a time at Springfield, Illinois. When Jasper was returning from this last circuit of his self-appointed mission the Black Hawk war had begun again. He came one day, after long wanderings, to Bushville, in Schuyler County, Illinois, and found the place in a state of great excitement. The town was filling with armed men, and among them were many faces that he had seen at New Salem, when Waubeno was his companion.

He recognized a Mr. Green, whom he had known in New Salem, and said to him:

" My friend, what does this armed gathering mean?"

" Black Hawk has crossed the Mississippi and is making war on the settlers. The Governor has called for volunteers to defend the State."

" What has led to this new outbreak?" said Jasper, although few knew the cause better than he.

" Oh, sentiment—Indian sentiment. Black Hawk wants the old Indian town on the bluff again. He says it is sacred to his race; that his ancestors are buried there, and that there is no place like it on earth, or none that can take its place in his soul. He claims that the chiefs had been made drunk by the white men when they signed the treaty that gave up the town; that he never sold his fathers' graves. His heart is full of revenge, and he and all his tribe cling to that old Sac village with the grasp of death."

" The trouble has been gathering long ? "

" Yes. The settlers came up, under the treaty, to occupy the best lands around the Sac town and compel the Indians to live west of the Mississippi. Then the Indians and settlers began to dispute and quarrel. The settlers brought whisky, and Black Hawk demanded that it should not be sold to his people. He violently entered a settler's claim, and stove in a barrel of whisky before the man's eyes. Then the Indians went over the Mississippi sullenly, and left their cabins and corn-fields. But hard weather came, and the women would come back to the old corn-fields, which they had planted the year before, to steal corn. They said that the corn was theirs, and that they were starving for their own food. Some of them were killed by the settlers. Black Hawk had become enraged again. He has been trying to get the Indian tribes to unite and kill all of the whites. He has violated the old Indian treaty, and is murdering people on every hand, and the Governor has asked for volunteers to protect the lives and property of the settlers. He had to do it. Either the whites or the Indians must perish. The settlers came here under a legal treaty; they must be protected. It is no time for sentiment now."

14

"Are nearly all of the men of New Salem here?" said Jasper.

"Yes; Abraham Lincoln was the first to enlist, and he is our leader. He ought to be a good Indian fighter. His grandfather was killed by the Indians."

"So I have heard."

"But Lincoln himself is not a hard man; there's nothing revengeful about him. He would be more likely to do a good act to an Indian than a harmful one, if he could. His purpose is not to kill Indians, but to protect the State and save the lives of peaceful, inoffensive people."

The men from the several towns in the vicinity gathered in the open space, and proceeded to elect their officers.

The manner of the election was curious. There were the two candidates for captain of the company. They were Abraham Lincoln and a man by the name of Fitzpatrick. Each volunteer was asked to put himself in the line by the side of the man of his choice.

One by one they stepped forward and arranged themselves by the side of Lincoln, until Lincoln stood at the head of a larger part of the men.

"Captain Lincoln!" said one, when he saw how the election was going. "Three cheers for Honest Abe! He is our man."

There arose a great shout of "Captain Lincoln!"

Jasper marked the delight which the election had given his old New Salem friends. Lincoln himself once said that that election was the proudest event of his life.

The New Salem Company went into camp at Beardstown,

and was disbanded at Ottawa thirty days after, not having met the enemy. Lincoln, feeling that he should be true to his country and the public safety at the hour of peril, enlisted again as a common private, served another thirty days, and then, the war not being over, he enlisted again. The war terminated with the battle of Bad Axe and the capture of Black Hawk, who became a prisoner of state.

One day, when the volunteers were greatly excited by the tales of Indian murders, and were beset by foes lurking in ambush and pirogue, a remarkable scene occurred in Lincoln's camp.

The men, who had been talking over a recent massacre by the Indians, were thirsting to avenge the barbarities, when suddenly the withered form of an Indian appeared before them.

They started, and an officer demanded:

"Who are you?"

"Main-Pogue."

"How came you here?"

"I am a friend to the white man. I'm going to meet my son, a boy whom I have made my own."

"You are a spy!"

"I am not a spy. I am Main-Pogue. I am hungry; I am old. I am no spy. Give an old Indian food, and I will serve you while you need. Then let me go and find my boy."

"Food!" said one. "You are a spy, a plotter. There is murder in your heart. We will make short work with you. That is what we are sent out to do."

"I never did the white man harm," said the old man, drawing his blanket around him.

" You shall pay for this, you old hypocrite !" said another officer. " Men, what shall we do with this spy ? "

" Kill him !" said one.

" Shoot him !" said another.

" Torture him, and make him confess !" said a third.

The old Indian stood bent and trembling.

" I am a wandering beggar, looking for my boy," said the Indian. " I never did the white man harm. Hear me."

" You belong to Black Hawk's devils," said an officer, " and you are plotting our death. You shall be shot. Seize him !"

The old Indian trembled as the men surrounded him bent on his destruction.

There came toward the excited company a tall young officer. All eyes were bent upon him. He peered into the face of the old Indian. The men rushed forward to obey the officer.

" Halt !" said the tall captain. " This Indian must not be killed by us."

That speaker was Abraham Lincoln. The men jeered at him, but he stood between the Indian and them, like a form of iron.

The Indian gave his protector a grateful look, and there dropped from his hand a passport, which in his confusion he had failed to give the officer. It was a certificate saying that he had rendered good service to the Government, and it was signed by General Cass.

" Why should you wish to save him ? " asked a volunteer of young Lincoln. " Your grandfather was killed by an Indian. You are a coward !"

"I would do what is right by any man," said Lincoln, fiercely. "Who says I am a coward? I will meet him here in an open contest. Now, let the man who says I am a coward meet me face to face and hand to hand."

He stood over the cowering Indian, dark, self-confident and defiant.

"I stand for justice. Let him come on. I stand alone for right. Let him come on.—Main-Pogue, go!"

Out of the camp hobbled the Indian, with the long, strong arm of Abraham Lincoln lifted over him. The eyes of the men followed him in anger, disappointment, and scorn. Hard words passed from one to the other. He felt for the first time in his life that he stood in this matter utterly alone.

"Jeer on," he said. "I would shield this Indian at the cost of my life. I would not be a true soldier if I failed in my duty to this old man. In every event of life it is right that makes might; and the rights of an Indian are as sacred as those of any other man, and I would defend them, at whatever cost, as those of a white man.—Main-Pogue, go hence! Here will I stand between you and death."

"Heaven bless you for protecting a poor old man! I have been a runner for the whites for many years, but I have never met a man like you. I will tell my boy of this. Your name is Lincoln?"

"Yes—Abraham Lincoln, though the name matters nothing."

CHAPTER XIX

THE FOREST COLLEGE.

ELL, how time flies, and the clock of the year does go round! Here's the elder again! It's a bright day that brings ye here, though I shouldn't let ye sleep in the prophet's chamber, if I had one, 'cause ye ain't any prophet at all. But ye are right welcome just the same. Where is yer Indian boy?"

"He's gone to his own people, Aunt Olive."

"To whet his tommyhawk, I make no doubt. Oh, elder, how ye have been deceived in people! Ye believe that every one is as good as one can be, or can be grafted to bear sweet fruit, but, hoe-down-hoe, elder, 'taint so. Yer Aunt Indiana knows how desperately wicked is the human heart. If ye don't do others, others will do ye, and this world is a warfare. Come in; I've got somethin' new to tell ye. It's about the Linkens' Abe."

The Tunker entered the cheerful cabin in the sunny clearing of the timber.

"I've been savin' up the news to tell ye when ye came. Abe's been to war!"

"He has not been hurt, has he?"

"*Hurt!* No, he hasn't been hurt. A great Indian fighter he proved! The men were all laughin' about it. He'll live to fight another day, as the sayin' goes, and so will the enemy. Well, I always thought that there was no need of killin' people. Let them alone, and they will all die themselves; and as for the enemy, let them alone, and they will come home waggin' their tails behind them, as the ditty says. Well, I must tell ye. Abe's been to war. He didn't see the enemy, nor fight, nor nothin'. But a wild Indian came right into his camp, and the soldiers started up to kill him, and what do ye suppose Abe did?"

"I think he did what he thought to be right."

"He let him go! There! what do you think of that? He just went to fightin' his own company to save the Indian. There's a warrior for ye! And that wasn't all. He talked in such a way that he frightened his own men, and he just gave the Indian some bread and cheese, and let him off. And the Indian went off blessin' him. Abe will never make a soldier or handle armies much, after all yer prophecies. Such a soldier as that ought to be rewarded a pinfeather."

"His conduct was after the Galilean teaching—was it not? —and produced the result of making the Indian a friend. Was not that a good thing to do? Who was the Indian?"

"It was old Main-Pogue. He was uncle, or somethin', to that boy who used to travel about with you, teachin' you the language—Waubeno; the old interpreter for General Cass's men. He'll go off and tell Waubeno. I wonder if Main-Pogue knew who it was that saved him, and if he will tell Waubeno that?"

"Lincoln did a noble act."

"Oh, elder, ye've got a good heart, but ye're weak in yer upper story. That ain't all I've got to tell ye. Abe has failed, after all yer prophecies, too. He and another man went to keepin' store up in New Salem, and he let his partner cheat' him, and they *failed ;* and now he's just workin' to pay up his debts, and his partner's too."

"And his partner's too? That shows that he saved an honest purpose out of losses. The greatest of all losses is a loss of integrity of purpose. I'm glad to hear that he has not lost that."

"Oh, elder, ye've allus somethin' good to say of that boy. But I'm not agin him. He's Tom Linken's son, just as I told ye ; and he'll never come to anythin' good. He all runs to books and gabble, and goes 'round repeatin' poetry, which is only the lies of crazy folks. I haven't any use for poetry, except hymns. But he's had real trouble of late, besides these things, and I'm sorry for that. He's lost the girl what he was goin' to marry. She was a beautiful girl, and her death made him so downhearted that they had to shut him up and watch him to keep him from committin' suicide. They say that he has very melancholy spells. He can't help that, I don't suppose. His mother what sleeps over yonder under the timber was melancholy. How are all the schools that you set to goin' on the Wabash ?"

"They are all growing, good woman, and it fills my heart with delight to see them grow. They are all growing like gardens for the good of this great country. It does my heart good, and makes my soul happy, to start these Christian schools. It's my mission. And I try to start them right—character first, true views of things next, and books last; but the teaching of young children to think and act right spiritually is the highest education of all. This is best done by telling stories, and so I travel and travel telling stories to schools. You do not see my plan, but it is the true seed that I am planting, and it will bear fruit when I am gone to a better world than this."

"Oh, ye mean well," said Aunt Olive, "but ye don't know more than some whole families—pardon my plainness of speech. I don't doubt that ye are doin' some good, after a fashion; but don't prophesy—yer prophecies in regard to Abe have failed already. He'll never command the American army, nor run the nation, nor keep store. Yer Aunt Indiana can read character, and her prophecies have proved true so far."

"Wait—time tells the whole truth; and worth is worth, and passes for the true gold of life in time."

"Ye don't think that there's any chance for him yet, do ye, elder, after lettin' the Indian go, and failin', and havin' that melancholy spell?"

"Yes, I do. My spiritual sense tells me so."

"Yer spiritual sense! Elder, ye ought to go to school. Ye are nothin' but a child yerself. And let me advise ye never to have anythin' more to do with that there Indian boy. Fishes don't swim on rocks, nor hawks go to live in a cage. An Indian is an Indian, and, mark my words, that boy will have yer scalp some day. He will, now—he will. I saw it in his eye."

The Tunker journeyed toward the new town of Springfield, Illinois, along the fragrant timber and over the blooming

prairies. Everywhere were to be seen the white prairie schooner
and the little village of people that followed it.

Springfield was but a promising village at this time, in a very
fertile land. Probably no one ever thought that it would become
a capital city of an empire of population, the hub of that great
wheel of destiny rimmed by the Wabash, the Mississippi, Rock
River, and the Lake; and still less did any one ever dream
that it would be the legislative influence of that tall, laughing,
sad-faced boy, Lincoln, who would produce this result.

Jasper preached at Springfield, and visited the log school-
house, and told stories to the little school. He then started to
walk to New Salem, a distance of some eighteen or twenty
miles.

It was a pleasant country, and all things seemed teeming
with life, for it was now the high tide of the year. The prairies were billows of flowers, and the timber was shady and cool,
carpeted with mosses, tangled with vines, with its tops bright
with sunshine and happy with the songs of birds.

About half-way between the two towns Jasper saw some
lofty trees, giants of the forest, that spread out their branches
like roofs of some ancient temple. There were birds' nests
made of sticks in their tops, and a cool stream ran under
them. He sought the place for rest.

As he entered the great shadow, he saw a tall young man
seated on a log, absorbed in reading a book. He approached
him, and recognized him as young Lincoln.

"I am glad to meet you here, in this beautiful place," he
said.

"This is my college," said Lincoln.

" What are you studying, my friend ? "

" Oh, I am trying my hand at law a little. Stuart, the Springfield lawyer, lends me his law-books, and I walk over there from New Salem to get them, and when I get as far back as this I sit down on this log and study. I can study when I am walking. I once mastered forty pages of Blackstone in a walk. But I love to stop and study on this log. It is rather a long walk from New Salem to Springfield—almost twenty miles—and when I get as far back as this I feel tired. These trees are so grand that they look like a house of Nature, and I call them my college. I can't have the privileges of better-off young men, who can go to Philadelphia, New York, or Boston to study law, and so I do the best I can here. I get discouraged sometimes, but I believe that right is might, and do my best, and there is something that is leading me on."

" I am glad to find you here, Abraham Lincoln. I love you in my heart, and I wish that I might help you in your studies. But I have never studied law."

" But you do help me."

" How ? "

" By your faith in me. Elder, I have been having a hard row to hoe, and am an unlucky fellow. Have been keeping a grocery, and we have failed—failed right at the beginning of life. It hurt my pride, but, elder, it has not hurt my honor. I've worked and paid up all my debts, and now I am going to pay *his*. I might make excuses for not paying his part of the debts, but, elder, it would not leave my name clear. I must live conscience free. People call me a fool, but they trust me. They have made me postmaster at New Salem, though that ain't much of an office. The mail comes only once a week, and I carry it in my hat. They'll need a new post-office by and by."

"My friend, you are giving yourself a moral self-education that has more worth than all the advantages of wealth or a famous name or the schools of Boston. The time will come when this growing people will need such a man as you to lead them, and you will lead them more grandly than others who have had an easier school. You have learned the first principles of true education—it is, the habit that can not do wrong without feeling the flames of torment within. Every sacrifice that you have made to your conscience has given you power. That power is a godlike thing. You will see all one day, as I do now."

"Elder, they call me a merry-maker, but I carry with me a sad heart. I wish to tell you, for I feel that you are my true friend. I loved Ann Rutledge. She was the daughter of James Rutledge, the founder of our village and the owner of the mill on the Sangamon. She was a girl of a loving heart, gentle blood, and her face was lovely. You saw her at the tavern. I loved her—I loved her very name; and she is dead. It has all happened since you were here, and I have wished to meet you again and tell you all. Such things as these make me melancholy. A great darkness comes down upon me at times, and I am tempted to end all the bright dream that we call life. But I rise above the temptation. Elder, you don't know how my heart has had to struggle. I sometimes think of my poor mother's grave in the timber in Indiana, and I always think of *her* grave—Ann Rutledge's—and then it comes over me like a cloud, that there is no place for me in the world.

Do you want to know what I do in those hours, elder? I repeat a long poem. I have said it over a hundred times. It was written by some poet who felt as I do. I would like to repeat it to you, elder. I tell stories—they only make me more melancholy—but this poem soothes my mind. It makes me feel that other men have suffered before, and it makes me willing to suffer for others, and to accept my lot in life, whatever it may be."

"I wish to hear the poem that has so moved you," said the Tunker.

Abraham Lincoln stood up and leaned against the trunk of one of the giant trees. The sunlight was sifting through the great canopy of leaves, boughs, and nests overhead, and afar gleamed the prairies like gardens of the sun. He lifted his long arm, and, with a sad face, said :

"Elder, listen.

> "'Oh, why should the spirit of mortal be proud?
> Like a swift-fleeting meteor, a fast-flying cloud,
> A flash of the lightning, a break of the wave,
> He passeth from life to his rest in the grave.

> "'The leaves of the oak and the willow shall fade,
> Be scattered around, and together be laid;
> And the young and the old, and the low and the high,
> Shall molder to dust, and together shall lie.

> "'The infant a mother attended and loved,
> The mother that infant's affection who proved,
> The husband that mother and infant who blest—
> Each, all, are away to their dwellings of rest.

> "'[*The maid on whose cheek, on whose brow, in whose eye,
> Shone beauty and pleasure, her triumphs are by ;*

And the memory of those who loved her and praised,
Are alike from the minds of the living erased.]

" ' The hand of the king that the scepter hath borne,
The brow of the priest that the miter hath worn,
The eye of the sage, and the heart of the brave,
Are hidden and lost in the depths of the grave.

" ' The peasant whose lot was to sow and to reap,
The herdsman who climbed with his goats up the steep,
The beggar who wandered in search of his bread,
Have faded away like the grass that we tread.

" '[The saint who enjoyed the communion of Heaven,
The sinner who dared to remain unforgiven,
The wise and the foolish, the guilty and just,
Have quietly mingled their bones in the dust.]

" ' So the multitude goes, like the flower or the weed
That withers away to let others succeed;
So the multitude comes, even those we behold,
To repeat every tale that has often been told.

" ' For we are the same our fathers have been;
We see the same sights our fathers have seen;
We drink the same stream, we view the same sun,
And run the same course our fathers have run.

" ' The thoughts we are thinking our fathers would think;
From the death we are shrinking our fathers would shrink;
To the life we are clinging they also would cling;
But it speeds from us all like a bird on the wing.

" ' They loved, but the story we can not unfold;
They scorned, but the heart of the haughty is cold;
They grieved, but no wail from their slumber will come;
They joyed, but the tongue of their gladness is dumb.

" ' They died, ay, they died: we things that are now,
That walk on the turf that lies over their brow,
And make in their dwellings a transient abode,
Meet the things that they met on their pilgrimage road.

> "'Yea, hope and despondency, pleasure and pain,
> Are mingled together in sunshine and rain;
> And the smile and the tear, the song and the dirge,
> Still follow each other like surge upon surge.

> "''Tis the wink of an eye, 'tis the draught of a breath,
> From the blossom of health to the paleness of death,
> From the gilded saloon to the bier and the shroud—
> Oh, why should the spirit of mortal be proud?'"

He stood there in moody silence when he had finished the recitation, which was (unknown to him) from the pen of a pastoral Scotch poet. The Tunker looked at him, and saw how deep were his feelings, and how earnest were his desires to know the true way of life and to do well his mission, and go on with the great multitude, whose procession comes upon the earth and vanishes from the scenes. But he did not dream of the greatness of the destiny for which that student was preparing in the hard college of the woods.

"My education must always be defective," said the young student. "I can not read law in great law-offices, like other young men, but I can be just—I can do right; and I would never undertake a case of law, for any money, that I did not think right and just. I would stand for what I thought was right, as I did by the old Indian, and I think that the people in time would learn to trust me."

"Abraham Lincoln, to school one's conscience to the habit of right, so that it can not do wrong, is the first and the highest education. It is what one is that makes him a knight, and that is the only true knighthood. The highest education is that of the soul. Did you know that the Indian whom you saved was Main-Pogue?"

" Yes."

" And that Main-Pogue is the uncle and foster-father of my old guide, Waubeno ? "

" No. Waubeno was the boy who came with you to the Wabash ? "

" Waubeno's father was killed by the white people. He was condemned to death. He asked to go home to see his family once more, and returned upon his honor to die. That old story is true. Does it seem possible that an English soldier could ever take the life of an Indian like that ? "

" No, it does not. Will Main-Pogue tell Waubeno that it was I who saved him ? "

" Does Main-Pogue know you by name ? I hope he does."

" He may have forgotten. I would like for him to remember it, because the Indian boy liked me, and an Indian killed my grandfather. I liked that Indian boy, and I would do justice, if I could, by all men, and any man."

" Lincoln, I came to love and respect that Indian boy. There was a native nobility in him. But my efforts to make him a Christian failed, for he carried revenge in his heart. I wish that he could know that it was you who did that deed ; your character might be an influence that would strike an unknown cord in the boy's heart, for Waubeno has a noble heart—Waubeno is noble. I wish he knew who it was that spared Main-Pogue. Acts teach where words fail, and the true teacher is not lips, but life. The boy once said to me that he would cease to seek to avenge his father's death if he could find a single white man who would defend an Indian to his own harm, because it was right. Now, Lincoln, you have done just the act that would change his heart. But he has gone with the winds. How will he ever hear of it? How will he ever know it?

"When Main-Pogue meets him, if he ever does again, he may tell him all. But does Main-Pogue understand the relations that exist between you and me, and us and that boy? O Waubeno, Waubeno, I would that you might hear of this!"

He thought, and added: "He *will* hear of it, somehow, in some way. Providence makes golden keys of deeds like yours. They unlock the doors of mystery. Let me see, what was it Waubeno said—his exact words? '*When I find a single white man who defends an Indian to his own hurt, because it is right, I will promise.*' Lincoln, he said that. You are that man. Lincoln, may God bless you, and call you into his service when he has need of a man!"

15

CHAPTER XX.

MAKING LINCOLN A "SON OF MALTA."

HEN Jasper, some years later, again met Aunt Eastman, she had a yet more curious story to tell about Abraham.

It was spring, and the cherry-trees were in bloom and musical with bees. In the yard a single apple-tree was red with blooms, which made fragrant the air.

"And here comes Johnnie Apple-seed!" said Aunt Olive. "Heaven bless ye! I call ye Johnnie Apple-seed because ye remind me so much of that good man. He was a good man, if he had lost his wits; and ye mean well, just as he did. Smell the apple-blossoms! I don't know but it was *him* that planted that there tree."

To explain Aunt Olive's remarks, we should say that there once wandered along the banks of the Ohio, a poor wayfaring man who had a singular impression of duty. He felt it to be his calling in life to plant apple-seeds. He would go to a farmer's house, ask for work, and remain at the place a few days or weeks. After he had gone, apple-seeds would be found sprouting about the farm. His journeys were the beginnings of many orchards in the Middle, West, and prairie States.

"I love to smell apple-blossoms," said Aunt Olive. "It reminds me of old New England. I can almost hear the bells ring on the old New England hills when I smell apple-blooms. They say that Johnnie Apple-seed is dead, and that they filled his grave with apple-blooms. I don't know as it is so, but it ought to be. I sometimes wish that I was a poet, because a poet fixes things as they ought to be—makes the world all over right. But, la! Abe Linken was a poet. *Have* ye heard the news?"

"No. What?—nothing bad, I hope?"

"*He's* hung out his shingle."

"Where?"

"In Springfield."

"In Springfield?"

"Yes, elder, I've seen it. I have traveled a good deal since I saw you—'round to camp-meetin', and fairs, rightin' things, and doin' all the good I can. I've seen it. And, elder, they've made a mock Mason on him."

In the pioneer days of Illinois the making of mock Masons, or *pseudo* Sons of Malta, was a popular form of frolic, now almost forgotten. Young people formed mock lodges or secret societies, for the purpose of initiating new members by a series of tricks, which became the jokes of the community.

"Yes," said Aunt Olive, "and what do ye think they did? Well, in them societies they first test the courage of those who want to be new members. There's Judge Ball, now; when they tested his courage, what do you think? They blindfolded him, and turned up his blue jean trousers about the ankles, and said, 'Now let out the snakes!' and they took an elder-bush squirt-gun and squirted water over his feet; and the water was cold, and he thought it was snakes, and he jumped clear up to the cross-beams on the chamber floor, and screamed and screamed, and they wouldn't have him."

Jasper had never heard of these rude methods of making jokes and odd stories in the backwoods.

"What did they do to test Abraham's courage?" he asked.

"I don't know—blindfolded him and dressed him up like a donkey, and led him up to a lookin'-glass, and made him promise that he would never tell what he saw, and then *un*bandaged his eyes—or something of that kind. His courage stood the test. Of course it did; no matter what they might have done, no one could frighten Abe. But he got the best o' them."

"How?"

"He took up a collection for a poor woman that he had met on the way, and proposed to change the society into a committee for the relief of the poor and sufferin'."

"That shows his heart again."

"I knew that you would say that, elder."

"Everything that I hear of Lincoln shows how that his character grows. It is my daily prayer that Waubeno may hear of how he saved Main-Pogue. It would change the heart of Waubeno. He will know of it some day, and then he will fulfill his promise to me."

The Tunker sat down in the door under the blooming cherry-trees, and Aunt Olive brought a tray of food, and they ate their supper there.

Afar stretched the prairies. The larks quivered in the air, happy in the May-time, and gurgling with song. In the sunny

SARAH BUSH LINCOLN, ABRAHAM LINCOLN'S STEP-MOTHER.

After photograph taken in 1865.

outlines were seen a train of prairie schooners winding over the plain.

These were rude times, when all things were new. Men were purchasing the future by hardship and toil. But the two religious enthusiasts presented a happy picture as they sat under the cherry-trees and talked of camp-meetings, and the inner light, and all they had experienced, and ate their frugal meal. Odd though their views and beliefs and habits may seem in some respects, each had a definite purpose of good; each lived in the horizon of bright prospects here and hereafter, and each was happy.

CHAPTER XXI.

PRAIRIE ISLAND.

HE beautiful country between Lake Michigan, or old Fort Dearborn, and the Mississippi, or Rock Island, was once a broad prairie, a sea of flowers, birds, and bright insects. The buffaloes roamed over it in great herds, and the buffalo-birds followed them. The sun rose over it as over a sea, and the arched aurora rose red above it like some far gate of a land of fire. Here the Sacs and Foxes roamed free; the Iowas and the tribes of the North. It was one vast sunland, a breeze-swept brightness, almost without a dot or shadow.

Almost, but not quite. Here and there, like islands in a summer sea, rose dark groves of oak and vines. These spots of refreshment were called prairie islands, and in one of these islands, now gone, a pioneer colony made their homes, and built a meeting-house, which was also to be used as a school-house. Six or more of these families were from Germantown, Pennsylvania, and were Tunkers. The other families were from the New England States.

To this nameless village, long ago swept away by the prairie fires, went Jasper the Parable, with his cobbling-tools, his stories, and his gospel of universal love and good-will. The

Tunkers welcomed him with delight, and the emigrants from New England looked upon him kindly as a good and well-meaning man. There were some fifteen or twenty children in the settlement, and here the peaceful disciple of Pestalozzi, and friend of Froebel, applied for a place to teach, and the school was by unanimous consent assigned to him.

So began the school at Prairie Island—a school where the first principles of education were perceived and taught, and that might furnish a model for many an ambitious institution of to-day.

"It is life that teaches," the Parable used to say, quoting Pestalozzi. "The first thing to do is to form the habits that lead to character; the next thing is to stamp the young mind with right views of life; then comes book-learning—words, figures, and maps—but stories that educate morally are the primer of life. Christ taught spiritual truths by parables. I teach formative ideas by parables. The teacher should be a story-teller. In my own country all children go through fairy-land. Here they teach the young figures first, as though all of life was a money-market. It is all unnatural and wrong. I must teach and preach by stories."

The school-house was a simple building of logs and prairie grass, with oiled paper for windows, and a door that opened out and afforded a view of the vast prairie-sea to the west. Jasper taught here five days in a week, and sang, prayed, and exhorted on Sunday afternoons, and led social meetings on Sunday evenings. The little community were united, peaceful, and happy. They were industrious, self-respecting people, who were governed by their moral sense, and their governing principle seemed to be the faith that, if a person desired and sought to follow the divine will, he would have a revelation of spiritual light, which would be like the opening of the gates of heaven to him. Nearly every man and woman had some special experience of the soul to tell; and if ever there was a community of simple faith and brotherhood, it was here.

Jasper's school began in the summer, when the sun was high, the cool shadows of the oaks grateful, and the bluebells filled the tall, wavy grasses, and the prairie plover swam in the air.

Jasper's first teaching was by the telling of stories that leave in the young mind right ideas and impressions.

"My children, listen," said the gracious old man, as he sat down to his rude desk, "and let me tell you some stories like those Pestalozzi used to tell. Still, now!"

He lifted his finger and his eyebrows, and sat a little while in silence.

"Hark!" he said. "Hear the birds sing in the trees! Nature is teaching us. When Nature is teaching I listen. Nature is a greater teacher than I, or any man."

The little school sat in silence and listened. They had never heard the birds sing in that way before. Presently there was a hush in the trees.

"Now I will begin," said he.

PESTALOZZI'S STORIES.

"Did you ever see a mushroom? Yes, there are mushrooms under the cool trees. Once, in the days when the plants and flowers and trees all talked—they talk now, but we have ceased to hear them, a little mushroom bowed in the winds, and said to the grass :

"'See how I grow ! I came up in a single night. I am smart.'

"'Yes,' said the grass, waving gently.

"'But you,' said the smart little mushroom, 'it takes you a whole year to grow.'

"The grass was sorry that it took so long for it to grow, and hung its head, and thought, and thought.

"'But,' said the grass, 'you spring up in the night, and in a day or two you are gone. It takes me a year to grow, but I outlive a hundred crops of mushrooms. I will have patience and be content. Worth is of slow growth.'

"In a week the boastful little mushroom was gone, but the grass bloomed and bore seed, and left a lovely memory behind it. Hark! hear the breeze in the trees! Nature is teaching now. Listen !

"Now I will tell you another little story, such as I used to hear Pestalozzi relate. I am going to tell this story to myself, but you may listen. I have told a story to you, but now I will talk to myself.

"There once was a king, who had been riding in the sun, and he saw afar a lime-tree, full of cool, green leaves. Oh, how refreshing it looked to him ! So he rode up to the lime-tree, and rested in the shadow.

"The leaves all clung to the branches, and the winds whispered among them, but did not blow them away.

"Then the king loved the tree, and he said :

"'O tree, would that my people clung to me as thy leaves do to thy branches !'

" The tree was pleased, and spoke :

" ' Would you learn from me wisdom to govern thy people?'

" ' Yes, O lime-tree! Speak on."

" ' Would you know, then, what makes my leaves so cling to my branches?'

" ' Yes, O Lime Tree! Speak on.'

" ' I carry to them the sap that nourishes them. 'Tis he that gives himself to others that lives in others, and is safe and happy himself. Do that, and thy kingdom shall be a lime-tree.' "

A child brought into the room a bunch of harebells and laid them upon the teacher's desk.

" Look!" said Jasper, " Nature is teaching. Let us be quiet a little and hear what she has to say. The harebells bring us good-will from the sun and skies. There is goodness everywhere, and for all. Let us be grateful.

" Now I will give you another little Pestalozzian story, told in my own way, and you may tell it to your fathers and mothers and neighbors when you go home.

" There was once a man who had two little ponies. They were pretty creatures, and just alike. He sold one of them to a hard-hearted man, who kicked him and beat him; and the pony said :

." ' The man is my enemy. I will be his, and become a cunning and vicious horse.'

" So the pony became cunning and vicious, and threw his rider and crippled him, and grew spavined and old, and every one was glad when he was dead.

" The man sold the other pony to a noble-hearted man, who treated him kindly and well. Then the pony said :

" ' I am proud of my master. I will become a good horse, and my master's will shall be my own.'

" Like the master became the horse. He became strong and beautiful. They chose him for the battle, and he went through the wars, and the master slept by his side. He bore his master at last in a triumphal procession, and all the people were sorry when he came to die. Our minds here are one of the little colts.

" So we will all work together. The lesson is ended. You have all the impressions that you can bear for one day. Now we will go out and play."

But the play-ground was made a field of teaching.

" There are plays that form right ideas," said Jasper, " and plays that lead to an evil character. I teach no plays that lead to cruelty or deception. I would no sooner withhold amusements from my little ones than water, but my amusements, like the water, must be healthy and good."

There was one odd play that greatly delighted all the children of the Prairie Island school. The idea of it was evolved in the form of a popular song many years afterward. In it the children are supposed to ask an old German musician how many instruments of music he could play, and he acts out in pantomime all of the instruments he could blow or handle. We think it was this merriment that became known in America as the song of Johnnie Schmoker in the minstrel days.

Not the children only, but the parents also all delighted to see Jasper pretend to play all the instruments of the German band. Often at sunset, when the settlers came in from the corn-fields and rested under the great trees, Jasper would delight the islanders, as they called themselves, with this odd play.

"The purpose of education," Jasper used to repeat over and over to his friends in this sunny island of the prairie sea, "is not to teach the young how to make money or get wealth by a cunning brain, but how to live for the soul. The soul's best interests are in life's highest interest, and there is no poverty in the world that is like spiritual poverty. In the periods of poetry a nation is great; and when poetry fails, the birds cease to sing and the flowers to bloom, and divinities go away, and the heart turns to stone."

There was one story that he often repeated to his little school. The pupils liked it because there was action in it, as in the play-story of the German musician. He called it "CHINK, CHINK, CHINK"—though we believe a somewhat similar story is told in Germany under the name of "The Stone-cold Heart."

He would clasp his hands together and strike them upon his knee, making a sound like the jingling of silver coin. Any one can produce this curious sound by the same action.

"Chink, chink, chink," he would say. "Do you hear it? Chink, chink, chink. Listen, as I strike my hands on my knees. Money? Now I will open my hands. There is no money in them; it was fool's gold, all.

"There lived in a great German forest a poor woodman. He was a giant, but he had a great heart and a willing arm, and he worked contentedly for many years.

"One day he chanced to go with some foresters into the city. It was a festival day. He heard the jingle of money, just like that" (striking his clasped hands on his knee). "He saw what money would buy. He thought it would buy happiness. He did not know that it was fool's gold, all.

"He went back to his little hut in the forest feeling very unhappy. His wife kissed him on his return, and his children gathered around him to hear him tell the adventures of the day, but his downcast spirit made them all sad.

"'What has happened?' asked his wife. 'You always seemed happy until to-night.'

"'And I was always happy until to-day. But I have seen the world to-day, and now I want that which will buy everything.'

"'And what is that?' asked his wife.

"'Listen! It sounds like that,' and he struck his clasped hands on his knee—chink, chink, chink. 'If I had that, I would bring to you and the little ones the fine things I saw in the city, and you would be happy. You are contented now because you do not know.'

"'But I would rather that you would bring to me a happy face and loving heart,' said his wife. 'You know that the Book says that "a man's life consisteth not in the abundance of the things which he possesseth." Love makes happiness, and gold is in the heart.'

"The forester continued to be sad. He would sit outside of his door at early evening and pound his hands upon his knees so—chink, chink, chink—and think of the gay city.

Then he would strike his hands on his knees again. He did not know that it was fool's gold, all.

"He grew more and more discontented with his simple lot. One day he went out into the forest alone to cut wood. When he had become tired he sat down by a running stream to hear the birds sing and to strike his hands on his knees.

"A shadow came gliding across the mosses of the stream. It was like the form of a dark man. Slowly it came on, and as it did so the flowers on the banks of the stream withered. The woodman looked up, and a black giant stood before him.

"'You look unhappy to-day,' said the black giant. 'You did not use to look that way. What is wanting?'

"The woodman looked down, clasped his hands, and struck them on his knees—chink, chink, chink.

"'Ah, I see—money! The world all wants money. Selfishness could not thrive without money. I will give you all the money that you want, on one condition.'

"'Name it.'

"'That you will exchange your heart.'

"'What will you give me for my heart?'

"'Your heart is a human heart, a very simple human heart. I will put in its place a heart of stone, and then all your wishes shall turn to gold. Whatever you wish you shall have.'

"'Shall I be happy?'

"'Happy! Ha, ha, ha! are not people happy who have their wishes?'

"'Some are, and some are happy who give up their wishes and wills and desires."

"The woodman leaned his face upon his hands for a while,

and seemed in great doubt and distress. He thought of his wife, who used to say that contentment was happiness, and that one could be rich by having a few wants. Then he thought of the city. The vision rose before him like a Vanity Fair. He clasped his hands again, and struck them on his knees—chink, chink, chink—and said, 'I will do it.'

"Suddenly he felt a heart within him as cold as stone. He looked up to the giant, and saw that he held his own good, true heart in his hands.

"'I will put it away in a glass jar in my house,' he said, 'where I keep the hearts of the rich. Now, listen. You have only to strike your locked hands on your knees three times—chink, chink, chink—whenever you want for gold, and wish, and you will find your pockets full of money.'

"The woodman struck his palms on his knees and wished, then felt in his pockets. Sure enough, his pockets were full of gold.

"He thought of his wife, but his thought was a cold one; he did not love her any more. He thought of his little ones, but his thoughts were frozen; he did not care to meet them any more. He thought of his parents, but he only wished to meet them to excite their envy. The stream no longer charmed him, nor the flowers, nor the birds, nor anything.

"'I will dissemble,' he said. He hurried home. His wife met him at the door. He kissed her. She started back, and said :

"'Your lips are cold as death! What has happened?'

"His children kissed him, but they said :

"'Father, your cheeks are cold.'

" He tried to pray at the meal, but his sense of God was gone; he did not love God, or his wife, or his children, or any-thing any more—he had a stone-cold heart.

" After the evening meal he told his wife the events of the day. She listened with horror.

" ' In parting with your heart you have parted with every-thing that makes life worth having,' said she. But he an-swered:

" ' I do not care. I do not care for anything but gold now. I have a stone-cold heart.'

" ' But will gold make you happy?' she asked.

" He started. He went forth to work the next day, but he was not happy. So day by day passed. His gold did not make his family happy, or his friends, or any one, but he would not have cared for all these, for he had a stone-cold heart. Had it made him happy? He saw the world all happy around him, and heavier and heavier grew his heart, and at last he could endure it no longer.

" One day he was sitting in the same place in the woods as before, when he saw the shadowy figure stealing along the mosses of the stream again. He looked up and beheld the giant, and exclaimed:

" ' Give me back my heart!' "

" Have you learned the lesson? "

CHAPTER XXII.

THE INDIAN PLOT.

NE sultry August night a party of Sac and Fox Indians were encamped in a grove of oaks opposite Rock Island, on the western side of the Mississippi. Among them were Main-Pogue and Waubeno.

The encampment commanded a view of the burial hills and bluffs of the abandoned Sac village.

As the shadow of night stole over the warm, glimmering twilight, and the stars came out, the lights in the settlers' cabins began to shine; and as the Indians saw them one by one, their old resentment against the settlers rose and bitter words passed, and an old warrior stood up to rehearse his memories of the injustice that his race had suffered in the old treaties and the late war.

"Look," he said, "at the eyes of the cabins that gleam from yonder shore. The waters roll dark under them, but the lights of the canoes no more haunt the rapids, and the women and children may no more sit down by the graves of the braves of old. Our lights have gone out; their lights shine. Their lights shine on the bluffs, and they twinkle like fireflies along the prairies, and climb the cliffs in what was once the Red

16

Man's Paradise. Like the fireflies to the night the white settlers came.

"Rise up and look down into the water. There—where the stream runs dark—they shot our starving women there, for crossing the river to harvest their own corn.

"Look again—there where the first star shines. She, the wife of Wabono, floated there dead, with the babe on her breast. Here is the son of Wabono.

"Son of Wabono, you ride the pony like the winds. What are you going to do to avenge your mother? You have nourished the babe; you are good and brave; but the moons rise and fall, and the lights grow many on the prairie, and the smoke-wreaths many along the shore. Speak, son of Wabono."

A tall boy arose, dressed in yellow skins and painted and plumed.

"Father, it is long since the rain fell."

"Long."

"And the prairies are yellow."

"Yellow."

"And they are food for fire."

"Food for fire."

"I would touch them with fire—in the east, in the west, in the north, and in the south. The lights will go out in the cabins, and the white woman will wander homeless, and the white man will hunger for corn. They shot our people for harvesting our corn. I would give their corn-fields to the flames, and their families to the famine in the moons of storms."

"Waubeno, you have heard Wabono. What would *you* do?"

"I would punish those only who have done wrong. The white teacher taught so, and the white teacher was right."

"Waubeno, you speak like a woman."

"Those people should not suffer for what others have done. You should not be made to bear the punishments of others."

"Would you not fire the prairies?"

"No. I may have friends there. The Tunker may be there. He who spared Main-Pogue may be there. Would I burn their cabins? No!"

"Waubeno, who was your father?"

"I am the son of Alknomook."

"He died."

"Yes, father."

"There was neither pity nor mercy in the white man's heart for him. You made your vow to him. What was that vow, Waubeno?"

"To avenge his enemies—not our friends."

"Brothers, listen. The white men grow many, and we are few. In war we are helpless—only one weapon remains to us now. It is the thunderbolt—it is fire.

"Warriors, listen. The moon grows. Who of you will cross the river and ride once more into the Red Man's Paradise, and give the prairies to the flames? The torch is all that is left us now."

Every Indian raised his arm except Main-Pogue and Waubeno, and signified his desire to unite in the plan for the desolation of the prairies.

"Main-Pogue, will you carry your torch in the night of fire?"

"I have been saved by the hand of a white man, and I will not turn my hand against the white man. I could not do it if I were young. But I am old—my people are gone. Leave me to fall like the leaf."

"Son of Alknomook, what will you do?"

"I will follow your counsel for my father's sake, but I will spare my friends for the sake of the arm that was stretched out over the head of Main-Pogue."

"Then you will go."

"I would that I were dead. I would that I could live as the white teacher taught me—in peace with every one. I would that I had not this blood of fire, and this memory of darkness, and this vow upon my head. The white teacher taught me that all people were brothers. My brain burns—"

Late in the evening Waubeno went to Main-Pogue and sat down by his side under the trees. The river lay before them with its green islands and rapid currents, serene and beautiful. The lights had gone out on the other shore, and the world seemed strangely voiceless and still.

"How did *he* look, Waubeno?"

"Who look?"

"That man who saved you—stretched his arm over you."

"His arm was long. His face was as sad as an Indian's; and he was tall. He was a head taller than other men; he rose over them like an oak over the trees. The men laughed at him; then his face looked as though it was set against the people—he looked like a chief—and the men cowered, and

jeered, and cowered. I can see how he looked, but I can not
tell it—I can see it in my mind. I told him that I would tell
Waubeno, and he seemed to know your name. Did you never
meet such a man?"

"Yes, in the Indiana country. He was journeyed from
the Wabash."

The Indians, after the council we have described, began to
cross the Mississippi by night, and to make stealthy journeys
into the Rock River country, once known as the Red Man's
Paradise. Rock River is a beautiful stream of the prairies.
It comes dashing out of a bed of rocks, and runs a distance
of some two hundred miles to the Mississippi. Here once
roamed the deer and came the wild cattle in herds. Here
rose great cliffs, like ruins of castles, which were then, as
now, cities of the swallows. Eagles built their nests upon
them, and wheeled from over the flowers of the prairies. The
banks in summer were lined with wild strawberries and wild
sunflowers. Here and there were natural mounds and park-
like woods, and oaks whose arms were tangled with grape-
vines.

Into this country ran Black Hawk's trail, and not far from
this trail was Prairie Island, with its happy settlers and new
school. The German school-master might well love the place.
Margaret Fuller (Countess Ossoli) came to the region in 1843,
and caught its atmosphere and breathed it forth in her Summer in the Lakes. Here, in this territory of the Red Man's
Paradise, " to me enchanting beyond any I have ever seen,"
where " you have only to turn up the sod to find arrow-heads,"
she visited the bluff of the Eagles' Nest on the morning of the

Fourth of July, and there wrote "Ganymede to his Eagle," one of her grandest poems.

"How happy," says this gifted soul, "the Indians must have been here! I do believe Rome and Florence are suburbs compared to this capital of Nature's art."

Black Hawk's trail ran from this region of perfect beauty to the Mississippi; and long after the Sacs and Foxes were compelled to live beyond the Mississippi, the remnants of the tribes loved to return and visit the scenes of the land of their fathers.

The Indians who had plotted the firing of the prairies made two stealthy journeys along the Rock River and over the old trail under the August moon. In one of these they rode round Prairie Island, and encamped one night upon the bluff of the Eagles' Nest, under the moon and stars. Waubeno went with them, and gazed with sad eyes upon the scenes that had passed forever from the control of his people.

He saw the new cabins and corn-fields, the prairie wagons and the emigrants. One evening he passed Prairie Island, and saw the lights glimmering among the trees, and heard the singing of a hymn in the school-house, where the people had met to worship. He wished that his own people might be taught these better ways of living. He reined up his pony and listened to the singing. He wished that he might join the little company, though he did not know that Jasper was there.

He rode away amid the stacks and corn-fields. He saw that the fields were dry as powder.

Out on the prairie he turned and looked back on the lights of the settlement as they glimmered among the trees. Could he apply the torch to the dry sea of grasses around the peaceful homes?

Once, revenge would have made it a delight to his eyes to see such a settlement in flames. But Jasper's teaching had created a new view of life and a new conscience. He felt what the Tunker taught was true, and that the young soldier who had spared Main-Pogue had done a nobler deed than any act of revenge. What was that young man's motive? He pondered over these things, and gave his pony a loose rein, and rode on under the cool cover of the night under the moon and stars.

CHAPTER XXIII.

FOR LINCOLN'S SAKE.

"THE prairie is on fire!" So cried a horseman, as he rode by the school.

It was a calm, glimmering September day. Prairie Island rose with red and yellow and crisping leaves, like a royal tent amid a dead sea of flowers. The prairie grass was dry, though still mingled with a green undergrowth. Prairie chickens were everywhere, quails, and plover.

At midday a billowy cloud of smoke began to wall the eastern horizon, and it slowly rolled forward, driven by the current of the air.

"O-o-oh!" said one of the scholars! "Look! look! What the man said is true—the prairie *is* on fire!"

Jasper went to the door. The blue sky had turned to an ashy hue, and the sun was a dull red. An unnatural wind had arisen like a draft of air.

"Teacher, can we go out and look?" asked several voices.

"Yes," said Jasper, "the school may take a recess."

The pupils went to the verge of the trees, and watched the billowy columns of smoke in the distance.

The world seemed to change. The air filled with flocks of

(236)

frightened birds. The sky became veiled, and the sun was as red as blood.

Since the great snow of 1830 but few buffaloes had been seen on the prairie. But a dark cloud of flesh came bounding over the prairie grass, bellowing, with low heads and erect tails. The children thought that they were cattle at first, but they were buffaloes. They rushed toward the trees of Prairie Island, turned, and looked behind. Then the leader pawed the earth, and the herd rushed on toward the north.

The fire spread in a semicircle, and seemed to create a wind which impelled it on with resistless fury.

"O-o-oh, look! look!" exclaimed another scholar. "See the horses and the cattle—droves of them! Look at the sky—see the birds!"

There were droves of cattle hurrying in every direction. The men in the fields near Prairie Island came hurrying home.

"The prairie is on fire!" said each one, not knowing what else to say.

"Will it reach us?" asked Jasper of the harvesters.

"What is to hinder it? The wind is driving it this way. It has formed a wall of fire that almost surrounds us."

"What can we do?" asked Jasper. The harvesters considered.

"We are safer here than elsewhere, let what will come," said one. "If the fire sweeps the prairie, it would overtake us before we could get to any great river, and the small creeks are dry."

The afternoon grew darker and darker. The sun went out;

under the black smoke rolled a red sea whose waves grew nearer and nearer. The children began to cry and the women to pray. An old man came hobbling out to the arch of the trees.

"I foretold it," said he. "The world is on fire. The Day of Judgment has come! A time and times time, and a half."

He had been a Millerite.

"It will be here in an hour," said a harvester.

But there arose a counter-wind. The wall of fire seemed to be stayed. The smoke columns rose to the heavens like Babel towers.

Afar, families were seen fleeing on horseback toward the bed of a creek which they hoped to find flowing, but which had run dry.

"This is awful!" said Jasper. "It looks as though the heavens were in flames."

He shaded his hands and looked into the open space.

"What is that?" he asked.

A black horse came running toward the island, bounding through the grass as though impelled by spurs. As he leered, Jasper saw the form of a human being stretched at his side. Was the form an Indian?

On came the horse. He leered again, exposing to view a yellow body and a plumed head.

"It's an Indian," said Jasper.

The fire flattened and darkened for a time, and then rolled on again. Animals were fleeing everywhere, plunging and bellowing, and the air was wild and tempestuous with the cries of birds. The little animals could be seen leaping out of the prairie grass. The earth, air, and sky seemed alive with terror.

The black horse came plunging toward the island.

"How can a horse run that way and live?" asked Jasper. "He is bearing a messenger. It is friendly or hostile Indian that is clinging to his side."

Jasper bent his eyes on the plunging animal to see him leer, for whenever the sidling motion was made it brought to view the tawny horizontal form that seemed to be clinging to the bridle, as if riding for life. Suddenly there arose a cry from the islanders:

"Look! look! Who has done it? There is a counter-fire ahead. *They* will all perish!"

A mile or more in front of the island, and in the opposite direction from the other fire, another great billow of smoke arose spirally into the air. The people and animals who had been fleeing toward the creek, which they thought contained water, but which was dry, all turned and came running toward the island grove. Even the birds came beating back.

"*That* fire was set by the Indians," said the harvesters. "It is started across the track of the other fire to destroy us all. An Indian set the fires."

"That is an Indian skirting around us on the back of a horse," said another. "He is holding on to the horse by the mane with his hands, and by the flanks with his feet. The Indians have done this!"

"The other fire will run back, though against the wind. The prairie is so dry that the fire will run everywhere. We must set a counter-fire."

"Set a counter-fire!" exclaimed many voices.

The purpose of the counter-fire was to destroy the dry grass, so that when the other fires should reach the place it would find nothing to burn.

"But the people!" said Jasper. "See them! They are hurrying here; a counter-fire would drive them away!"

An awful scene followed. Horses, cattle, animals of many kinds came panting to the island. Many of them had been fleeing for miles, and sank down under the trees as if ready to perish. There was one enormous bison among them. The tops of the trees were filled with birds, cawing and uttering a chaos of cries. The air seemed to rain birds, and the earth to pour forth animals. The sky above turned to inky blackness. Men, women, and children came rushing into the trees from every direction, some crying on Heaven for mercy, some begging for water, all of them exhausted and seemingly ready to die. The island grove was like a great funeral pyre.

Jasper lifted his hands and called the school and the people around him, knelt down, and prayed for help amid the cries of distress that rose on every hand. He then looked for the black horse and the plumed rider again.

They were drawing near in the darkening air. The figure of the rider was more distinct. The people saw it, and cried, "An Indian!" Some said, "It is a scout!" and others, "It is he who set the fire!"

The wind rose and changed, caused by the heated air in the distance. The currents ran hither and thither like drafts in a room of open doors. One of these unnatural drafts caused a new terror to spread among the people and animals and

THE APPROACH OF THE MYSTERIOUS INDIAN.

birds. It drew up into the air a great column of sparks and, scattered them through the open space, and a rain of fire filled the sky and descended upon the grove.

It was a splendid but terrible sight.

"The end of all things is at hand," said the old Millerite. "The stars are beginning to fall."

But the rain of fire lost its force as it neared the earth, and it fell in cinders and ashes.

"An Indian! an Indian!" cried many voices.

The black horse came plunging into near view, and rushed for the trees and sank down with foaming sides and mouth. The people shouted. There rolled from his side the lithe and supple form of a young Indian, plumed, and dressed in yellow buckskin. What did it mean? The Indian lay on the ground like one dead. The people gathered around him, and Jasper came to him and bent over him, and parted the black hair from his face. Suddenly Jasper started back and uttered a cry.

"What is it?" asked the people.

"It is my old Indian guide—it is Waubeno. Bring him water, and we will revive him, and he will tell us what to do. —Waubeno! Waubeno!"

The Indian seemed to know that voice. He revived, and looked around him, and stared at the people.

"Give him water," said Jasper.

A boy brought a cup of water and offered it to the Indian. The latter started up, and cried:

"Away! I am here to die among you. My tongue burns, but I did not come here to drink. I came here to die. The white man killed my father, and I have come back with the

avengers, and we have brought with us the Judgment Day."
He stood and listened to the cries of distress.

" Hear the trees cry for help—all the birds of the prairie—
but they cry for naught. My father hears them cry. The cry
is sweet to his ears. He is waiting for me. We are all about
to die. When the wheat-fields blaze and the stacks take fire,
and the houses crackle, then we shall all die. So says Waubeno." He listened again.

" Hear the earth cry—all the animals. My father hears—
his soul hears. This is the day that I have carried in my soul.
My spirit is in the fire."

He listened again. The prairie roared with the hot air,
the flames, and the clouds of smoke. There fell another rain
of fire, and women shrieked for mercy, and children cried on
their mothers' breasts.

" Hear the people cry! I have waited for that cry for a
hundred moons. I have paid my vow. We have kindled the
fire of the anger of the heavens—it is coming. I will die with
you like the son of a warrior. The souls of the warriors are
gathering to see me die. I am Waubeno."

The people pressed upon him, and glared at him.

" He set the fire!" they cried. " The Indian fiend!"

" I set the fire," he said ; " I and Black Hawk's men.
They have escaped. I have done my work, and I want to
die."

Jasper lifted his hat, and with bared head stood forth in the
view of the Indian.

" Waubeno, do you want to see *me* die?"

He started with a cry of pain. His eyes burned.

"My father—I did not know that you were here. Heaven pity Waubeno now!"

"Waubeno, this is cruel!"

"Cruel? This country was once called the Red Man's Paradise. Cruel? The white man made the red man drunk with fire-water, and made him sign a false treaty, and then drove him away. Cruel? Think of the women the whites shot in the river for coming back to their own corn-fields starving to gather their own corn. Cruel? Why is the Red Man's Paradise no longer ours? Cruel? The Rock River flows for us no more; the spring brings the flowers to these prairies for us no more; the bluff rises in the summer sky, but the red man may no longer sit upon it. Cruel? Think how your people murdered my father. Is it more cruel for the Indian to do these things than for the white man to do them? You have emptied the Red Man's Paradise, and Waubeno has fulfilled the vow that he made to his father. The clouds are on fire. I would have saved you had I known, but you must perish with your people. I shall die with you. I am Waubeno. I am proud to be Waubeno. I am the avenger of my race.'

"But, white brother, listen. I tried to prevent it. I remembered your teaching, and I tried to prevent it by our council-fires over the Mississippi. Main-Pogue tried to prevent it. I thought of the man who saved him in the war, and I wondered who he was, and tried to prevent it for *his* sake.

"Then said they to me : 'We go to avenge the loss of our country, the Red Man's Paradise. The grass is feathers. We go to burn. Waubeno, remember your father's death. You are the son of Alknomook!'

"White brother, I have come. I tried to prevent it, but this hand has obeyed the voice of my people. I have kindled the fires of the woe. The world is on fire. I tried to prevent it, but it has come."

"Waubeno, do you remember *Lincoln?*"

"Lincoln? The Indians killed his father's father. I have often thought of that. He said that he would do right by an Indian. I have thought of that. I love that man. I would die for such a man."

"Waubeno, who saved the life of Main-Pogue?"

"I don't know, father. I would die for *that man.*"

"Did Main-Pogue not tell you?"

"He told me 'twas a white captain saved him. Is the white captain here?"

"No. Waubeno, listen. That white captain was Lincoln."

"Lincoln? Whose father's father the red man killed? Was it he who saved Main-Pogue? Lincoln? He forced his men to do right. He did himself harm."

"Yes, he did himself harm to do right. Waubeno, do you remember your promise that you made to me? You said that you would never avenge the death of your father, if you could find one white man who would do himself harm for the sake of an Indian."

Waubeno leaped upon his feet, and his black eye swept the clouds, and the circle of fire, and the distressed people on every hand.

"Father, I can save you now. I know how. I will do it *for Lincoln's sake.*

"Ho! ho!" he cried. "Kill me an ox, and Waubeno will

save you. Kill me six oxen, and Waubeno will save you. Give me raw hides, and do as I do, and Waubeno will save you. Ho! ho! The gods have spoken to Waubeno. A voice comes from the sky to Waubeno. It has spoken here. Ho! ho!"

He put his hand upon his heart, then rushed in among the oxen. A company of men followed him.

He slew an ox with his knife, and quickly removed the hide. The people looked upon him with horror; they thought him demented. What was he doing? What was he going to do?

He tied the great hide to his horse's neck, so that the raw side of it would drag flat upon the ground, and, turning to Jasper, he said:

"That will smother fire. Ho! ho! How?"

The fire was fast approaching some stacks of wheat on the edge of the settlement. Waubeno saw the peril, and leaped upon his horse.

"Kill more cattle. Get more hides for Waubeno," he said.

He rode away toward the stacks, guiding the horse in such a way that the raw hide swept the ground. The people watched him. He seemed to ride into the fire.

"He is riding to death!" said the people. "He is mad!"

But as he rode the fire was stayed, and a rim of black smoke rose in its stead. Near the stacks the fire stopped.

"He is the Evil One himself," said the old Millerite. "That Indian boy is no human form."

Out of the black came the horse plunging, bearing the boy, who waved his hands to the people. Then the horse plunged away, as though wild, toward the outer edge of the great sea of fire.

17

The horse and rider rushed into the flames, and the same strange effects followed. The running flame and white cloud changed into black smoke, and the destruction was arrested.

The people watched the boy as he rode half hidden in rolling smoke, his red plumes waving above the verge of the flaming sea. What a scene it was as he rode there, round and round, like the enchanted form of a more than human deliverer! But the effect of his movements at last ceased.

"He is coming back," said the people.

Out of the fire rushed the horse and rider toward the island grove again.

"Give me new hides!" he cried, as, singed and blackened, he swept into the trees. "The hide is dead and shriveled. Give me new hides. Ho! ho!"

New hides were provided by killing oxen. He tied two together like a carpet, with the raw side upon the earth. He attached them by a long rope to the horse's neck, and dashed forth again, crying:

"Do the same, and follow me."

The horse seemed maddened again. It flew toward the fire as if drawn by a spell, and plunged into it like a bather into the sea. Waubeno tried to deaden the fire in the whole circle. Round and round the island he rode, in the tide of the advancing flames. The people understood his method now, and the men secured new hides and attached them to horses, and followed him. He led them, crying and waving his hands. Round and round he led them, round and round, and where they rode the white smoke changed into black smoke and the fire died.

The people secured raw hides by killing the poor cattle, and came out to the verge of the fiery sea and checked the progress of the flames in places. In the midst of the excitement a roll of thunder was heard in the sky.

" 'Tis the trumpet of doom," said the old Millerite.

The people heard it with terror, and yet with hope. It might be an approaching shower. If it were, they were saved.

The fire in front of them was checked. Not the great sea, but the current that was rolling toward the island grove. The fire at the north was rushing forward, but it moved backward toward the place slowly. The women began to soak blankets and clothing in water, and so prepared to help the men fight the flames. An hour passed. In the midst of the crisis the riding men, the hurrying women, the encircling fire, the billows of smoke, a flame came zigzagging down from the sky. The people stood still. Had the last day indeed come?

Then followed a crash of thunder that shook the earth. The people fell upon their knees. The sky darkened, and great drops of rain began to fall.

Waubeno had checked the current of the flame that would have destroyed the settlement in an hour, and had taught the men how to arrest an advancing tide of flame. The people began to have hope. All was now activity on the part of the people. Smoke filled the sky.

"There is a cloud above the smoke," said many. "God will save us all."

Waubeno came flying back again to the grove.

"It thunders," he cried. "The Rain-god is coming. If I

can keep back the fire an hour, the Rain-god will come. Hides! hides! Quick, more hides! Ho! ho!"

New hides were provided, and he swept forth again.

The island grove was now like a vast oven. The air was stifling. The animals laid down and rolled their tongues from their mouths. But the fire in front did not advance. It seemed deadened. The river of flame forked and ran in other directions, but it was stayed in front of the grove, houses, corn-fields, and stacks, and it was the hand that had set flames that had broken its force in the road to the settlements.

There were sudden dashes of rain, and the smoke turned into blackness everywhere. Another flash of lightning smote the gloom, followed by a rattling of thunder that seemed as if the spirit of the storm was driving his chariot through the air. Then it poured as though a lake was coming down. In an hour the fire was dead. The cloud parted, the slanting sun came out, revealing a prairie as black as ink.

The people fled to the shelter of the houses and sheds at the approach of the rain. The animals crowded under the trees, and the birds hid in the boughs. After the rain-burst the people gathered together again, and each one asked;

"Where is the Indian boy?"

He was not among them.

Had he perished?

A red sunset flamed over the prairies and the birds filled the tree-tops with the gladness of song. It seemed to all as if the earth and sky had come back again.

In the glare of the sunset-fire a horse and rider were seen slowly approaching the island grove.

"It is Waubeno," said one to the other. "The horse is disabled."

The people went out to meet the Indian boy. The horse was burned and blind, and staggered as he came on. And the rider! He had drawn the flames into his vitals; he had been internally burned, and was dying.

He reeled from his blind horse, and fell before the people. Jasper laid his hand upon him.

"Father, I have drunk the cup of fire. I have kept my promise. I am about to die. The birds are happy. They are singing the death-song of Waubeno."

His flesh quivered as he lay there, and Jasper bent over him in pity.

"Waubeno, do you suffer?"

"The stars do not complain, white brother. The clouded sun does not complain. The winds complain, and the waters, and women and children. Waubeno does not complain."

A spasm shook his frame. It passed.

"White brother, go beyond the Mississippi and teach my people. You do pity them. This was once their paradise. They loved it. They struggled. Go to them with the Book of God."

"Waubeno, I will go."

"The sun sets over the Mississippi. 'Tis sunset there. You will go to the land of the sunset?"

"Yes, Waubeno. I feel in my heart the call to go. I love and pity your people."

"Pour water upon me; I am burning. I shall go when the moon comes up, when the moon comes up into the shady sky.

My father suffered, but he did not complain. Waubeno does not complain. Don't pity me. Pity my poor people. I love my people. Teach my people, and cover me forever with a blanket of the earth."

He lay on the cool grass under the trees for several hours in terrible agony, and the people watched by his side.

"When the moon rises," he said, "I shall go. I shall never see the Red Man's Paradise again. Tell me when the moon rises. I am going to sleep now."

The great moon rose at last, its disk hanging like a wheel of dead gold on the verge of the horizon in the smoky air.

"Waubeno," said Jasper, "the moon is rising."

He opened his eyes, and said;

"We kindled the fire for our fathers' sake, and I smote it for him who protected Main-Pogue. What was his name, father? Say it to me."

"Lincoln."

"Yes, Lincoln. He had come for revenge, but he did what was right. He forgave. I forgive everybody. I drank the fire for Lincoln's sake."

The moon burned along the sky; the stars came out; and at midnight all was still. Waubeno lay dead under the trees, and the people with timid steps vanished hither and thither into the cabins and sheds.

They killed the poor blind horse in the morning, and laid Waubeno to rest in a blanket, in a grave under the trees.

Nancy Lincoln was born Feby
10th 1807 —
Abraham Lincoln, son of Thomas &
Nancy Lincoln was born Feby
12th 1809 —

Sarah Bush first married to
Daniel Johnston, and afterwards
married with Thos Lincoln,
was born the Dec 13th 1788 —

Jno D. Johnston, son of Daniel &
Sarah Johnston, was born May
1815 afterward to Mary Ann

October 13th 1834 — wedding —
born July 22nd 1816 —
Thomas L. D. Johnston, Son of Jno
& Nancy Johnston, was born
of Orong January 10 E 1837 —

Abraham L. D. Johnston, son of Jno &
Nancy, was born March 29th 1858 —
Another Sarah Jane Johnston daughter
James Sarah, was born January 2
1840 —
James H. A Luster son of James Luster

Thomas Lincoln married to April
Johnston Feby 2 1815 —
Sarah Lincoln daughter of Thos
Lincoln, was married to
Lincoln, was Aug —

Abraham Lincoln, son of Thos
Lincoln, was married to Mary
died Novr 4th 1842 —
John D. Johnston married to
Nancy Kelly, Nancy Jane Williams
March 5 1851

John D Johnston born
of Jno D Nancy Nancy
Jane Johnston 1791—1772)
born April Dec 11 1854

1696
1616

(1696)

CHAPTER XXIV.

"OUR LINCOLN IS THE MAN."

IFTEEN years have passed since the events described in the last chapter. It is the year 1860. A great political crisis is upon the country, and Abraham Lincoln has been selected to lead one great party of the people, because he had faith in the principle that right is might. The time came, as the Tunker had prophesied, when the people wanted a man of integrity for their leader—a man who had a heart that could be trusted. They elected him to the Legislature when he was almost a boy and had not decent clothes to wear. The young legislator walked over the prairies of Illinois to the Capitol to save the traveling fare. As a legislator he had faith that right is might, and was true to his convictions.

"He has a heart that we can trust," said the people, and they sent him to Congress. He was true in Washington, as in Illinois.

"He has a heart we can trust," said the people; "let us send him to the Senate."

He failed of an election, but it was because his convictions of right were in advance of the public mind at the time; but he who is defeated for a principle, triumphs. The greatest victors are those who are vanquished in the cause of truth, justice, and right; for the cause lives, and they live in the cause that must prevail.

Again the people wanted a leader—all the people who represented a great cause—and Illinois said to the people:

"Make our Lincoln your leader; he has a heart that we can trust," and Lincoln was made the heart of the people in the great cause of human rights. Lincoln, who had defended the little animals of the woods. Lincoln, who had been true to his pioneer father, when the experience had cost him years of toilsome life. Lincoln, who had pitied the slave in the New Orleans market, and whose soul had cried to Heaven for the scales of Justice. Lincoln, who had protected the old Indian amid the gibes of his comrades. Lincoln, who had studied by pine-knots, made poetry on old shovels, and read law on lonely roads. Lincoln, who had had a kindly word and pleasant story for everybody, pitied everybody, loved everybody, and forgave everybody, and yet carried a sad heart. Lincoln, who had resolved that in law and politics he would do just right.

John Hanks had brought some of the rails that the candidate for the presidency had split into the Convention of Illinois, and the rails that represented the hardships of pioneer life became the oriflamme of the leader from the prairies. He who is true to a nation is first true to his parents and home.

That was an ever-to-be-remembered day when, in August, 1860, the people of the great West with one accord arranged to visit Abraham Lincoln, the candidate for the presidency, at

Springfield, Illinois. Seventy thousand strangers poured into the prairie city. They came from Indiana, Iowa, and the lakes. Thousands came from Chicago. Men came in wagons, bringing their wives and children. They brought tents, camp-kettles, and coffee-pots. Says a graphic writer who saw the scene:

"Every road leading to the city is crowded for twenty miles with vehicles. The weather is fine, and a little overwarm. Girls can dress in white, and bare their arms and necks without danger; the women can bring their children. Everything that was ever done at any other mass-meeting is done here. Locomotive-builders are making a boiler; blacksmiths are heating and hammering their irons; the iron-founders are molding their patterns; the rail-splitters are showing the people how Uncle Abe used to split rails; every other town has its wagon-load of thirty-one girls in white to represent the States; bands of music, numerous almost as those of McClellan on Arlington Heights in 1862, are playing; old men of the War of 1812, with their old wives, their children, grandchildren, and great-grandchildren, are here: making a procession of human beings, horses, and carriages not less than ten miles in length. And yet the procession might have left the town and the people would scarcely be missed.

"There is an immense wigwam, with galleries like a thea-tre; but there are people enough not in the procession to fill a dozen like it. Half an hour is long enough to witness the moving panorama of men and women, horses, carriages, rep-resentatives of trades, mottoes, and burlesques, and listen to the bands."

And among those who came to see the great procession, the rail-splitters, and the sights, were the Tunker from the Indian schools over the Mississippi, and Aunt Indiana from Indiana.

There was a visitor from the East who became the hero of the great day. He is living now (1891) in Chelsea, Mass., near the Soldiers' Home, to which he often goes to sing, and is known there as "Father Locke." He was a natural minstrel, and songs of his, like "Down by the Sea," have been sung all over the world. One of his songs has moved thousands of hearts in sorrow, and pictures his own truly loving and beautiful soul:

> " There's a fresh little mound near the willow,
>   Where at evening I wander and weep;
> There's a dear vacant spot on my pillow,
>   Where a sweet little face used to sleep.
> There were pretty blue eyes, but they slumber
>   In silence, beneath the dark mold,
> And the little pet lamb of our number
>   Has gone to the heavenly fold."

This man, with the approval of President Lincoln, went as a minstrel to the Army of the Potomac. We think that he was the only minstrel who followed our army, like the war-singers of old. In a book published for private use, entitled Three Years in Camp and Hospital, "Father Locke" thus tells the story of his interview with President Lincoln at the White House:

"Giving his hand, and saying he recollected me, he asked what he could do for me.

"'I want no office, Mr. President. I came to ask for one, but have changed my mind since coming into this house. When it comes to turning beggar, I shall shun the places where all the other beggars go. I am going to the army to sing for the soldiers, as the poets and balladists of old sang in war. Our soldiers must take as much interest in songs and singing as did those of ancient times. I only wished to shake hands with you, and obtain a letter of recommendation to the commanding officers, that they may receive and treat me kindly.'

" 'I will give you a letter with pleasure, but you do not need one; your singing will make you all right.'

" On my rising to leave, he gave his hand, saying: ' God bless you; I am glad you do not want an office. Go to the army, and cheer the men around their camp-fires with your songs, remembering that a great man said, "Let me but make the songs of a nation, and I care not who makes its laws." ' "

The President then told him how to secure a pass into the lines of the army, and the man went forth to write and to sing his inspirations, like a balladist of old.

His songs were the delight of many camps of the Army of the Potomac in the first dark year of the war. They were sung in the camp, and they belonged to the inside army life, but were little known outside of the army. They are still fondly remembered by the veterans, and are sung at reunions and camp-fires.

We give one of these songs and its original music here. It has the spirit of the time and the events, and every note is a pulse-beat:

We are Marching on to Richmond.

WORDS AND MUSIC BY E. W. LOCKE.

Published by the permission of the Composer.

1. Our knapsacks sling and blithely sing, We're marching on   to
2. Our foes are near, their drums we hear, They're camped a-bout in

Rich-mond; With weap-ons bright, and hearts so   light, We're
Rich-mond; With pick-ets   out, to   tell the   route Our

march-ing on   to Rich-mond; Each wea-ry   mile with
Ar-my takes   to Rich-mond; We've craft-y   foes to

song be-guile, We're marching on   to Richmond; The roads are
meet our blows, No doubt they'll fight for Richmond; The brave may

rough, but smooth e-nough To take   us safe   to Richmond.
die,   but nev-er fly, We'll cut   our way   to Richmond.

CHORUS.

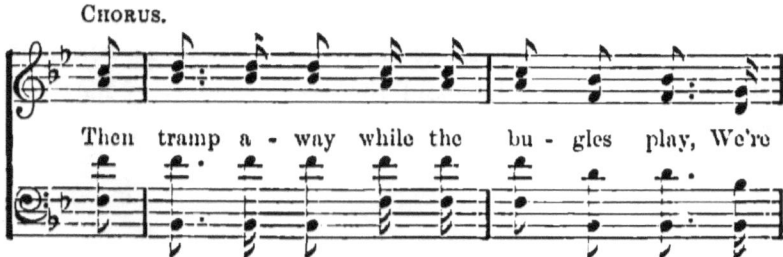

Then tramp a-way while the   bu-gles play, We're

march-ing on to Rich-mond; Our flag shall gleam in the

morn-ing beam, From man-y a spire in Rich-mond.

3.

"But yesterday, in murderous fray,
  While marching on to Richmond,
We parted here from comrades dear,
  While marching on to Richmond;
With manly sighs and tearful eyes,
  While marching on to Richmond,
We laid the braves in peaceful graves,
  And started on to Richmond.

4.

"Our friends away are sad to-day,
  Because we march to Richmond;
With loving fear they shrink to hear
  About our march to Richmond;
The pen shall tell that they who fell
  While marching on to Richmond,
Had hearts aglow and face to foe,
  And died in sight of Richmond.

5.

"Our thoughts shall roam to scenes of home,
    While marching on to Richmond;
The vacant chair that's waiting there,
    While we march on to Richmond;
'Twill not be long till shout and song
    We'll raise aloud in Richmond,
And war's rude blast will soon be past,
    And we'll go home from Richmond."

This song-writer had brought a song to the great Spring-field assembly. He sang it when the people were in a recep-tive mood. It voiced their hearts, and its influence was electric. As he rose before the assembly on that August day under the prairie sun, and sang : "Hark ! hark ! a signal-gun is heard," a stillness came over the great sea of the people. The figures of the first verse filled the imagination, but the chorus was like a bugle-call :

"*THE SHIP OF STATE.*

"(Sung at the Springfield Convention.)

"Hark ! hark ! a signal-gun is heard,
    Just out beyond the fort ;
The good old Ship of State, my boys,
    Is coming into port.
With shattered sails, and anchors gone,
    I fear the rogues will strand her ;
She carries now a sorry crew,
    And needs a new commander.

"Our Lincoln is the man !
Our Lincoln is the man !
    With a sturdy mate
    From the Pine-Tree State,
Our Lincoln is the man !

" Four years ago she put to sea,
　　With prospects brightly beaming ;
　Her hull was strong, her sails new-bent,
　　And every pennant streaming ;
　She loved the gale, she plowed the waves,
　　Nor feared the deep's commotion ;
　Majestic, nobly on she sailed,
　　Proud mistress of the ocean.

" There's mutiny aboard the ship ;
　　There's feud no force can smother ;
　Their blood is up to fever-heat ;
　　They're cutting down each other.
　Buchanan here, and Douglas there,
　　Are belching forth their thunder,
　While cunning rogues are sly at work
　　In pocketing the plunder.

" Our ship is badly out of trim ;
　　'Tis time to calk and grave her ;
　She's foul with stench of human gore ;
　　They've turned her to a slaver.
　She's cruised about from coast to coast,
　　The flying bondman hunting,
　Until she's strained from stem to stern,
　　And lost her sails and bunting.

　　　　" Old Abram is the man !
　　　　Old Abram is the man !
　　　　　And he'll trim her sails,
　　　　　As he split the rails.
　　　　Old Abram is the man !

" We'll give her what repairs she needs—
　　A thorough overhauling ;
　Her sordid crew shall be dismissed,
　　To seek some honest calling.
　Brave Lincoln soon shall take the helm,
　　On truth and right relying ;
　In calm or storm, in peace or war,
　　He'll keep her colors flying.

" Old Abram is the man!
Old Abram is the man !
With a sturdy mate
From the Pine-Tree State,
Old Abram is the man !"

These words seem commonplace to-day, but they were
trumpet-notes then. " Our Lincoln is the man!" trembled on
every tongue, and a tumultuous applause arose that shook the
air. The enthusiasm grew; the minstrel had voiced the people,
and they would not let him stop singing. They finally mounted
him on their shoulders and carried him about in triumph, like
a victor bard of old. Ever rang the chorus from the lips of the
people, " Our Lincoln is the man !" " Old Abram is the man !"

Lincoln heard the song. He loved songs. One of his
favorite songs was " Twenty Years ago." But this was the
first time, probably, that he had heard himself sung. He was
living at that time in the plain house in Springfield that has
been made familiar by pictures. The song delighted him, but
he, of all the thousands, was forbidden by his position to express
his pleasure in the song. He would have liked to join with the
multitudes in singing " Our Lincoln is the man !" had not the
situation sealed his lips. But after the scene was over, and the
great mass of people began to melt away, he sought the minstrel, and said :

" Come to my room, and sing to me the song privately. I
want to hear you sing it."

So he listened to it in private, while it was being borne over
the prairies on tens of thousands of lips. Did he then dream
that the nations would one day sing the song of his achieve-
ments, that his death would be tolled by the bells of all lands,

and his dirge fill the churches of Christendom with tears? It
may have been that his destiny in dim outline rose before him,
for the events of his life were hurrying.

Aunt Indiana was there, and she found the Tunker.

"The land o' sakes and daisies!" she said. "That we
should both be here! Well, elder, I give it up! I was agin
Lincoln until I heard all the people a-singin' that song; then
it came over me that I was doin' just what I hadn't ought to,
and I began to sing 'Old Lincoln is the man!' just as though
it had been a Methody hymn written by Wesley himself."

"I am glad that you have changed your mind, and that I
have lived to see my prophecy, that Lincoln would become the
heart of the people, fulfilled."

"Elder, I tell you what let's we do."

"What, my good woman?"

"Let's we each get a rail, and go down before Abe's win-
der, and I'll sing as loud as anybody:

> "'Old Abram is the man!
> Old Abram is the man!
> And he'll trim her sails
> As he split the rails.
> Old Abram is the man!'

I'll do it, if you will. I've been all wrong from the first. Why,
even the Grigsbys are goin' to vote for him, and I'm goin' to
do the right thing myself. Abe always had a human heart,
and it is that which is the most human that leads off in this
world."

Aunt Indiana found a rail. The streets of Springfield were
full of rails that the people had brought in honor of Lincoln's

18

hard work on his father's barn in early Illinois. She also found a flag. Flags were as many as rails on this remarkable occasion. She set the flag into the top of the rail, and started or the street that led past Lincoln's door.

"Come on, elder; we'll be a procession all by ourselves."

The two arrived at the house where Lincoln lived, the Tunker in his buttonless gown, and Aunt Indiana with her corn-bonnet, printed shawl, rail, and flag. The procession of two came to a halt before the open window, and presently, framed in the open window, like a picture, the face of Abraham Lincoln appeared. That face lighted up as it fell upon Aunt Indiana.

She made a low courtesy, and lifted the rail and the flag, and broke forth in a tone that would have led a camp-meeting :

> "'Our Abram is the man!
> Our Abram is the man!
> With a sturdy mate
> From the Pine-Tree State,
> Our Abram is the man!'

"Elder, you sing, and we'll go over it again."

Aunt Indiana waved the flag and sang the refrain again, and said :

"Abe Lincoln, I'm goin' to vote for ye, though I never thought I should. But you shall have my vote with all the rest.—Lawdy sakes and daisies, elder—I forgot; I can't vote, can I? I'm just a woman. I've got all mixed up and carried away, but

> "'Our Abram is the man!'"

ABRAHAM LINCOLN.

From a photograph by Alexander Hesler, Chicago, 1853.

Six years have passed. The gardens of Washington are bursting into bloom. The sky is purple under a clear sun. It is Wednesday morning, the 19th of April, 1865.

All the bells are tolling, and the whole city is robed in black. At eleven o'clock some sixty clergymen enter the White House, followed by the governors of the States. At noon comes the long procession of Government officers, followed by the diplomatic corps.

In the sable rooms rises a dark catafalque, and in it lies a waxen face.

Toll!—the bells of Washington, Georgetown, and Alexandria! Minute-guns boom. Around that dead face the representatives of the nation, and of all nations, pass, and tears fall like rain.

A funeral car of flowers moves through the streets. Abraham Lincoln has done his work. He is on his journey back to the scenes of his childhood! The boy who defended the turtles, the man who stretched out his arm over the defenseless Indian in the Black Hawk War, and who freed the slave; the man of whom no one ever asked pity in vain—he is going back to the prairies, to sleep his eternal sleep among the violets.

Toll! The bells of all the cities and towns of the loyal nation are tolling. In every principal church in all the land people have met to weep and to pray. Half-mast flags everywhere meet the breeze.

They laid the body beneath the rotunda of the Capitol, amid the April flowers and broken magnolias.

Then homeward—through Baltimore, robed in black;

through Philadelphia, through New York, Cleveland, Indianapolis, and Chicago. The car rolls on, over flowers and under black flags, amid the tolling of the bells of cities and the bells of the simple country church-towers. All labor ceases. The whole people stop to wonder and to weep.

The dirges cease. The muffled drums are still. The broken earth of the prairies is wrapped around the dead commoner, the fallen apostle of humanity, the universal brother of all who toil and struggle.

The courts of Europe join in the lamentation. Never yet was a man wept like this man.

His monument ennobles the world. He stands in eternal bronze in a hundred cities. And why? Because he had a heart to feel; because to him all men had been brothers of equal blood and birthright; and because he had had faith that "RIGHT MAKES MIGHT."

CHAPTER XXV.

AT THE LAST.

ROM the magnolias to the Northern orchards, from the apple-blooms to the prairie violets! The casket was laid in the tomb. Twilight came; the multitudes had gone. It was ended now, and night was falling.

Two forms stood beside the closed door of the tomb; one was an old, gray-haired woman, the other was a patriarchal-looking man.

The woman's gray hairs blew about her white face like silver threads, and she pushed it back with her withered hand.

"Sister Olive," said the old man, "*he* loved others better than himself; and it is not this tomb, but the great heart of the world, that has taken him in. I felt that he was called. I felt it years ago."

"Heaven forgive a poor old woman, elder! I misjudged that man. See here."

She held up a bunch of half-withered prairie violets tha she had carried about with her all the day, and then went and laid them on the tomb.

" For Lincoln's sake! for Lincoln's sake!" she said, crying like a child.

The two went away in the shadows, talking of all the past, and each has long slept under the violets of the prairies.

THE END.